Y040130   KU-303-314

COLLATERAL DAMAGE

Steve Howell

Published by Quaero Publishing

Quaero Publishing
Cilhaul
Guilsfield
Welshpool
SY21 9NH

Copyright © Steve Howell 2021

The moral right of Steve Howell to be identified as the author of this work has been asserted by him in accordance with the Copyright, Designs and Patents Act 1988.

All rights reserved. No part of this publication may be reproduced, stored in a retrieval system or transmitted, in any form or by any means (electronic, mechanical, photocopying, recording or otherwise), without the prior written permission of the author.

This is a work of fiction. Names, characters and incidents are either the product of the author's imagination or are used fictitiously. Any resemblance to actual persons, living or dead, businesses, companies or events is entirely coincidental.

ISBN: 978-0-9931607-1-4

Cover design: Simon John, Freshwater UK

For Kim

*"If the Prime Minister is right in
accepting America's bombing of Libya
as legitimate self-defence, that would
certainly justify the Nicaraguan
Government, if it had the capacity,
bombing the CIA headquarters at
Langley in Virginia."*

Denis Healey, MP, House of Commons, 16.4.86

CHAPTER ONE
29 APRIL 1987

Jed has never been to a funeral. Somehow, he's reached the age of twenty-seven without ever going to one, or having any contact with death. His mother's mother is still going strong, and her husband was lost to philandering long ago, whereabouts unknown. His paternal grandparents were both American and died while he was a small child. Even his father didn't go to their funerals, for reasons that still aren't altogether clear to him.

Yet, here he is now, at a crematorium, witnessing the arrival of a hearse bearing the corpse of a man his own age who he's never met, a man whose name – Tom Carver – meant nothing to him only eight days ago.

As he stands there on a grassy bank, watching the immaculate black vehicle roll slowly into the narrow drive alongside the chapel, followed by a stretch Jaguar jammed with people, he thinks of the photographs he's seen of Tom and imagines his deathly face in the coffin. But he doesn't feel he really knows what Tom was like, even though his death has sent his own life hurtling into chaos.

There's a crowd of a hundred or more gathered under the porch of the crematorium, sheltering from a light drizzle. They begin shuffling back to allow the undertakers, two men, to get out, put their top hats on and open the Jaguar's rear doors for the close family to scramble awkwardly onto the pavement either side.

The undertakers march slowly to the hearse, where its driver is waiting with the tailgate open. From among the mourners, four men appear and crouch behind the vehicle

1

in pairs to allow the undertakers to slide the dark oak coffin from its berth onto their shoulders.

Everyone falls silent as the pallbearers carry Tom into the chapel. Some are looking at their feet, perhaps to hide tears. Others stare gravely at the coffin as it goes slowly past, wobbling slightly on its uneven carriage. It's so quiet that Jed can – even from the good distance he's keeping – hear the gentle splashing sound of the small fountain by the chapel entrance.

Keen to do the right thing, and wearing his black lawyer's suit and a borrowed black tie, Jed had arrived at the crematorium early. He'd walked the pathway circling the building, noting how it was laid out to channel people in on one side and out on the other. As he passed the exit, another service had ended and the mourners emerged to piped music and spent a few minutes in muffled conversation before going to their cars. As a first-timer, it struck him as an industrial operation, a conveyor belt, operating to a strict timetable with little margin for spontaneity or an outpouring of emotion.

Jed doubts Tom's father, Major Carver, as he likes to be called, would want that anyway. As he follows his son's coffin into the chapel now, he looks like a man with his feelings completely under control. Tall and walking with military bearing in an immaculate black overcoat, he seems oblivious to his distraught wife who's a yard behind, stooped and struggling to complete each step, supported by two women of a similar age.

As the crowd forms an orderly procession behind the coffin, Jed continues to keep his distance. His sense of not belonging is growing. He's there solely for Tom's girlfriend, Ayesha, but she hasn't arrived yet and may not turn up at all. If she does come, she will be shunned by Tom's family.

Major Carver has already refused to allow her to see Tom's body. He blames her for Tom's death.

When Jed saw Ayesha the previous day, she hadn't made her mind up. She said she'd call him if she needed a lift. But she didn't and, when he couldn't get hold of her, he felt he had no choice but to come, just in case.

He scans the crowd one more time. There's still no sign of her, and she'd easily stand out. Not only is she tall and strikingly good looking, she would double the number of non-whites among the mourners.

Jed feels a growing sense of exasperation at her no-show. He doesn't blame her for not wanting to suffer doubly – endure both her grief and the hostility of Tom's father – but he's annoyed she didn't let him know.

It's not unexpected though. In the short time he's known her, she has sprung more than a few surprises. He's had to learn fast that Ayesha is someone who defies prediction and appears to act on impulse. But that's not to say her actions are irrational – they usually have, he's discovered, an inner logic. It's just not always clear what it is.

Apart from Tom's father, the only people he knows at the funeral are Hannah and Gavin. He's spotted them standing at the far end of the crowd, and Hannah has exchanged nods with him, but he doesn't feel at all inclined to make his way over to them.

Hannah looks tired and subdued. Her normally radiant blue eyes have retreated into grey hollows, and she's leaning on Gavin, who towers above her, as most people do. It reminds him of the times he would tease her about her height when they were students, ridiculously pretending not to see her in a packed bar when she was right in front of him. They'd been lovers, in an on and off

3

way, but he hadn't seen her for months until she turned up with Ayesha in his office eight days ago.

With the last of the mourners squeezing into the back of the chapel, and still no sign of Ayesha, Jed is tempted to slip away. But that now feels disrespectful to Tom, and he fears it might not go unnoticed by his family.

He makes his way tentatively across to the entrance as the organ starts playing a stirring hymn that he doesn't recognise, the mourners not helping by singing at different paces and not knowing the words.

When everyone is seated, apart from Jed and a few others at the back, a woman describing herself as the celebrant takes charge. She admits she didn't know Tom but, on a mission to live up to her title, she enthuses about how missed he will be and how many wonderful things family and friends have said about him.

Her description of Tom is nice, though Ayesha might call it sanitised. The celebrant speaks of his love of his home village in rural Hertfordshire, of his school days at Haberdashers and the pranks he played on teachers, of his passion for rugby, of how – but for an injury – he would have won an Oxford Blue for cricket, and of the way he had made a great start to a career in journalism only for it to be cut short by a tragic accident.

It is meticulously crafted, but she doesn't mention the location of the accident, nor would you have known that his "blossoming" in journalism had been for a radical magazine, or that he was someone of such strong convictions that he had – more than once – run into trouble with the authorities. The passionate, rebel Tom – as Ayesha had portrayed him to Jed – is airbrushed from this version.

The celebrant's eulogy is followed by an uncle reading 'The Lord's My Shepherd'; a female schoolfriend reciting a mercifully short poem about not weeping at the grave because "I am not there, I do not sleep"; and a speech by an old family friend who hardly mentions Tom but speaks fulsomely of the "fortitude" of his parents, saying: "I yield to no one in my admiration for the strength and dignity shown by the Carvers in the face of this tragedy – they're an example to us all."

Just as Jed is trying to suppress his own less-than-warm feelings about the Major, the organist launches into the opening chords of 'Abide With Me', bursting the emotional blockage inside him so completely that he can't stop the tears flowing. The suppressed frustrations and fears of the last few days come brimming to the surface, catching him by surprise and worrying the woman to his right, who hands him a tissue and says, sympathetically, how lovely Tom was and how much we would all miss him.

Jed can't bring himself to say they'd never even met. The truth, he's ashamed to admit, is that this outpouring is really all about him and the torrid time he's had since first hearing Tom's name. As they leave the chapel, he thanks her fulsomely and begins to stride briskly towards the car park before she asks any questions.

The drizzle has given way to sunshine so powerful that the puddles are visibly shrinking and a steamy fog is rising from the grass. Most of the mourners are ahead of Jed, gathering in groups to look at the flowers and wreaths laid out neatly on a patio opposite the exit.

Jed sees Hannah and Gavin and thinks he ought to say 'goodbye' as he passes them. He pauses momentarily. But Tom's father is nearby, talking to a young couple. Jed decides to forgo the goodbyes in the hope of making a quiet exit – but he isn't quite quick enough.

"You've got a nerve," Major Carver says, stepping in front of him.

They are face to face, only inches apart. His pre-funeral composure has gone. Looking much older than the dapper 50-something Jed had first met only a few days earlier, his thin lips are quivering and his bushy brows are so tightly clenched they almost completely conceal his eyes. Grief has visibly taken its toll.

Jed steps sideways, but the Major moves in tandem. "What are you doing here?"

It plainly isn't a question, and Jed would have no idea how to reply even if it was. Most of the obvious, trite phrases don't apply, and mentioning Ayesha would be like detonating a bomb.

"I'm sorry for your loss," he says feebly, adding "sir" like he's back at school.

The Major stands there still blocking Jed's path. He's chewing his lips, as if mulling what punishment to dish out to a mutinous soldier.

Jed senses hostile eyes on his back as mourners stop their conversations to watch the confrontation.

"I'm sorry for your loss, I really am," he repeats with genuine sincerity.

To his right, there's movement. A hand touches his arm. "Jed, let's go," a familiar voice says.

It's Hannah.

Without taking his eyes off Tom's father, Jed edges in the direction she's gently tugging him to go in. As he does, the Major turns and marches away, back towards the chapel, where his wife and the celebrant are waiting.

"Come on Jed," Hannah whispers. "There's nothing you could have said that would have made any difference. He blames us. He's not going to change his mind."

Jed and Hannah walk towards Gavin, who's waiting a few yards further along the drive.

"Wanker," he says, nodding towards the Major.

Taken aback, Jed checks over his shoulder to see if anyone else has heard. He might not like Tom's father, but he has just seen the curtains, literally, close on his son. The smoke from Tom's burning flesh is puffing out of the crematorium chimney as they stand there.

Hannah senses Jed's unease and changes the subject. "Where's Ayesha?"

"No idea," Jed says, feeling suddenly angry that Ayesha's put him in this position.

They fall silent. Jed can't muster the motivation for conversation.

"I'm going, I'll see you," he says, not giving them a chance to reply.

As he walks up the drive to the car park, he hears footsteps behind him. He's too wary of another encounter with an angry relative to look over his shoulder. The person is breathing heavily with the effort of the hill. Somehow, it sounds like a woman.

"Young man," she shouts. "Slow down. I want a word with you."

Her voice is determined but not angry. Jed stops and turns to see a tall, slender woman of about sixty closing the gap between them with bold confident strides. He recognises her as one of the two women helping Tom's mother make her way into the chapel.

"Goodness you walk quickly, Jed. It is Jed? I hope I'm talking to the right person."

"Yes, I'm Jed," he says. "I'm sorry. I shouldn't have come."

"Don't be so silly. Why do you say that?"

"Only because Tom's father doesn't seem very happy about it…"

"The Major? Oh, goodness, don't mind him. Henry's a prick. He always has been."

She laughs, and Jed allows himself a tentative smile as they stand there for a moment taking stock of each other. He can see a resemblance to Tom, blond with a thin face and intense grey-blue eyes. She's wearing a plain black trouser suit, but he suspects from her weathered complexion that she'd be more at home dressed casually, hiking or horse-riding.

"Look," she says. "I won't hold you up. I've been asked to pass on a message, from Elizabeth, Tom's mother. I'm her sister. She's too upset to talk to anyone. It's a message for you to give to Ayesha. Just tell her… Put it this way, Liz wants to know the truth too. Tell her that, would you? And give her this. She can contact me at any time if she wants to talk or if there are any developments."

Tom's aunt hands Jed a card.

"I'm Dorothy," she says, shaking his hand with the firm grip of a woman who's used to doing business with men.

Jed wants to ask what she thinks the truth might be but, before he can say anything, she's striding away, and he's left reading her card:

> **Dorothy Willis**
> **Partner and Head of Practice**
> **Forensic Accountancy**
> **Ogilvy and Archer**
> **King William Street**
> **London EC4**

Tucking the card into his wallet, he watches Dorothy continue her descent towards the rest of the mourners.

The funeral had an air of unreality from the moment he arrived. Now he's been told that the mother of the deceased is – unlike her husband – not convinced of the official version of how her son died.

Jed may not have known Tom or had any previous experience of bereavement, but he can understand why the truth would be so important. What he's not sure about is whether or not there's any more he can do to find it.

CHAPTER TWO
EIGHT DAYS EARLIER

Jed puts the receiver down and munches the last mouthful of his bacon sandwich. He'd been in the office for barely five minutes when Hannah phoned. Like so often in the past, she needs his help. Only, this time, she was in too much of a hurry to go through their usual ritual of flirting, teasing and small talk. She got straight to the favour. It's for her friend, Ayesha, a post graduate at LSE. Ayesha has a problem that Hannah didn't want to discuss over the phone. They need to meet. Right away.

Jed could do without the hassle. He's nursing a hangover from a long bank holiday drinking session in The Prince Regent. He'd walked briskly to work to shake it off, taking his usual route through the backstreets of Islington. The fresh April breeze had helped. And, on reaching Chapel Market, he'd picked up a bacon sandwich from the greasy spoon immediately below the rambling offices of O'Brien and Partners.

O'Brien's is at the bottom end of the legal market, and Jed is at the bottom end of the firm's hierarchy, a junior solicitor hired to plough through routine immigration cases. He's contemplating the files piled precariously in his in-tray when this week's receptionist calls to say she's sending his two visitors up to see him.

Before he can tidy up, Hannah is breezing through the door without knocking and giving him a cheery smile. She's followed by the much taller Ayesha, whose face is tilted towards the floor and largely hidden by the thick dark hair flowing abundantly onto her shoulders. Over the last few years, Hannah had often enthused about her new friend from Beirut, but Jed has never paid much attention.

"This is Ayesha," says Hannah.

Ayesha lifts her head and pushes her hair back. Jed stands up and nods awkwardly as their eyes meet. She smiles, but her full lips are quivering slightly and her eyes – a rich mahogany colour – are glistening as if tears could flow at any moment.

Jed is used to friends asking for favours – witnessing documents, providing free advice – and regarding their needs as urgent and important, but he senses this is different and serious. He gestures at the two chairs facing his desk in the small space between a filing cabinet and some dilapidated shelves packed with law books.

His office is about the size of a garden shed, and nearly as drafty. It doesn't help that the glass in his rickety sash window, which overlooks Chapel Market, still has a hole in it from an explosion a few years earlier. Jed is never sure whether his boss, Conor O'Brien, won't repair it because he's tight or because he gets a buzz from telling the story of how it was caused by a bomb South African agents planted at the nearby offices of the African National Congress. When one of their officials, a man called Thozamile, had come to see the damage, O'Brien had taken him around the building, introducing him to everyone like a celebrity. "These are the people rattling Botha's cage," he'd said.

With Ayesha still wrapped in a long black coat and Hannah shivering in her familiar mustard Parka, he's tempted to explain the reason for his heating problem, thinking two politically-active women would appreciate its origins more than most visitors. But, looking at the sadness in Ayesha's face, he realises this is no time for digressions.

"It's nice to meet you Ayesha, having heard so much..."

"Jed, we need to get straight to the point," Hannah says abruptly.

"Yes, yes... I know." Jed's indignant at not being allowed to finish his sentence and feels like telling her so – this is *his* office, after all – but Ayesha holds a hand up as if silencing two children.

"Thank you, Jed, for seeing us at such short notice," she says slowly, her tone clipped and controlled. "We're here about a friend of ours who went to Tripoli. To attend a conference. His name's Tom Carver. He was part of a delegation from Britain. And he was due back yesterday. I went to Heathrow to meet him. When I got there, the plane was delayed. By about two hours. I waited, of course. But when the other delegates came through customs, Tom wasn't with them."

Ayesha pauses. Jed waits for her to continue, but she's looking down at her hands, clasped tightly on her lap, as if in prayer. Hannah reaches out and rests a hand on the back of Ayesha's head and starts stroking her hair gently.

"The Libyans had detained him...?" Jed asks, tentatively.

Hannah breaks off from comforting Ayesha and looks solemnly at Jed. "No, not that."

"What then?"

"Not detained. Dead."

"You're kidding." Jed stares at her for a long moment.

"Why would we be kidding?"

"But how do you know? I mean, are you certain?"

"Ayesha knows some of the other delegates. When they came through customs, they told her."

Jed looks at Ayesha, whose face is hidden again by a dense veil of hair. She's sobbing softly and rocking in rhythm.

"Did they say how?" he says, turning back to Hannah.

"No. Apparently it was chaos yesterday morning when they were due to leave. A coach had arrived at the hotel to take them to the airport, but the police kept them there, and didn't explain why. Obviously, rumours started flying around and, eventually, one of the Libyan officials gathered them together and told them officially... that Tom was dead."

Hannah produces a newspaper cutting from the pocket of her Parka and hands it to Jed.

"This was in the *Guardian,* this morning," she says.

The report adds a few details: the body of Tom Carver was found early on Monday morning on a beach at a coastal resort near Tripoli; he was one of forty delegates from Britain attending a conference to mark the first anniversary of the US bombing of Libya; delegations had also come from across Europe and north America; the family had been notified; the Foreign Office was investigating the circumstances of his death.

Jed lays the cutting on his desk, chews his lip for a moment, and picks it up again. The report doesn't say the death was suspicious, nor does it say it wasn't. Either way, he's not sure what they imagine a junior solicitor with no experience at all of criminal work could do to help.

"I'm really sorry about Tom." Jed hears his words echo and knows they sound feeble.

Ayesha lifts her head and leans forward slowly, as if in anticipation, expecting Jed to say more.

"You'll help, then?" she says.

Jed slumps back in his chair, trying to give himself some space and perspective on what is being asked of him.

"But how? I'm an immigration lawyer. I do visas, I try to stop deportations..." He looks to Hannah for confirmation, but sees only irritation in her face. "I'm just saying I really don't have any experience of this kind of thing."

"Don't be a dick," Hannah says.

Jed bristles, anticipating what's coming. Throughout their relationship, in its various guises, Hannah often accused him of dodging difficult issues and wanting an easy life. And she was right, basically.

He had met her during fresher's week at Bristol University. It was 1979, and he'd gone along to the Labour Club, feeling vaguely curious to know what other left-leaning students thought Margaret Thatcher had in store for them. And there was Hannah – this small, slender 18-year-old with mousy blond hair and animated blue eyes – brimming with ideas, talking confidently and taking command. He'd tagged along afterwards when she'd said 'who's coming to the bar?'

And that set the pattern: she would lead, he would follow. She became the students' union campaigns officer. If there was a protest, she organised it. If volunteers were needed, she expected Jed to be one of them. Occasionally, he'd push back, put a game of football or a drink with his mates first. When he did, she would berate him for his lack of commitment. Mostly, Jed admired her. At times, he was in love with her.

Now, he's ready for one of her verbal onslaughts.

But Ayesha steps in again. "I need someone I can trust to help me look into this, to find out how he died. What kind of lawyer you are doesn't matter. If you phone the Foreign Office, you'll have more chance of getting some answers. They won't even take a call from me."

"Why not? You and Tom were… together, right?"

"He was my *boyfriend*, my partner, yes."

"But not married?"

"No, but we'd talked about it."

"How long had you been together?"

"Just over a year."

"What's that got to do with anything?" Hannah interjects impatiently.

Jed sighs. "Do you want my help or not? I'm trying to clarify the situation. The law's inconsistent. Social security can treat you as cohabiting regardless of time. With immigration, there's a two-year rule. I'm looking for a line of argument that might work with the Foreign Office."

"Okay," Hannah says. "If a year's enough for social security, why not use that?"

"We could, but what about his family? Can't you approach the Foreign Office with them?"

Ayesha laughs bitterly. "I've met Tom's parents. He arranged for us to have tea with them at a hotel in Victoria, The Goring. It was very formal, very English. He was worried how they would react. He thought they'd have to be on their best behaviour in a place like that. But it didn't go well. His mother was okay. She didn't say much but she was polite and smiled nicely at me once or twice. But his father – the Major – was frosty and so patronising, so rude, I felt like walking out. And, in the end, we more or less did. Tom cut it short, and we left."

Jed starts, out of habit, to make notes. But he stops himself, still wary of getting too involved.

"So, I take it, from that, that you haven't spoken to Tom's parents about this?"

"No, and I can't see any point in trying. His father didn't approve of him going to the conference. And his mother thought it was dangerous."

"And it turns out she was right."

Ayesha flinches and, for the first time, sounds angry. "You say that like you think the Libyans are to blame. That's so typical."

15

"I only meant…" Jed stops himself. He's not really sure what he meant, and he realises it's a pointless discussion when they don't even know how Tom died. He looks at Hannah hoping she'll help him out, tell Ayesha he isn't the kind of person who believes everything he reads about Libya.

"Whatever you think of Gaddafi," Hannah says. "This happening isn't in his interests. Why would he invite people who opposed the air strikes to Libya and then not look after them?"

Jed is tempted to say 'but he didn't look after them' and to suggest that having hundreds of Westerners around on the anniversary of a Western attack that killed dozens of his own citizens, innocent civilians, was asking for trouble – feelings must have been running very high. But he doesn't say any of that. He bites his lip and turns towards the window to avoid eye contact, trying to give himself time to think.

"Look," he says finally. "I can make some calls but, because you aren't – technically – family, they probably won't tell me anything either. And I'm not sure where we go from there."

The room falls silent. Jed doodles on his notepad, conscious that looks are being exchanged on the other side of his desk.

"To Tripoli, that's where we go."

When Ayesha says this, Jed gasps and Hannah gives him a dark don't-be-so-useless look.

Ayesha ploughs on. "Jed, I have to know what happened. None of it makes any sense. What was he doing on the beach? Why did he go there? How did he die? Someone must have seen something. I'm going to get some answers – whatever it takes. But I don't want to go on my own, and…" Ayesha looks across at Hannah. "And we don't think two women will get very far. I don't like admitting it but I'm realistic: we need a man. And we need someone who knows where we stand legally."

"Where you stand legally? Under *Libyan* criminal law? How would I know that? I didn't do that course at Bristol."

Jed regrets his sarcasm instantly. He didn't mean to sound flippant. But the reality is he's not sure what her rights would be in British law — if any — never mind in a country he had never visited and knew next to nothing about.

"Jed, you are…" Hannah starts.

"A dick. Yes, you said earlier."

"I wasn't going to say that. I was going to say, you're the most conscientious person I know. And I trust you completely, and we're here because we really need your help. We really do."

Jed finds Hannah's flattery even more annoying than her attacks. But he's looking at Ayesha, whose eyes are imploring him to say he'll go with her to Tripoli.

"Look, I *do* want to help. It's just I'm pretty junior here and I can't take on something so big, so serious, and just up sticks and bugger off to Libya without asking the firm…"

"We can pay, my family will help," Ayesha says, sounding desperate.

As if on cue, someone's footsteps crunch across the floor above. Jed looks up at the ceiling, and Ayesha and Hannah's eyes follow.

"It's O'Brien, the boss. He likes to pace."

They sit there for a long moment staring upwards like three people in a prayer meeting. Eventually, Jed breaks the silence.

"Look, let me make some inquiries. The Foreign Office must know more than what's being reported in the *Guardian*. But I don't want any money. I couldn't take it anyway, because then you'd actually have to be a client of the firm, and I'd have to do everything by the book or be told I couldn't help you at all. I'll make the calls in my own time, as a friend."

"And then you'll come with me to Libya? I can book the flights, arrange everything... I have a contact in Tripoli who will meet us at the airport."

Jed looks levelly into those mahogany eyes again. He gets why Ayesha wants to go to Tripoli. He would be desperate to find out what happened if he was her. But he can't see how he could be of any more use than Hannah, or what, realistically, it would achieve.

And there's something else holding him back. He feels anxious. His heart is pumping a little faster than usual. His body is telling him something, and he knows what it is but finds it hard to admit to himself, and impossible to admit to Ayesha and Hannah. The truth is that this idea – of going to a place he doesn't understand, where he doesn't know a word of the language, to probe into an unexplained death – scares him. And he's annoyed with Hannah for putting him in this position and making him feel like a coward.

"I don't know. I'll have to think about it. But one step at a time. If I'm going to make some calls, I'll need a few more details. And if I'm doing this as a friend, I don't want to discuss things on the firm's premises. Let's go and get a cup of tea downstairs."

Jed picks up his notebook and pen, without giving Ayesha or Hannah a chance to argue. He wants more time to think about going to Tripoli, and he wonders if there is actually a good chance of getting answers for Ayesha from the Foreign Office. He played this down because O'Brien had taught him never to over-promise, but he has a contact there – an old university friend – and is hopeful he'll be able to help.

They leave O'Brien's to find Chapel Market quiet after the bank holiday. Some teenagers are mooching around enjoying being off school. Stallholders hover ready to pounce if anyone comes along who appears to have money to spend. In the café, the tables are empty apart from three elderly women sitting together who Jed vaguely recognises as fellow regulars.

As Hannah goes to the counter to order, Jed waits for Ayesha, who's standing in front of him scanning the room. She heads for the table furthest away, in a gloomy rear corner, and takes a seat with her back to the wall. Jed sits opposite, opens his notebook and – as he would with a client – starts by asking for Tom's full name and date of birth. Ayesha answers each question in a hushed voice, her eyes looking over his shoulder warily watching as other customers arrive.

By the time Hannah returns with the teas, Jed has filled a page. Tom William Carver was twenty-seven – younger than he expects considering Ayesha looks to be in her thirties – and grew up in Hertfordshire, where his parents still live. He went to a private school that Ayesha thinks is called Haberdashers – Jed knows the one, in Elstree – and then got a degree in English at Cambridge. His father had wanted him to join the long line of other Carver males and go into the army or get a job in the City. But Tom had defied him to take a job as a trainee on the *Watford Observer* and then made matters worse by joining a magazine called *Third World Voice*. Ayesha had met Tom when he spoke at a conference on the Middle East at LSE, which she and Hannah had organised.

"That was early in 1986," Hannah interjects, squeezing Ayesha's hand. "He spoke well. He'd just come back from visiting a Palestinian refugee camp in Jordan."

"That must have thrilled his father."

"I bet it did. I've never met him but, from what Tom and Ayesha have said, he's anti-Arab in general. Apparently, he was in Aden when Britain got kicked out."

Jed puts his pen down and reads through his notes, trying to think what his friend at the Foreign Office might ask him.

"So, you got together not long after that conference, and actually lived together?"

Jed detects a slight nod from Ayesha, but he sees her eyes filling up and turns to Hannah with a plaintiff look, hoping she'll continue the story.

"That's right," she says. "Ayesha lives in Kentish Town. Tom was living at home – in Wheathampstead – but he moved in with her a few weeks after they started dating. This might sound a bit weird but it was linked to the bombing of Libya. A group of us were staying in Aldeburgh for a few days, having a break, and we were walking on the beach, throwing stones into the water, when these US planes came from behind us. The roar made us jump. We didn't think much of it at first – there are so many US bases around Suffolk, you often see fighters flying low, deafening everyone – but these were flying high and in formation. There were more of them than usual. I remember thinking it was odd. And the next morning, driving back to London, we heard the news that the Americans had bombed Tripoli. Kate Adie's reports on the attack were chilling. And it had been launched from Britain. We'd actually seen the planes, and we were all so incensed we went straight to the US embassy to join the protests. Afterwards, Tom threw himself into helping to

organise a big march and didn't have time to go home –
he stayed at Ayesha's… and, well, never moved out. Did
he?"

Ayesha smiles at the memory, but her cheeks are
drenched with tears.

"I had to buy some clothes for him – he had nothing,
only the clothes from our trip, and no clean underpants,"
she says with a hollow laugh.

They both look at Jed, as if expecting him to comment,
but he doesn't know how to react to Ayesha's gallows
humour. And he's eager to get back to the details he might
need for his call to the Foreign Office.

"So, when he left for Tripoli, he was still working for the
magazine, the two of you were living together, and
everything was fine?"

The question comes out clumsily, and Ayesha looks
indignant at the implication that some problem between
them might have a bearing on Tom's death.

"Yes, why wouldn't they be?" she says.

"Just checking, that's all. I don't want any surprises
when I talk to the Foreign Office."

"Yes, things could not have been better. He was due to
meet my parents this weekend. We had the flights
booked."

"To Beirut?"

"Yes. We were going to spend a week with my parents
and then see Lebanon, or at least the bits that aren't
occupied. It's very beautiful, and Tom had never been
there."

Jed grits his teeth. He knows how clinical his questions
must sound, but the café is filling up, it's become noisy and
hard to talk, and he wants to get finished.

"Just a few more things, then. I need your full name and
nationality?"

"Ayesha with a Y and an E and then Khoury – that's K-H-O-U-R-Y. And I'm half Palestinian and half Lebanese."

Jed looks up from his notebook, knowing the important issue is which half.

"Luckily, my Lebanese half came from my father. As an immigration lawyer, you'll probably understand that I'd be stateless otherwise..."

He nods, and they exchange smiles. He's relieved to see a sign that she doesn't hold these questions against him.

"And how did Tom going to Tripoli come about?"

Ayesha looks at Hannah as if she can't remember.

"These opportunities often come up," Hannah says. "There are so many events and delegations you could spend half your life travelling. And some people do. But this one seemed more important than most when we were approached – the peace group at LSE, I mean."

"Who by?"

"A guy from CND who was in touch with the Libyans and trying to get a delegation together from Britain. I can't remember his name."

"Why didn't you both go too?"

Ayesha takes over. "There was so much going on. I was speaking at a teachers' conference on Saturday. Hannah was running a fund-raiser. Most people had commitments. You know how it is, there aren't enough activists. And there was no point in duplicating. So, we discussed it in the group at LSE and decided Tom would be best because he could also write something for his magazine."

"But he wasn't at LSE."

"No, but we'd made him an honorary member. Everybody loved Tom."

Jed puts his pen down and closes the notebook. Hannah is hunched over the table, digging a spoon into a bowl of sugar spotted with tea drops.

Ayesha seems to be mulling something she wants to say. "Gavin went as well, in the end."

Hannah flinches slightly but carries on poking the sugar, her hair hiding most of her face.

"Gavin?"

"He's another guy in our group," Ayesha explains. "At the last minute, he wanted to go."

"But I thought there was no point in duplicating?"

"Someone from another group dropped out at the last minute, and he was really keen to go."

"So, have you spoken to him about Tom?"

Hannah lifts her head and shakes the hair from eyes. Jed has a momentary memory of her doing that when they were together. It usually meant she was about to tell him something he might not want to hear.

"I have," she says, looking sheepish. "I spoke to him last night, on the phone. Jed, we're together, not living together, but seeing each other."

She pauses to let that sink in. Jed is taken aback. He feels a pang of jealousy. He hasn't actually seen Hannah since December. They'd met for a drink just before Christmas and slept together afterwards. They'd both known it was a mistake. But she was the one to say so the next morning. And the only time they'd spoken since was when – a few weeks ago – she'd called to ask after his father, whose life falters from one stroke to another.

She hadn't mentioned Gavin then. Jed probably would have been jealous, but that's the least of it now. Now, he's angry that she's been guilt-tripping him about needing a man to go to Tripoli with Ayesha when, surely, Gavin is the obvious person for the job. He looks at his watch. It's gone eleven. They arrived at his office at nine-thirty.

"Why has it taken you an hour and a half to mention this?"

Hannah shrugs and shifts to a more upright, combative posture.

"It's not a big deal, Jed. He was there, but he doesn't know any more than the other delegates Ayesha spoke to at the airport."

"But why can't he go back to Tripoli with Ayesha? You're asking me to do it, when he's the obvious person. He already knows the lie of the land, literally."

"He can't go. His father's seriously ill, and he's going home tomorrow to help his mother look after him."

Jed falls silent, thinking of his mother struggling to lift his father in and out of a wheelchair in their small house in Golders Green. He often goes round to help, and he empathises with Gavin, but he resents Hannah looking at him now like he'd be selfish not to drop everything and go with Ayesha.

"Okay, well, like I say, I will think about Tripoli, but, in the meantime, I'll call the Foreign Office to see what I can find out." He taps his notebook. "I think I've got everything I need."

As he starts to get up, he notices Ayesha looking forlorn and realises she's been getting the backdraft from his irritation with Hannah. Her hands are clasped together, resting on the table. He reaches forward and squeezes them.

"I will do my best, I promise," he says.

Chapter Three

Hannah is standing on Jed's doorstep. She knows it's the right house. In the pocket of her Parka is the card he sent her with his new address when he moved there just after Christmas. It was formal, the details printed on white card inside a white envelope. No personal note. No invitation to come round. She'd felt hurt at the time. 'So, this is what it's come to,' she'd thought.

She found the house easily. It's in a Georgian terrace on a back street just behind Caledonian Road, only ten minutes' walk from King's Cross. It's not one of the houses that's been done up – the paint is peeling and the brickwork needs pointing – but she can tell from the cars that money is coming into the area. It won't be long before it's worth double whatever Jed paid. She's surprised he's done so well for himself. At university he was hopeless with money. He was always up to his overdraft limit, and his parents couldn't afford to bail him out.

She's been waiting for a while now. She's not sure for how long because she was so preoccupied that morning, still reeling from the news of Tom's death, that she'd left her watch at home. She thinks she's been there half an hour. It must be at least six thirty. The sun is low in the sky, and she's shivered a few times.

She's passed some of the time doing a little weeding in the narrow space between the front window and an overgrown hedge. She can't help herself. It's a habit she picked up at an early age. She and her mother lived just outside Brighton in a small house with a garden that seemed to a six-year-old as big as a football pitch. Not that you could see from one end to the other because it was so overgrown.

When her father left for the last time, Hannah's mother had lost herself – sometimes literally – among the neglected shrubs and out of control fruit bushes. The weeds seemed to come back as fast as her mother cleared and planted, and it was Hannah's job to dig them out as soon as they reappeared. Eventually, her mother was supplementing her salary as teaching assistant by selling fruit, vegetables and jam, which was just as well because they never saw Hannah's father again.

Now Hannah can't see weeds without feeling compelled to pull them out.

She'd decided she had to talk to Jed again after spending the afternoon with Ayesha at her flat in Kentish Town. Ayesha had been beside herself. She couldn't settle. One minute she was crying, the next she was raging about Tom's father and how she has a right to know what was going on. And she was worrying about Jed too, fearing he'll refuse to go to Tripoli with her. "Why should he? He doesn't know me," she kept saying as Hannah tried to reassure her, while herself thinking she might be right.

As Hannah watched Ayesha drink umpteen cups of mint tea, her hand shaking as she took each sip, she'd grown more and more anxious about her ever coming to terms with Tom's death if she didn't go to Tripoli. She'd been through so much. It had taken her three or four years to find an equilibrium of sorts after leaving Beirut. It might help her this time, with this bereavement, if she could at least see where he died and find out what had happened.

She hadn't wanted to leave Ayesha on her own in the flat, but she thought it was more important to see Jed, to use whatever was left of whatever they'd meant to each other to put pressure on him.

She didn't tell Ayesha where she was going because she wasn't optimistic about persuading him. He seemed to have become so set in his ways these days.

At university, he'd been adventurous, sometimes to the point of being reckless. He was not only one of the first to join overseas students in occupying Senate House, he'd volunteered to hang the banner from the balcony in full view of the Vice-Chancellor and the police. When his faculty sent him a warning letter, he gave it to the student newspaper and told them he had no regrets.

After university, he'd gone to central America when it was in turmoil with Jonathan, a friend who could be just as blasé about the risks, and they'd ended up stumbling into Nicaragua just as Reagan started arming the Contras. When he came back, six months and only one letter later, he'd phoned her suggesting they go for a drink and told her a story about gunshots being fired while they were out drinking, somewhere – she couldn't remember where.

Hannah had started her Masters by then and was sharing a house in Belsize Park with three other women on the course. Jed was living at home again with his parents in Golders Green and applying for articled clerk jobs around north London. They'd met for a drink in Hampstead – her choice because it was halfway – and he'd behaved as if they were picking up where they'd left off. When she said she was seeing someone else, he'd acted hurt like she'd dumped him. It wasn't that the man she was dating at the time meant much to her – she just didn't like Jed taking her for granted.

But it wasn't long before she'd relented and, inevitably, they'd started seeing each other so often that Jed was sleeping at her flat more nights than not, and she suggested going down to Brighton for the weekend to see her mother.

'What a fucking mistake that was,' she's thinking now – and not for the first time. As she wrestles with the last of the weeds, she can still picture Jed's face across the dinner table through a clutter of empty wine and lager bottles, looking panic-stricken as her mother rabbited on about them getting a nice little flat together with a spare room so she'd have somewhere to stay when she comes to London.

"Stupid cow. What was she thinking?" she says out loud as the weed comes away with a lump of dark earth. Jed was freaked. He didn't say anything until the next day when he told Hannah he was saving to buy a house, and it was obvious his plans didn't include her. After that, she knew her place – the girl on tap, two stops away on the Tube. Their date before Christmas was the last straw. She felt so shit the next morning, she told herself 'never again'. Gavin, who'd asked her out a few times, was so much more attentive and thoughtful than Jed. She realised she was clinging to something with Jed that was never going to happen, and started seeing Gavin.

Hannah tosses the weed on a small pile she's built up and wipes a tear from her cheek. It's bad enough that Tom's dead without having to grovel to Jed. But she's thought this through. She accepts Gavin's got to put his parents first, and Jed is the only other male she'd trust to go with Ayesha. He's sensible, and he'd be sensitive to the politics. He wouldn't throw his weight around like most Westerners in an Arab country. And maybe his caution about going is a good sign because Ayesha can be impetuous. But what will it take to persuade him? Every line she rehearsed on the way there sounded clumsy and feeble.

And now it's too late – she'll have to rely on instinct – because she can see Jed's familiar mop bouncing above a high hedge further down the street. His face and shoulders come into view. He's hunched, looking down at the pavement. His brow is furrowed like he's deep in thought. She hopes this is a good sign, that he's thinking about going to Libya.

Jed's so preoccupied he doesn't see her until he's turning onto the front path. He pulls up, surprised but not in a good way.

"Hi," she says breezily. "So, this is it then?"

She waves at the house behind her. Jed looks knowingly at the weeds at her feet.

"So, you were just passing, and thought you'd do a spot of weeding."

His tone is abrupt. She feels hurt and looks down at the weeds, making a muted awkward laughing sound. She can feel herself flushing and continues staring at the ground until it passes. She would really like to thump him, but she reminds herself, she's here for Ayesha.

Jed starts rummaging in his trouser pocket and pulls out a key. She stands back to give him room and follows him into the house.

It's small. There's a staircase at the far end of a dark passage and a door to the left that leads into a living room with a beige Berber carpet, a new three-seater navy settee, a tatty wooden table with two hard-backed chairs, two bookcases, a TV on a pine cabinet and what looks like the original fireplace but with an ugly sky blue and chrome gas fire plonked on the hearth.

"Nice place," she says, meaning the house rather than how the living room looks. "You're doing well for yourself."

Jed has gone through another door to a kitchen. He grunts in a surly way in reply to her compliment and puts the kettle on. Hannah stays in the living room browsing his books. She shudders slightly at the memory they trigger of his bedroom in Bristol and turns away to look at the photographs on the mantelpiece.

She's surprised to see he's taken the trouble to have some of them framed. There's one of him and his brother, Rusty, with his parents on a windswept beach somewhere in Britain. They're all fully clothed and look as if they'd rather be somewhere else. There's a picture of him and Jonathan with their backpacks in the market square of a Latin American-looking town, somewhere on their travels. And, in the centre, there's one of her with him after his graduation when she saw him wearing a suit and tie for the first time. His wavy brown hair was long, much longer than now, but it was combed back to show fully his square jaw, wide brow and weathered skin. He'd looked so handsome in smart clothes she wouldn't let him change after his parents had gone.

"It's nice to see I haven't been cropped," she says.

"Cropped?" he replies, bringing two steaming mugs of tea into the room.

"The picture of the two of us after your graduation."

"Why would I do that?"

He sounds defensive. Hannah wishes she hadn't mentioned it. She takes one of the mugs from him. It's just the right colour. They stand facing each other on either side of the fireplace.

"I was just teasing."

"No, you weren't."

"Okay, I wasn't. I suppose I meant, it's not like you to be sentimental. You never took anything all that seriously – not us, anyway."

Jed frowns. "Of course I took you seriously."

"We must have different definitions of serious. That's not how it felt." Hannah sips her tea. "Or maybe my mother scared you off."

Jed smiles at that and Hannah smiles back, though she has no idea any more what Jed's thinking and she's not sure she ever did.

"How is your mum?"

"Still in love with you, but apart from that she has all her faculties."

"I like your mum."

"She likes you. I know she came on a bit strong that time, but she really wanted us to get together."

"We were together."

"No, I mean properly. Not just shagging when you fancied it."

'Shit,' she thinks, 'that sounded whiny and bitter.' She's wanted to say something like that to Jed for a long time, but she hadn't meant to throw the past at him now. 'Forget the photograph – concentrate on Ayesha,' she tells herself. 'You're here to persuade him to help her for God's sake.'

"So, you're with Gavin *properly*, are you?" Jed asks.

Hannah shrugs, knowing anything she says now won't help matters.

"Are you living together?" he continues, his lips twitching like he's suppressing a smirk. "Has he taken you to meet his parents?"

"I've moved to a new place of my own actually." She can hear her voice like it belongs to someone else. It sounds flat and inexpressive. She wants it that way now. It's safer, less likely to provoke him. "And, no, I haven't met his parents yet. They're very elderly and, like I told

31

you, his father's not in the best of health. And, besides, they live in Kent."

Jed smirks, this time not attempting to hide it. "It's not Timbuktu, you know."

Hannah sips her tea again. She needs a pause to get this on track.

"Talking of places in north Africa," she says. "Ayesha's in bits. She's desperate to go to Tripoli to find out what happened. She feels she has to *do* something. Tom's family has shut her out. The Foreign Office won't talk to her because they weren't married. Her only hope is to go there. But I'm no use to her – two women won't be taken seriously. And I'm worried, really worried, she won't ever get over this if she doesn't…"

"I know, you said all that this morning…"

"Okay, sorry, I'm repeating myself. Did you…?"

"Yes, I phoned the Foreign Office."

"And?"

"And, no joy. I tried to speak to a friend, to get an inside line, but he's away on holiday until next week. So they put me through to someone who deals with Libya, and he couldn't have been less helpful. Basically told me it was none of my business."

Jed shakes his head and sits down on one of the hard-backed chairs. Hannah stops herself saying that's exactly what she expected and slumps onto the settee at the end furthest away from Jed. She watches him anxiously. He's staring down at the carpet. After a moment he lets out a long sigh.

"I sympathise, I really do, Hannah, but you shouldn't have put me on the spot like that. It was unfair, just turning up without warning and then expecting me to drop everything and go to Tripoli. Tripoli, I mean, for fuck's sake."

Hannah starts to reply but Jed isn't finished.

"And I still don't get why Gavin can't go. Is his father really so ill that a couple of days away would matter?"

"Apparently, yes," Hannah insists. "He is very frail. He's been having chemo. But it doesn't sound like there's much hope."

"So why did Gavin go to the conference in that case?"

"That's his point. He now feels he shouldn't have gone – he shouldn't have left his mother on her own to cope."

Jed shakes his head again. The room is so quiet Hannah can hear his steady breathing. She wants to tell him he owes her this. But she grips her mug of tea and lets the burning feeling distract her.

"Going to Tripoli just seems so crazy. And so risky. What if Tom was actually murdered? The Libyans – ordinary people, I mean – they've got plenty of reasons to hate Westerners. What if it was revenge, angry relatives of people killed in the air strikes?"

Hannah shrugs. "But you've taken risks before. What about Nicaragua? You and Jonathan got caught in the middle of a civil war."

"But that was an accident. I didn't plan it. And, anyway, we didn't actually see any fighting."

"But you said you heard gunfire."

"Only in Managua, and that was just some crazy drunk people firing into the air." Jed chuckles and shakes his head at the memory. "We panicked, hit the deck. The Nicaraguans we were with were laughing at us. Two Brits scared shitless. But it was only people celebrating the anniversary of the revolution. It was their idea of fun."

Hannah doesn't remember him telling the story like that when he came back. He made a big deal out of being there when the war was on, everyone carrying guns. But she isn't going to argue now.

"Okay, but there's no civil war in Libya, Gaddafi's got an iron grip," she says.

"But not enough of an iron grip to host a conference without one of the delegates ending up dead on a beach."

"Come on, Jed. You know things like that can happen anywhere. Muggings, accidents... You've probably got as much chance of getting killed in New York. Everywhere has its risks. And, besides, it's likely this was just an accident."

Jed gives her a puzzled look. "What are you basing that on?"

"Just something Gavin said when I spoke to him last night." Hannah hesitates. She feels disloyal to Ayesha, but it's too late now. Jed's waiting for her to explain what she means. And she knows he needs to know. "Apparently, Tom was drunk. Gavin says he was in a bad way when he went onto the beach. He'd drunk some of the local spirit, Bokha. It's illegal but someone had some."

"Why didn't you mention this earlier?"

"Because when I told Ayesha, before we came to your office, she had a fit. Tom doesn't drink, at all, and she doesn't believe he would in Libya, because he's very respectful about things like that."

"And what do you think?"

"She's right – it is out of character – but everyone makes mistakes. Maybe he tried it and didn't realise how strong it would be. If you don't drink, it doesn't take much..."

"And so, you think he was so drunk he fell off a cliff or something?"

"I don't know, obviously. But it makes the accident option more likely, I suppose."

"And Gavin hasn't spoken to Ayesha himself?"

"No, he missed her at Heathrow. He was rushing to catch the Tube."

Hannah studies Jed intently as he sits silently gazing at the fireplace. He seems to have shed his grumpiness. He's asking questions, talking like he's interested.

"So, who's this contact Ayesha has?"

Hannah straightens up. She knows Jed wouldn't ask a question like that unless he was seriously considering going.

"He's a faculty dean at the university there. An engineer, I think. And quite influential – good connections, she says."

"But is he reliable? How does she know him?"

"He used to lecture in Beirut, apparently. At the American University. He was a friend of the family or something. I'm not sure. Ask her, she'll tell you. But go steady with her – she's very fragile. Tom was so important to her. When she first came here from Beirut, she was in a really bad way. It was after the Israeli invasion in 1982, and she was in bits, completely traumatised. I was the first real friend she made. Then Tom came along. And he was really good, and gradually she opened up to him and they became so close. And now this – she really can't believe that he's dead. She's still in shock."

Jed nods and leans forward, elbows on his knees, head in his hands, his fingertips pressing into his forehead, making the skin ripple, as if the pressure will force an answer to pop out of his head. Hannah's seen this before. She waits.

"Oh, fuck, okay," Jed says, standing up abruptly. "You win, as always."

Win? She's incredulous. She can't believe he sees it like that, and she has an urge to tell him, until images come to mind of Ayesha looking heartbroken, and she starts to cry, her shoulders heaving with each sob.

She has never cried in front of Jed like this before. He steps hesitantly towards her and puts a hand on her shoulder, squeezing it gently.

After a few moments, her sobbing subsides and she stands up, facing him, close enough to feel his breath on her skin. She avoids his eyes and wipes the tears from her cheeks with the sleeve of her Parka. She feels embarrassed and begins to edge backwards towards the open doorway to the hall.

"Thank you, Jed. I'll tell Ayesha. It will mean a lot to her."

"I'll speak to O'Brien," Jed says in a formal tone. "I'm owed a shedload of leave. It shouldn't be a problem."

Hannah's within touching distance of the front door, but she's reluctant to leave without making a firm arrangement.

"Would you like to speak to Gavin before you go? He'll be at Ayesha's tomorrow morning for a meeting of our peace group at eleven. If you come an hour beforehand, I'll get him to come early."

"And what about the travel arrangements, booking flights and stuff?"

"Don't worry about that. I think, just assume you'll be flying on Thursday. Ayesha will arrange everything. She'll want to go as soon as possible."

Hannah starts to reach for the door handle and then turns back to face Jed.

"What's up?" he asks.

Hannah isn't really sure what's up, beyond a vague feeling that she wants Jed to know that she doesn't take him for granted and that she wouldn't have asked for his help if Ayesha wasn't so important to her.

"I'm sorry I put you on the spot," she says. "It's just that Ayesha's the closest friend I've ever had, and she's been through so much…"

Jed doesn't let her finish. "It's okay, Hannah. Don't worry, I get it."

Hannah smiles, feeling a weight lifting, and leaves hurriedly before she says anything to spoil it.

CHAPTER FOUR

The clock on her bedside table says 05.16. Ayesha's surprised. She was expecting the time to be nearer to six. It feels to her like at least an hour since she last looked, yet barely twenty minutes have passed.

She's been awake at least since 02.54. She knows that because the clock was facing her, and she saw it as soon as she opened her eyes. At 03.27, she turned the clock towards the wall, hoping that would help her get back to sleep. It didn't. It made matters worse because she then had to stretch to turn the clock around whenever she wanted to check the time.

'It's only the second night,' Ayesha tells herself. It's only 34 hours since she heard the words *Tom is dead*. Only five nights before that, she'd been lying there in the warm, woolly pyjamas he'd bought her, and he was beside her, asleep, in a grey T-shirt and white boxer shorts, lying on his back, snoring softly.

She always felt his snoring was in character – steady and gentle. Far from wanting to nudge him, to get him to stop, she found the rhythmic sound and his reassuring presence helped her sleep after the insomnia of her first few years in Britain.

Now, once again, she's a creature of the dead hours of the night when she knows morbid thoughts will eat away at her like invisible parasites. She tries to keep them at bay, but they always overwhelm her. In between checking the time, she's been counting people she's known who have died and trying to remember their faces. She's got to twenty-seven – not counting Tom – and just three of them were from natural causes. That, she feels, is an awful lot of death for a 34-year-old.

As a maths teacher in Beirut, one of the most difficult concepts she'd had to teach was probability. Most of the children in the elementary school where she worked during the day were too young to grasp it. But the Palestinian girls she'd taught at the Shatila refugee camp in the evenings were mostly eleven or twelve, and she'd get them to think about probability using dice, coins and playing cards. At first, she'd met a sea of blank faces. But then the brightest and most confident of them, Samira, stood up and explained what Ayesha was saying by relating it to the chance of being killed by a bomb. After that, they'd all argued passionately over whether it was fifty per cent like tossing a coin or one in six like throwing dice. Everyone thought it was hilarious until one girl silenced them by saying: "A coin's no good because the chances of it happening are more than fifty-fifty."

Ayesha was horrified. The brutal truth of the girl's words was sickening, and she'd felt awful for days afterwards for allowing the ever-present risk of death they faced to be treated so lightly.

The thought of it now makes her cringe. She shakes her head vigorously as if the jerking movement will fling it away.

Closing her eyes, she tries to distract herself by listening to the noises outside of a city coming to life. There's already a constant hum from the traffic on Kentish Town Road and the occasional sound of trains clattering along the London North line. After a while, she thinks it really must be after six and turns the clock around. It's 5.48. She decides to get up, even if it means disturbing her temporary lodger, Simon, who she's allowed to sleep on a mattress in the living room while he looks for a place of his own. He asked just after Christmas, and he's still there.

The flat, occupying the top floor of a palatial Victorian house, has two bedrooms, the one Ayesha uses and another reserved for her elderly great aunt Amirah who now lives most of the time in Paris with her son's family. Aunt Amirah is the family celebrity, a violinist who spent her younger days touring and becoming affluent enough not to think twice about paying Ayesha's tuition fees and giving her a home when she was desperate to leave Beirut in 1983.

Ayesha arrived in London in the middle of January to find a blizzard swirling around the streets. She was used to seeing snow on distant mountaintops, not hitting her horizontally like shrapnel. The temperature had been in the seventies when she left Beirut. In the taxi from Heathrow, Aunt Amirah had — as if wanting to reassure Ayesha that the weather was abnormal — asked the driver if he'd ever seen anything like it. When they reached the flat, she'd insisted on them watching the weather forecast so Ayesha could hear for herself the presenter say it was the coldest spell London had had since 1740.

But, once the snow had gone, Ayesha found herself facing another unexpected problem. On her first attempt at using the Tube, she'd felt herself becoming more and more breathless as the crowded escalator descended into the gloomy rush hour chaos below. At the bottom she'd hurried straight to the upward-moving side and left the station. The next day, she made another attempt and forced herself to board a packed train, only to feel nauseous and faint when the doors closed. She'd jumped off as soon as the train reached Camden Town and walked back to the flat furious with herself, thinking of how she'd once walked the busy streets and used the crowded buses of Beirut without the slightest trouble, and disturbed at how, in the months before she decided to move to London, something seemed to have invaded her body and taken control of her nervous system. It would be months before she could cope with the Tube or be in any crowded confined space.

Hannah had helped. They'd met waiting for their interviews for the same Masters course at LSE and gone for a coffee afterwards. When they were both offered places, they'd celebrated together, and Hannah had soon appointed herself Ayesha's London guide, taking her everywhere, mostly on foot but occasionally using the Tube, starting with the less claustrophobic Circle Line.

On their outings, they would talk about the Middle East, and Hannah would surprise Ayesha with her insight and how much she knew about what had happened in Beirut the previous summer. But Ayesha usually steered the conversation onto other things. She wasn't ready for that. She couldn't imagine ever going back to Beirut.

It was Tom who gave Ayesha the confidence to change her mind. He was eager to meet her parents and see the places where she'd grown up, but he was sensitive enough to let her come to the decision in her own time. That moment came unexpectedly only a few weeks before he went to Tripoli. Ayesha had suddenly said "let's go to see my parents," as they were walking along the canal near the flat. The words just came out. She hadn't consciously made a decision. But, once she'd said it and seen Tom's smile, she was determined to go through with it. She'd phoned home as soon as they got back to the flat. Her mother was so overcome she couldn't speak and had to hand the phone to her father. A week later, Ayesha received a letter from her mother saying how thrilled she was and reeling off all the things she'd already planned.

As she gets out of bed now, the letter is lying next to the clock. She picks it up and reads again about how her sisters were planning a family party and how nice it would be to go to her cousin's winery in the Beqaa Valley, adding 'if the situation is stable'. Her mother had desperately wanted to impress 'the English boy', Ayesha could tell because the winery was actually owned by the husband of a relative so distant that she had never met them. But it's all irrelevant now. The flights are cancelled, and the half-packed suitcase would have to be emptied. She'll only need a smaller one for Tripoli.

Ayesha puts on some slippers and a dressing gown and steps softly into the hall. She notices the door to the living room is ajar and pulls it shut before going into the kitchen. She doesn't want to wake Simon, the flat needs one person who's had some sleep. Sitting down at the large oak breakfast table, she reads again the list she made after Hannah had called to say Jed would go to Tripoli. From experience, she knows she has to keep herself busy.

Phone Eleni is the top item, and she'd done that straight away. Eleni was aunt Amirah's travel agent in her touring days and had become a friend. Ayesha knew she would know the best way to get to Tripoli and wouldn't ask any questions.

"You'll have to go via Charles de Gaulle, and then transfer to Orly," she'd said without needing to check.

When Ayesha added that she wanted two returns leaving on Thursday, there was a moment's hesitation as if Eleni was deciding whether or not to ask why. But all she said was, "leave it to me, darling" and hung up. An hour later, she'd phoned back to say Stavros – her son who'd taken over the business – had fixed everything, and she could collect the tickets from his office at Tufnell Park, any time after nine the next morning. This time, though, she did ask if everything was okay, and Ayesha had wept and told her about Tom and made her promise not to call her aunt. "I will do it myself, after I've phoned my mother," she'd insisted.

Ayesha looks at the list. She will make the family calls this afternoon. The other items are: phone Gibran to tell him their arrival time, delay an appointment with her supervisor to discuss her thesis, give apologies for having to miss a Medical Aid For Palestinians meeting. She picks up a pen and adds one more item: *buy a small suitcase*.

It's getting light now. The dawn sunshine is making the kitchen's net curtains glow. She goes back into her bedroom and puts on a navy tracksuit and some trainers. She's decided she needs some fresh air. She'll walk to Parliament Hill Fields, right to the top, where the previous summer she and Tom had spent hours reading and talking and watching the London skyline change with the weather. She could then walk over to Tufnell Park to pick up the tickets and be back in time to see Jed, Hannah and Gavin at the flat.

The walk took her much longer than expected, though. She'd underestimated the distances, and Stavros didn't help by chatting her up sleazily and coming so close she'd had to push him away. But the main problem had been on Parliament Hill, where the reality of Tom's death struck so painfully that she'd felt like wailing to release the agony of it and had to sit down on a bench to stop herself scaring the early joggers. It took her a long time to gather herself and overcome a strong reluctance to leave. She was certain that spot was where Tom would have wanted his ashes to be scattered, but she knew that would never happen.

By the time Ayesha arrives back at the flat, perspiring from having run the last mile, Hannah is waiting on the landing peering down at her over the bannisters. She's groomed and gleaming and wearing slim-fit jeans and a plunging V-necked navy jumper like she's ready to go out on a date. Ayesha smiles and Hannah waves back with a tweak of her wrist that suggests she's impatient and wants her to hurry. But Ayesha's too tired now to rush up the three flights of stairs.

"What's up?" she says, on finally reaching the landing.

Hannah nods towards the doorway. "Jed and Gavin are here, but Gavin's got to go in ten minutes."

"So, he's not staying for the meeting? You can't be serious. Why?"

"Because of his father. You know, he's very ill. He's having some more treatment today, at short notice apparently."

"But everyone's coming round to talk about what happened, about Tom. They're expecting Gavin to be here. Can't he go later?"

"He says not. I've only just found out myself – we were going to go out for lunch." Hannah waves a hand at what she's wearing to emphasise she's been let down too.

"But it does sound serious," she says in a hushed voice. "Sounds like his father's on his last legs. So, it's good of him to run over here specially, just to meet Jed, but then he's going back to his flat to change, pick up his things and head straight to London Bridge to catch a lunchtime train down to Kent."

Ayesha finds it hard to imagine that Gavin's father is so ill that going an hour later would make any difference, but she tries not to let it show. She follows Hannah into the hallway but can't face going straight into the living room where the others are sitting. She turns into the kitchen, fills a glass with water and drinks it with deep gulps, trying to calm herself. The surges of panic she had when she first arrived in London are coming back. The thought of facing a room full of people is making her anxious. She refills the glass, braces herself, and goes into the living room.

Hannah is now curled up on the settee next to Gavin, who looks relaxed but sweaty in a running vest and shorts, his legs stretched out under the coffee table. Jed is facing them in the only armchair, smartly dressed in a black suit, white shirt and a garish tie, a notebook on his lap. Simon, his blond hair dishevelled, is sitting cross-legged on a double mattress in one corner wearing a tent-like grey sweat shirt that covers his knees.

Ayesha senses everyone is staring at her, but she can't see their faces clearly because of the glare from the sunlight streaming through the vast bay windows behind the settee.

"Anyone want a drink?" she says, suddenly wanting an excuse to leave the room again.

"I made tea, everyone's had some," Simon says, nodding towards the large silver tea pot and bone china cups and saucers scattered across the coffee table.

Ayesha isn't sure where to sit. There's room on the settee next to Gavin and Hannah, but that would be awkward. The only other chairs are the hard-backed ones around a dining table that fills the end of the room behind Jed's armchair. Ayesha opts to sit down next to Simon on the mattress. There's a moment of silence as everyone watches her arranging herself cross-legged like him.

Jed breaks it. "I was just asking Gavin about Tripoli."

45

Ayesha turns to Gavin, who straightens up, nudging Hannah aside. "And?"

"I was saying what a shock it was, Ayesha, when we were told about it yesterday morning. I couldn't believe it. I'm so sorry. You must be devastated."

Ayesha nods. She can't cope with sympathy. She'd fall apart again if she tried to speak. She'd rather let Jed do the talking and listen to what Gavin has to say, hoping it will shed some light on what happened. She looks across at Jed and is relieved to see his business-like pose, a pen poised ready to take notes.

She wasn't sure what to make of him at first. He'd seemed so young and unworldly. But he wasn't like some of the other London men she knows whose self-confidence is inversely proportional to their knowledge. Jed seemed unassuming and sensible, and she's reassured by the questions he'd asked and by him taking his time to make a decision, despite it inflicting an afternoon of emotional agony on her. Now, he's her advocate, and she realises she should let him get on with it.

"Let's start at the beginning," he says. "I'd like a clearer picture of the whole thing."

Gavin wriggles into a position where he's directly looking at Jed and slightly away from Ayesha, who's to his right.

"Okay, so we got there on Wednesday, just in time for a big rally for the anniversary, and then they took us to where we were staying - this resort-type place on the outskirts of Tripoli. The next day was the conference, if you can call it that – it was just some speeches, mainly in Arabic, in a theatre. And then, on the Friday we went to see Gaddafi's bombed-out house, what was left of it. The rest of the time we were treated like tourists. On Saturday, we went to see some Roman ruins along the coast."

"That would be Sabratha," Ayesha says, more pointedly than she intended. "One of three Roman cities... hence, *Tripoli*."

"Yeah, that was it, Sabratha. Massive amphitheatre. Very impressive. And on Sunday, we drove up into the Atlas Mountains for this bizarre picnic – God knows where we were. We were in the coach for about two hours and then we stopped on this grassy hilltop and had a barbecue. The food was great. But it was all a bit surreal – a bunch of Western activists munching kebabs and talking politics in the middle of nowhere in north Africa."

"And Tom was with you?"

"Yeah, yeah, everything was fine. He was there – talking to a Canadian guy, I think – and then we all got back on the coach and made our way down to Tripoli again."

"So, what happened when you got back?"

"It was getting late. Everyone went straight to this bar area where they'd laid on a buffet. More kebabs."

"Including Tom?"

"He was there, yes."

Jed pauses to make a few notes. In a silence that seems painfully long, Ayesha feels her heart pounding as she anticipates the questions moving to the final few hours of Tom's life.

"And they served alcohol?"

"It wasn't a bar as we'd know it. They only served soft drinks and tea. But some people had smuggled alcohol in, no one searched our luggage at the airport. And someone had got their hands on a couple of bottles of the local moonshine, Bokha or whatever it's called."

"And no one stopped you?"

"There weren't many Libyans around, just a few staff, and they didn't seem bothered or surprised."

"So, you were drinking with Tom?"

"No, he was still talking to the Canadians and a few Brits at another table."

"And then he left the bar?"

"That's right."

"At about what time?"

Gavin thinks about that for a moment "Pretty late. I'd say just before midnight. The bar was still busy. I was going for a slash, and he walked past me, heading for the doors out to the beach."

Jed is making more notes, slowly, like he's taking a formal statement. Ayesha holds herself in check. She doesn't know if Hannah's told Jed about Gavin claiming that Tom was drunk. She's waiting to see if Gavin mentions it. Jed lifts his head and seems to be hesitating about his next question.

Finally, he says: "And how did he seem, Tom, when you last saw him?"

Ayesha focuses on Gavin. His torso is vertical, not resting against the back of the settee. His biceps bulge from the running vest he's wearing. He looks nervous. She knows what he's about to say.

"Look, I'm sorry," he says, half turning in Ayesha's direction. "But it looked to me like he'd had a skin-full. He definitely seemed the worse for wear, from the way he staggered past me."

"Did you speak to him?"

Gavin shakes his head.

"And that was it, he went out to the beach, probably to walk it off?" Jed asks.

"I guess so."

"And anything could have happened out there. He could have fallen off a cliff, been mugged, attacked. Were you given any idea, by the Libyans?"

"No, we weren't told anything much. They were in a panic, and they just kept saying they thought it was an accident, but they didn't give any details. Nothing would surprise me. It's a strange place. There's a lot of poverty and bad feeling towards Westerners."

Jed nods and slides his pen into the wire spine of his notebook.

"Is that everything, Jed? Because I've really got to go," Gavin says.

"Of course. Let me know if you think of anything else."

Jed gives his business card to Gavin, who tucks it into the waistband of his shorts and inches forward on the settee ready to stand up.

"I'm sorry about having to miss the meeting," he says, addressing himself to Ayesha. "But my father is in a really bad way, and I can't leave my mother to cope on her own."

Ayesha tries to muster an understanding expression but she's put off by Simon stirring on the mattress next to her. He's been sitting there practically motionless, staring at the floor, as Jed quizzed Gavin, but now he lifts his head and catches everyone by surprise with his blunt tone.

"Can't you wait for the others, Gavin? They'll be here soon."

"No, I really can't," replies Gavin, on his feet now with Hannah by his side.

"But for fuck's sake, Gavin, Tom's dead, and you were there, and people are coming round today expecting to find out what happened."

Hannah pushes Gavin towards the door. "Give him a break, Simon," she says. "He's just told you everything he knows. Now he's got to put his parents first."

Ayesha stands up. She's as frustrated as Simon, but she feels she owes it to Hannah not to make a scene, and she doesn't know enough about Gavin's circumstances to be sure it isn't an emergency. She goes with them into the hall.

"I'm sorry things are so bad with your father, Gavin," she says.

"Thanks Ayesha, I appreciate that."

Hannah opens the door to leave. "I'll be back in five minutes," she tells Ayesha. "I'm only walking to the end of the road with him."

Ayesha gives her a smile and closes the door behind them. Once back in the living room, she pulls a cardboard wallet from the pocket of her tracksuit and hands it to Jed.

"Our flight is at twelve thirty tomorrow – we could meet at Heathrow."

Jed opens the wallet, takes out the long floppy ticket book and flicks through the faintly-typed sheets and smudged carbon copies.

"So, we have to transfer from Charles de Gaulle to Orly?" he says.

"Unfortunately, yes. There's nothing direct from the UK, and going via Paris means we have to change airports, but all the other options – Rome, Athens – would take even longer."

"And what about the visas for Libya, and for you for France."

"Libya is okay – my contact will arrange everything. And I've got one for France already. I have family in Paris and visited them a few months ago. The visa's still valid."

"Fingers crossed then."

Ayesha holds both hands up with fingers crossed. "I always have them crossed when I'm travelling, but it will be good also to have a lawyer by my side. Thank you so much for doing this. I can't tell you how grateful I am."

And she really means it. Since hearing about Tom – 39 hours ago now – she has felt utterly helpless, lost in a kind of void. When relatives and friends have died in Tripoli, she could keep herself busy with practicalities. So far, with Tom, most of those have been denied her. But now, the ticket in Jed's hand makes going to Tripoli tangible, a reality. She can get her passport out of the bedside drawer. She can go out and buy a suitcase. She can pack. And she will go there not only to search for the truth but also to be where Tom's life ended, to imagine him there and to touch the ground on which he took his final steps.

CHAPTER FIVE

Jed's father is on the commode when he lets himself in. For obvious reasons, he knows it before he cranes his neck around the door to what used to be the dining room. His mother is waiting for Charlie to finish, standing by a dishevelled bed that has replaced the table. Jed greets them with a silent nod. His father ignores him. Margaret smiles wearily and waves him away.

Jed goes into the kitchen and puts the kettle on. He's not fazed by the commode scene – he's seen it all before, even played carer a few times – but he knows it's best to leave his mother to it. One person is a necessity, two an audience. And he wouldn't want that. Poor sod.

Charlie's first stroke had come, as they do, out of the blue two years ago when he was doing a pre-season photo-shoot for Spurs. Pat Jennings drove him to the hospital, and Charlie would later joke that it was the best save he'd ever made. He was left with a weak arm, but he could still speak without much slurring and recovered enough to take on a few commissions again. Six months later, though, a massive second stroke has left him so weak on one side he needs a Zimmer frame to get around the house and a wheelchair on the rare occasions he goes anywhere with Margaret.

Jed tries to visit at least once a week. It's a bit of a trek from Islington but he likes going back to Golders Green and the house where he and his younger brother Rusty grew up. He knows too how much his mother relies on him now that Rusty has disappeared across the Atlantic, last heard from in San Antonio working as a chef. "Do they call them chefs when it's a diner?" Margaret had said when she read the card with a picture of the place.

Jed's expecting an inquisition from his mother about why, at short notice, he's visiting a day earlier than previously arranged. That afternoon, he'd told O'Brien he needed to take a couple of days leave and managed to get out of his office with only a gruff comment about making sure Adam – his fellow junior solicitor – had everything covered. O'Brien rarely shows any interest in what people do outside work, but Jed knows his mother won't let a change of plan pass so easily. She'll probe, especially if she suspects he's hiding something.

He goes into the kitchen, puts the kettle on and starts washing up the mugs lined up by the sink.

As he makes two mugs of tea, he decides that, if he can't get away without saying anything about Libya, he will at least keep it simple. It'll be bad enough that he's going to a country blacklisted by Britain with a woman he hardly knows to investigate the death of a man he's never met, without mentioning the rift between Ayesha and Tom's family or Ayesha's refusal to accept that Tom probably died in a drunken accident. Besides, what Gavin said had made sense. Moonshine can blow the mind of a hardened drinker, never mind a teetotaller like Tom.

In other respects, Jed doesn't know what to make of Gavin. After getting used to seeing Hannah fawning over him, he'd found him likeable enough, but he's surprised she would hook up with a man who's so athletic and obviously alpha male when she views running for the bus as an extreme sport. And physically they struck him as an odd couple – Gavin so tall and thick set, Hannah so petite – but that imagery isn't something he wants to dwell on.

"Are you done, Charlie?" Jed hears his mother say.

Dad grunts his assent and growls a few expletives. Jed knows this means she's cleaning him up and manoeuvring him into his wheelchair. She pushes him into the living room and turns the radio on. Then, there are footsteps as she goes back to the commode and carries it into the downstairs toilet.

Margaret looks pale and tired when she finally arrives in the kitchen. She brushes stray grey hairs from her face with the back of her hand and focuses on Jed, who's now sitting at the small breakfast table.

"You look miles away."

Jed laughs – thinking she's closer to the truth than she realises – and nods at the second steaming mug in front of him.

"I've made some tea. How's Dad today?"

"Grumpier than usual, but okay," she replies, washing her hands and sitting down. "There's some cricket on the radio. That helps."

"Of course, that's good news, the season's just starting."

Jed can see the relief in his mother's face at the prospect of months of a sport that can fill time like no other. Charlie's interest in cricket – almost unheard of for an American – started as a professional necessity: snapping pictures of cricketers for Fleet Street was what Margaret called his 'nice little earner' when he first arrived in Britain in the 1950s. She often jokes that it was thanks to Jim Laker taking 19 wickets at Old Trafford in 1956 that they could afford to get married.

After a few tentative sips of her tea, she asks the inevitable questions. "So, why the visit tonight rather than tomorrow? Have you got a date?"

Jed's mother likes to imagine that he leads an exciting social life, and he doesn't see any point in shattering her illusions.

"Sort of, but not of the kind you mean. I'm going away for a few days."

Margaret waits, expecting an explanation, but Jed isn't going to make this easy for her.

"For work?" she asks.

"Not exactly."

"Jed, what's this all about?"

"Nothing – it's confidential, that's all. Anyway, how's your work?"

"You mean the night shift…"

Jed pulls a pained expression to empathise. It isn't like his mother to play martyr. For as long as he can remember, she's taken running a book-keeping business from home in her stride, but lately there's been no time in the day for it and she has to work into the small hours to keep it going.

"That bad?" he says.

"Yes, that bad. He hasn't been doing anything much for himself last week or two. He rarely uses the Zimmer. Even when it was sunny over the weekend, he wouldn't go in the garden. He mostly watches TV or listens to the radio. Sometimes he doesn't get out of bed at all until lunchtime. I'm worried he's heading for another stroke…"

Jed is tempted to say 'it might be for the best – what sort of life is it for either of you?' But his mother starts to well up, and he gives her a hug. Only a few years ago, they'd have these conversations in the kitchen while Charlie was well and out on a job, and she'd talk about all the things they'd do when Charlie retired. None of that's ever mentioned now.

"Couldn't you give up the business?"

"You've got to be joking. It's our only income these days."

"But he must have earned a shedload of money over the years."

"Not really. It was tough when you were little, money was tight."

"But what about all those awards?"

"The glory days?" Margaret smiles and sighs in one movement.

"Those dinners you went to."

"Charlie in his Tux. He did look handsome. They were good years. Everyone wanted to talk to him. But it didn't last long. It's a tough, competitive business. There's always someone younger ready to fill your shoes. And it's demanding, physically, all those hours outdoors in all weathers."

"And all the drinking."

"Now Jed, don't judge him. Everyone drank. It was the culture in journalism. It was a wonder newspapers ever got produced. But at least he's given up the Marlboros and the Martinis now."

Jed stands up and goes into the living room where his father is sitting in his wheelchair, next to a flickering coal-effect gas fire, listening to the cricket on what he still calls the wireless. His right hand is holding an empty wine glass, the index finger caressing the stem. His left hand is resting on his lap, the motionless bent fingers looking like the claw of a dead eagle.

"Who's winning?"

"Essex. They just need to get this nineteen-year-old out, Atherton."

Charlie's voice sounds more like a Texan drawl than the smooth Californian voice that once charmed Jed's school friends. They would rave about it after visits to the house, but Jed never really understood why. He'd grown up with his father's accent. It didn't seem that pronounced or special to him, not like the East European and South African accents of some of the other parents. But this was the seventies, and all things American were cool. He didn't mind milking the kudos of it.

Jed stands next to his father now, listening to the over-excited commentator saying something about Essex beating Cambridge University by 249 runs. He can't muster any interest and wanders over to the bookshelves that fill an alcove to one side of the fireplace. It's almost exactly as it's been for as long as he can remember: some novels, a set of encyclopaedias, Charlie's award plaques. But one shelf is now devoted to neatly-labelled photo-albums.

He slides one of them out. It's filled with black and white images he's never seen before of his father in his younger days – at his parents' home in Mill Valley, with other college kids on the campus at Berkeley, on the pier at Paradise Park.

In one, Charlie is with his brother Jack. They look to be barely in their twenties, and they're on Stinson Beach, both in swimming trunks, skin speckled with water, arms round each other, laughing into the camera. Jack is tanned and athletic, his wild blond hair blowing in the breeze. Charlie is skinny, with the heavily Brylcreemed dark hair Jed remembers from his early childhood, but he looks happier and healthier than Jed's ever seen him.

On the radio, the news reader says: "A Swiss bank account may have been used by Lieutenant Colonel Oliver North to finance arms for Nicaraguan rebels. In Washington, Admiral Poindexter's been given immunity from prosecution by the Senate committee investigating the Iran-Contra affair..."

Charlie leans over and pushes the off button with a good finger. "You watch. That creep Reagan'll wriggle out of this, like he always has."

"Probably." Jed would like to say a lot more, but his mother has warned him not to wind Charlie up about politics. Instead, he shows him the album, open at the page with the photograph of him and Jack.

"I haven't seen this one before. Nice pic of you and uncle Jack. When would that be – just after the war, I'm guessing?"

Charlie squints at it. He has glasses but rarely wears them. "Forty-six, that would be or thereabouts. Jack was a hell of a swimmer."

Jed nods, remembering the time he rescued Rusty from a sinking Lilo on the first and only holiday they could afford to have in California, probably in Charlie's glory days.

"You heard from him lately?"

"Yep, he might…"

"Come over." Margaret arrives from the kitchen, with a wine bottle in one hand and a can of lager for Jed in the other.

"It would be great to see him again, seems like ages."

"It does but he phones quite often these days, every couple of weeks, he's worried about…" Margaret, standing slightly behind Charlie, nods in his direction as she gives Jed his lager and then fills Charlie's empty glass. "He says he'll try to get over here this summer, if he can. But he's busy – doing well, of course. You know what it's like over there, a rat race, no one takes any time off."

"Has he still got that house on Stinson Beach?"

Charlie's head jerks in an involuntary way, the paralysed left side of his face wobbling as he does. Margaret holds a shushing finger to her mouth. Jed guesses what the problem is and lets the subject drop.

He's noticed a stronger-than-average sibling rivalry before. Although Charlie had had his good years, there was no comparison with Jack's career as an architect so successful he could design for himself a house on stilts overlooking the Pacific.

Charlie puts his wine glass down on the table next to his wheelchair, reaches his right hand out for Jed to give him the album and rests it on his lap, slowly turning the pages.

Margaret smiles and throws her head sideways to signal to Jed that they should leave him to it. They retreat to the kitchen. It's become Margaret's refuge. Charlie can't even get through the narrow door, either with his Zimmer frame or in the wheelchair, and it's now the one place in the house where the air isn't tinged with the odours of a sick man.

"The boxes, Jed," Margaret says, sitting down at the breakfast table. "When are you going to get round to it?"

It's a question Jed always dreads. Margaret had first asked him nearly a year earlier, just after Charlie's second stroke, but crawling around a dusty attic to sort out sixty-odd years of memorabilia isn't a prospect that thrills him.

"Sorry, I know. I need to set aside some time to do it. I will get around to it."

"Time's marching on, Jed."

"What's the rush?"

"We'll have paid off the mortgage next year, and I want to put the house on the market. Prices are ridiculous now, so we may as well make the most of it, buy something smaller, a place more suitable for Charlie."

Jed's stunned. It's never occurred to him that this might happen. He was born in the house and still thinks of it as home.

"Wow, I didn't see that coming. Where might this smaller, more suitable place be?"

Margaret looks irritated, bordering angry. "I don't know yet. But I can't go on like this. The house is too big. There's only me using the upstairs, and I just need to clear some stuff out. I can do a lot of it myself – I've sorted quite a few of the photos out, as you've seen – but God knows what Charlie's got in those boxes in the loft. It's mainly stuff from before we were married. I've never looked. He wouldn't let me near it. And now I can't say I'm interested. But I want you to go through it while you can still get some sense out of him. I don't want to be left with it if, you know, something happens." She pauses and purses her lips, keeping her emotions in check. "And the dark room needs clearing out too. He's never going to use that again."

Jed's chastened by her bluntness. It's not out of character, but he's taken aback by the realisation that sorting out the boxes is preparation for the end of his father's life, not some routine chore.

They fall silent, the only sound the rumbling and screeching of trains coming and going at Golders Green station beyond the garden. For a moment, Jed is his much younger self, peering out of his bedroom window to watch the carriages disappearing into the tunnels like rabbits running for cover.

"I'll come over to do the boxes when I get back, definitely, that's a promise." And instantly he realises the words 'get back' are a reminder of his trip.

"So, what is this thing you're going on, Jed, if it's 'not exactly' work?"

"Oh, it's nothing, just a woman I'm helping out."

"In what way? Come on, Jed, what's the mystery. Don't tell me, it's Hannah."

There is more than a little cynicism in her tone, an unspoken 'again' at the end. Jed knows she thinks Hannah has given him the run around too many times.

"It's not Hannah. It's a friend of hers, Ayesha. Her boyfriend died, while he was abroad. It seems to have been an accident. He'd probably had too much to drink. I'm going over there with her to see if we can find out what happened."

"Going over where?"

Jed decides it's time to sit down. Margaret fixes her eyes on him in the way she always did when something had gone wrong at school. He avoids her gaze, but he knows she won't let it go.

"To Tripoli."

Margaret's jaw drops so far Jed gets a good view of her tonsils.

"Tripoli. Libya. For goodness sake, Jed, are you crazy? You're going there to look into the death of this girl's boyfriend. In Tripoli. And it might be an accident, but it might not. What does that mean? And who is this boy, and what was he doing there in the first place?"

Jed is not sure in what order to take the questions or whether to avoid some of them completely. His mother has a very low threshold for risk, especially when it comes to travel, and Libya is so far above that he doubts she'd ever understand.

"He was there for a conference – with hundreds of Westerners – and it looks like he had too much to drink on the last night, and probably went for a swim when he shouldn't have done..."

"And now he's dead. And you're going over there with Hannah's friend to annoy Gaddafi and probably get yourself into trouble. Hannah's put you up to be the fall guy as usual, by the sound of it."

Jed bristles at the idea that he's so easily manipulated. Part of him is still annoyed with Hannah, because of the way she turned up out of the blue and put him on the spot. But he doesn't regret his decision to help Ayesha. The more he's thought about it, the more he's felt good about it, and – when he's thinking rationally – he accepts that Hannah was turning to him out of desperation to help her friend.

"Look, Ayesha needs a lawyer and it has to be a bloke."

"And O'Brien doesn't mind you doing it?"

Jed gives himself a moment to find words that aren't a lie. "He's given me the time off."

"I'm surprised. I would have thought a man with his experience would have stopped you. At best, it sounds like a wild goose chase."

"I think I'm doing the right thing, Mum. What sort of person would I be if I'd refused to help?"

Margaret laughs. "Now you're sounding like your father. In his younger days, he got himself into serious trouble for doing what he thought was the right thing. But doing the right thing for someone else wasn't the right thing for his family. You've got to look after yourself in this world."

Jed is completely baffled by this. He doesn't see his father as someone who puts himself out for other people. In fact, he has hardly any idea what his father is really like because he was so often not around when Jed was growing up. Margaret would always defend him on that point, because she knew that weekends were when a sports photographer made most of their money. But his job meant that he seemed like a shadowy figure who came and went at strange times of the day and night and who, when he was in the house, was either in the dark room or too tired to talk.

"Hey, you two, what does a guy have to do to get a drink around here?"

Charlie's shout from the living room startles them. It's easy to forget he's there, and Jed worries that he might have heard what his mother had said.

They both reach for the wine bottle, Margaret getting there first and taking it into the living room. Jed follows her. He decides it's time to escape. The house is beginning to feel like a sealed box in which two people are slowly asphyxiating.

"I've got to go. I have to pack."

Jed's mother has switched the TV on and is turning Charlie's wheelchair so that he's facing it. Jed gives her a hug and a peck on the cheek.

"I'm only going for two nights. I'll come over on Sunday."

She nods with a grim look as if bracing herself for the next round of nursing.

Jed squeezes his father's shoulder and gives him a farewell wave. As he leaves the room, he turns to see his mother filling his father's glass and wiping his mouth and is filled with sadness that it's come to this.

Chapter Six

The Easter week crowds at Heathrow are noisy and chaotic. The mayhem overwhelms Ayesha as she emerges from the Underground. She puts her bag down to steady herself and opens the raincoat she's wearing to cool down.

People seem to be swirling around her in a milky haze. She often has a feeling of being detached, as if observing life through an unfocused camera lens, but this is much worse than usual. This is nearly as bad as it used to be when she first arrived from Beirut. She's cross with herself because she knows it's partly the after-effects of the sleeping pills Eleni gave her the night before.

Eleni had turned up at Ayesha's flat at just after eight the previous evening with a bottle of wine and two carrier bags of food in plastic containers. She'd been sent by aunt Amirah, who Ayesha had phoned to tell her about Tom that afternoon. Amirah had talked about flying back from Paris to London until Ayesha told her she'd be travelling in the opposite direction.

"I've been told to make sure you have a proper meal," Eleni had said as she bustled in. For a Cypriot that meant enough for a family feast. Simon was thrilled – he kept saying it was the best food he'd ever had – but Ayesha had no appetite and could only nibble at some Moussaka.

Eleni had stayed for two hours, talking incessantly and apologising for Stavros' advances. "It's my fault, he didn't know why you were going to Libya. He's a good boy really."

As she was leaving, after washing up and packing the fridge with half-full containers, she'd hugged Ayesha, grabbed her hand and pressed two pink tablets into her palm. "You must take them both – they'll help you sleep."

Ayesha was dreading the night ahead, but she ignored Eleni's advice at first. It was only after a restless few hours that she'd relented and swallowed them both. But it was a mistake. She nearly slept through the alarm, and now she's late and feeling dizzy – panic welling up inside her – as she tries to focus on faces in the crowd, desperate to pick Jed out.

They haven't arranged a specific meeting place. But, of course, he would go to the Air France check-in area. Ayesha picks her bag up and edges through the groups gathered between her and the nearest noticeboard. Air France has twenty desks. It doesn't say which ones are for Paris, but she finds the right area and walks past the queues until Jed's face suddenly appears, grinning at her over the shoulder of another person.

She was beginning to worry that she wouldn't recognise him. She's hardly thought about him at all, and she couldn't bring his face to mind, but now he's standing in front of her, looking earnest and eager, his brown eyes sparkling warmly and his hair neatly combed. She's pleased to see he's wearing a jacket – dark blue, herring bone – with some plain grey trousers and a white shirt. Smart enough not to insult our hosts, she thinks, as he holds a hand out to shake hers like a tour guide greeting a customer.

"I was beginning to worry, but we're just about okay for time. And most people have checked in, so there isn't much of a queue. Shall I take your bag?"

Ayesha laughs out loud at how British he sounds, but he looks hurt and she regrets it instantly. She takes his hand and smiles.

"That's very kind. But it's okay, thanks."

Ayesha goes through the opening to a roped off area where a handful of passengers are queuing for one counter. She pulls a navy Lebanese passport from the pocket of her raincoat and grips it firmly. At the desk, she takes Jed's British passport from him and discusses seats in fluent French. Ayesha doesn't check the bags in – they are small enough to carry on and it will save precious time in Paris.

Ayesha is still slightly drowsy but she can feel most of her anxiety ebbing away now that she's found Jed and is confident of not missing the flight.

"Your French was impressive," Jed says as they join the queues for security.

Ayesha shrugs. "That's colonialism for you."

Once in the Departure Lounge, the screen has the word 'boarding' flashing next to their flight. They reach the gate with only a few minutes to spare and are among the last to take their seats on the packed plane. Ayesha opts for being next to the window and starts reading a copy of the *International Herald Tribune* she picked up from a rack at the gate. The steward is offering other newspapers. Jed takes the *Guardian* as she passes and watches her unclipping a curtain across the aisle just behind him.

"Is this first class?" he says, turning to Ayesha.

"Yes, courtesy of my aunt, she knows how to travel."

"Your aunt?"

"My aunt Amirah. She lives in Paris now."

"And she paid for this?"

Ayesha looks at him sideways, trying to work out what's on his mind. "Not all Palestinians are poor, you know."

"Of course. Right. It's just I've never travelled first class before. And the flat's hers too?"

Ayesha throws her head back with a laugh. "Did you think it was mine?"

"I must admit, I was puzzled. It seemed a bit posh for students."

"My aunt's done well for herself. She was a classical violinist. One of the best. And she's very generous to me and my many cousins. But especially to me. Hannah calls her the coolest 80-year-old on the planet. She's very nice. You'd like her."

Ayesha senses Jed has more questions. She feels his unease, like a boy on a first date who doesn't really know what to say.

"Anything else you want to know?"

"How did your meeting go?"

Ayesha pauses for a moment. The truth is she can hardly remember it. People were talking about Tom, suggesting ideas for a memorial event, and then looking to her for approval, but she'd been consumed by her own thoughts and kept having to ask people to repeat themselves.

"It was good, the room was packed," she says. "People came who haven't been to a meeting for ages. We discussed a memorial event for Tom, at LSE. Hannah's going to arrange everything. It was originally Simon's job, but Hannah wants to do it because she's in a huff with Simon, she didn't like how he spoke to Gavin."

Ayesha looks at Jed wondering what he feels about Gavin and Hannah. Her impression of him – sincere and thoughtful – is very different to the one she got from

Hannah, but she knows what some relationships can be like – two good people, but together they are like an equation that's impossible to solve.

Jed's earnest expression has returned. "Simon did seem very wound up. And I suppose I didn't help by questioning Gavin like I did. All that aggro can't be much fun for you."

Ayesha's touched by his concern. "The aggro is just how things are between Simon and Gavin – they don't get on. But Simon had a point, and I wanted you to question Gavin and see what he had to say. For me, it was also the first time I'd heard his account of what happened. It's painful, of course, to go over these things but it was good you asked those questions, Jed. I like it that you're thorough."

The plane's engines drown Ayesha's last few words. The thrust as it starts to accelerate seems to press into her back. She peers out of the window and watches the hangars and hotels shrink as they leave the ground and begin to ascend through low, fluffy clouds.

As the plane levels, she returns to reading the paper. Her eyes are drawn to a feature on Libya saying life under Gaddafi has become 'an endurance test for educated, middle-class Libyans'. They are sustained by the hope that they will outlast him or that he will change. They think Libya's defeats in Chad will be 'the last straw'. A nameless 'bureaucrat' is quoted, saying, "Reagan or Gaddafi, one has to go". Ayesha laughs and shows Jed the article.

"Everything is through the prism of what suits America," she says.

His brow furrows. "Do you think there's anything in it?"

"Who knows, I've never been to Libya, but I bet Gaddafi outlasts Reagan. He's got plenty of enemies, but he has followers too. The Libyans I know in London remember how corrupt King Idris was. Even the ones opposed to Gaddafi give him some credit for spending the oil money to improve the country."

"What about this?" Jed has turned the page and is pointing at a report headlined 'PLO chiefs seem to be making up'.

Ayesha pulls the paper onto her lap and reads that 'Yasir Arafat's attempt to unite warring factions of the Palestine Liberation Organization met with some success at a conference in Algiers'.

She had heard the conference was taking place and was hoping that it would, finally, overcome some of the divisions that had beset the PLO since it was driven out of Beirut. But this is better than she had imagined possible. The three most popular Palestinian leaders – Arafat, George Habash and Nayef Hawatmeh – had stood together on the same platform, the report says. She feels a surge of relief. It looks like the scars of 1982 are healing at last.

Ayesha folds the paper up and sits back in her chair. She closes her eyes, hoping for sleep, and is relieved that, for once, the image is a happy one of her uncle, sitting at a table outside his favourite café in Beirut, the sun drenching his face, talking in his usual animated, optimistic way about the future and how liberation would come one day. She wanted always to think of him like that.

When she wakes, she's disorientated. Her dreams had taken her back to a different flight, four years earlier, the one she took from Beirut when she was escaping to London and feeling torn between guilt and relief. But now she sees the Normandy coast below and looks up to find Jed pulling his jacket out of the overhead locker.

"Sorry, did I wake you?" he says. "I wasn't sure where I'd put my passport. I always worry I've lost it at this point in a journey."

Jed produces the passport, closes the locker and gives Ayesha a self-mocking shrug as he sits down.

"A British passport," she says, taking it from him and flicking through the pages. "Hannah tells me your father's American."

"Yes. Came to Britain in the fifties."

"A sports photographer, she said. But don't they have different sports?"

"It doesn't make much difference. My father always says 'an action shot is an action shot regardless of the shape of the ball'."

"So, can you get a US passport too?"

"I have one, but I only use it for getting in and out of the US. When I was a kid, and going to go to the States with my family for the first time, the consulate said that either I had to have a US passport or I had to renounce my citizenship. My father thought dual nationality would come in handy, so I got the passport."

"So, you have two of the most sought-after passports in the world."

"I know, it does seem greedy." Jed taps the passport on his lap. "A lot of my clients have passports that look almost identical to this, but they're practically useless – they don't actually entitle them to live in Britain."

Ayesha smiles at the sheepish look on Jed's face. "Guilt is the new white man's burden, Jed. You just have to suck it up."

Ayesha is still enjoying her own joke as they follow the crowd along the underground walkways at Charles De Gaulle airport. Arriving at the vast passport control hall, she follows the channel for aliens while Jed goes into a queue for EEC citizens. The people ahead of her seem to be mainly American tourists, and she is soon face to face with an immigration official, a middle-aged woman with bleached blond hair and more make up than she needs. Ayesha hands over her navy Lebanese passport, the cover with its embossed cedar tree face up. The woman's face is inscrutable as she opens it, finds the page with a visa and holds it closer to check it. She silently turns to the page with the photograph and holds it up, looking back and forth from the image to Ayesha in a laboured way.

"How long are you staying in France?" the official asks in French.

"Only a few hours. I'm in transit. I have a flight from Orly this afternoon."

"To where?"

"Tripoli."

The woman nods slowly and waves to a male official standing nearby. He comes over. They whisper. She gives him the passport. He gestures to Ayesha to follow him. They walk along a channel that separates the queues from the passport control desks. Ayesha looks over her shoulder to try to see where Jed is, but the crowds are too dense. The official stops at a door, opens it and ushers her into a small, windowless interview room with a table and three chairs. A female official joins them.

"Put your bag on the table, please," she says in a formal, almost robotic voice.

Ayesha feels quite calm. She's done this before, probably in this same room, possibly with these same people. She's not sure. In their uniforms, they all look the same.

Ayesha grits her teeth. She knows what's coming. She chose to wear trousers, expecting to be stopped.

The woman steps forward, pats Ayesha's raincoat down, takes some keys and a purse from the pockets, and puts them on the table. As the male official picks up the purse and browses through it, the woman slides her hands inside the coat and feels under Ayesha's armpits and around her bra before moving to her lower body and pushing two fingers into her crutch.

Straightening up, without the slightest embarrassment, the woman turns to the brand-new suitcase on the table and, without asking, opens it. Ayesha likes to pack with care. Two blouses and a scarf are folded neatly on top. Under them are a T-shirt, a V-necked jumper, a cardigan and a sweat shirt. The bottom layer is a swimming costume, tights, socks and underwear squeezed alongside a toiletry bag, a box of Tampax, some sandals and a notebook. The woman lifts out the top two layers of clothes and lays them on the table. Then she rummages through the items underneath, feels around the sides of the suitcase and takes the notebook out. She flicks through it, sees it's all in English and sets it down on the table.

The man watches solemnly like someone assisting a medical procedure. "You are flying from Orly to Tripoli. May I see the ticket?" he says.

Ayesha hands him the ticket, which she has been holding firmly in her right hand. He flicks through the pages and pauses at the one showing the outbound flight from Orly.

"What's the purpose of your visit to Libya?"

"It's a personal matter."

The man frowns, making clear he wants to know more.

"My boyfriend died in an accident. I'm going there with a lawyer to find out what happened."

"This lawyer, where is he?"

"He's British. He was in the other queue."

The man points at one of the chairs and leaves. Ayesha doesn't sit down. She's taller than either of the officials and standing makes her feel less vulnerable.

The woman nods at the items on the table. "You may pack them again now."

Ayesha looks at her watch. The flight from Orly departs in just over two hours, and the bus there takes 75 minutes. She starts packing her suitcase hurriedly. Growing anxiety about missing the flight displaces the calm she's managed to maintain. Ayesha closes and zips the case.

"My flight's in two hours."

The woman nods, unmoved. They stand there, face to face for several long moments, the official avoiding eye contact. Eventually, the man returns.

"You can go."

Ayesha grabs her suitcase and rushes out to find Jed waiting nearby.

"Are you okay?"

Ayesha waves Jed's question away and points to the sign for taxis.

"Let's go. We'll have to get a taxi now. We can talk on the way to Orly."

Clutching their bags, they run across the vast Arrivals Hall, zigzagging through travellers dragging enormous suitcases and pushing luggage trolleys. The queue at the taxi rank is short and within minutes they are climbing into the back of a Peugeot that's seen better days. As the driver pulls away, they look at each other and laugh.

"It feels like we're on the run," Jed says.

Ayesha nearly says she's felt like that for five years, but she stops herself. She doesn't want to dredge all that up now. The nights are bad enough.

"Did they speak to you?" she says.

"Yes, they wanted to know why we were going to Tripoli. I told them about Tom. I couldn't see any reason not to. What happened to you in there?"

Ayesha shakes her head. "They searched me and went through my suitcase and then they asked me about Tripoli. I told them I was travelling with a lawyer. I assume that's why he went out to find you, to check our stories tallied."

"I'm sorry you had to go through that."

"Why? It's not your fault."

"No, but it's not nice. It happened to me once, in my gap year, when I arrived in LA from Mexico City. The FBI took me into a room and searched me, emptied my rucksack. They wanted to know where I was going, who I was staying with, names, everything."

Ayesha frowns, taken aback. "And you're a citizen. And white. I'm surprised."

"It's happened to my father too. More than once, I think."

The taxi reaches an elevated section of Peripherique, where it crosses the Seine, and they get a panorama of Paris. Ayesha spots Notre Dame peaking above the rooftops, the Eiffel Tower beyond.

"It's such a beautiful city," she says.

But Jed has dosed off, his forehead resting on his suitcase like someone who's had too much to drink on the first flight. The driver gives Ayesha a knowing smile in the mirror. She senses he's going to try some conversation, but she's not in the mood and fixes her eyes on the skyline and her thoughts on Tom and how they talked once of living in Paris.

At Orly, Ayesha nudges Jed and pays the driver with some Francs left over from her last visit. The official check-in deadline has passed, but the woman at the Libyan Arab Airlines desk has a note on her list saying they are government guests, and she accompanies them through the faster channel for security and all the way to the gate.

As they enter the gangway, Ayesha catches Jed's look of dismay at how old the plane looks. "God, it's like something out of a book I used to have a child, *Birth of the Jet Age*."

"They can afford new planes, but there's a US embargo. They can't even buy spare parts. They have to get them from old aircraft to keep the fleet in the sky."

Jed rolls his eyes. "Thanks for putting my mind at rest."

The plane's interior is a far cry from first-class on Air France. The upholstery is faded and panels that were obviously once white are now shades of grey and yellow.

They slump into their seats, and Ayesha is instantly overwhelmed by exhaustion. She is soon sleeping heavily, leaning on Jed, who – having missed the views of Paris from the taxi – is eager to stay awake long enough to spot some landmarks.

When Ayesha wakes, it's dark outside. She looks at Jed, who's reading *The Independent*, and feels a twinge of embarrassment for falling asleep on a man she hardly knows. She smiles sheepishly. He smiles back with a reassuring blink.

"We'll be landing soon," he says.

Ayesha peers out of the window. She can't make much out, apart from a ragged line of surf, sand and rock that separates the continuous dark grey of the Mediterranean from the yellow glow of a city spreading as far as she can see.

As the plane descends, Ayesha grabs Jed's right hand with her left and holds it tight. Her sense of panic isn't to do with flying. She is suddenly overwhelmed by the finality of Tom's death. This is the journey he made only a few days earlier. Tomorrow, she will be on the beach where he died. There is no escaping it now. She can't kid herself that it might not be true any longer. He's dead. Her life has changed abruptly once again.

The undercarriage drops with an alarming thud. She catches a glimpse of a well-lit runway, the plane surging and swaying towards it. Contact with the ground is sudden. With a few bumps and skids, the plane comes juddering to a halt and turns to taxi towards a terminal about the size of a motorway service station.

Ayesha slips her hand from Jed's and feels even more embarrassed than before. She wipes a tear from her cheek. Jed seems to be about to say something when a thick male voice shouts "Ayesha Khoury, Gerald McIntosh". Two uniformed men are pushing past passengers who've already started opening overhead lockers.

Their names are shouted again. Ayesha calls back in Arabic. They stop one row away. The nearest man is short, grey-haired and overweight, the navy cloth of his uniform pulling at its silver buttons. Behind him is a younger man, no taller but taut and lean.

"Please, come," the nearer man says. Ayesha and Jed stand and follow the two men down the aisle. The cabin is silent as everyone waits for them to pass before resuming their chaotic scramble for their belongings. At the exit, a stewardess thanks them in English for flying with Libyan Arab Airlines, completely unfazed by the manner of their departure.

Rattling down the steps, their warm breath is fogging in the cool evening air. Ayesha stops at the bottom, pulls a big embroidered scarf from her bag and wraps it around her head and shoulders.

They scan the arc of vehicles ahead of them – two buses, a fuel tanker, a truck pulling two baggage dollies and an unmarked black Mercedes. Three men in orange overalls are dragging a pipe from the tanker towards the plane. A woman in airline uniform is waiting by the buses. The plane's engines are deafening.

The two men have walked on and are standing by an open rear door of the Mercedes. The younger man is shouting something in Arabic. Ayesha strides off towards them, Jed following and looking anxious.

"What's going on?"

"They want us to hurry."

"I can see that, but where? Who are they?"

"Relax, Jed – my contact has arranged this. They're taking us to the hotel."

Ayesha steers Jed into the back of the car. The two chaperones get in, the older man taking the driver's seat. The younger man introduces himself as Ali and tells Ayesha in Arabic that Saleh Saeed Gibran is waiting for them at the hotel. She relays this to Jed to reassure him everything is as planned.

The road into Tripoli is paved but narrow and cluttered with vehicles of all kinds and vintages. The driver hoots his way through the traffic. A man on a scooter shouts abuse at them in Arabic. As they near the centre, the salty smell of the Mediterranean fills the car.

Ayesha feels a pang of nostalgia for Beirut, not as she left it but as it was when she was growing up. She expected to be emotional about Tom, but seeing Tripoli – even at night – reminds her that she hasn't been in an Arab city for five years.

They pull up outside an elegant, sandstone building overlooking a bay in what appears to be the city centre. A tall grey-haired man – wearing gold-rimmed glasses and an immaculate light brown suit – is waiting for them at the hotel entrance. He steps forward to greet Ayesha with a bow.

"As-salāmu ʿalayki."

"As-salāmu ʿalayka," she replies.

He turns and shakes hands with Jed. "Welcome to Tripoli, Mr McIntosh, and the Al Waddan. I'm Saleh Saeed Gibran, please call me Gibran."

They follow him into the hotel and across a foyer with a grey and blue marble floor and arched galleries above. He pauses to let them take in its faded grandeur.

"This hotel was built when we were an Italian colony. It was a gambling den in the Mussolini era. Then, after the war, it became a fashionable resort for Hollywood stars. Sophia Loren, Sinatra, Marilyn Munro... In those days Tripoli had the biggest American air base outside the United States."

Ayesha nods. "Wheelus."

"It was called Mehalla originally. The British captured it from the Germans in the war and then the Americans took it over and renamed it. They've never forgiven Gaddafi for throwing them out. But, of course, you know all this."

"Ayesha probably does, but not me. I vaguely remember a history lesson about Montgomery defeating Rommel at El Alamein..."

"That's in Egypt, along the coast, and it was undoubtedly the beginning of the end for the Axis forces. The British drove them back into Libya and then took Tripoli a few months later. That was early in 1943. I remember it. I was twelve at the time. There wasn't much fighting. Rommel had retreated, Montgomery's tanks rolled through the streets, and Churchill flew in for the victory parade. We are used to Westerners coming and going."

Gibran laughs and leads them through some double doors into a small meeting room with a circular walnut table and about a dozen chairs. Laid out on the table are bottled drinks, a glass bowl piled high with fruit, plates of sweets, a steaming coffee pot and cups, saucers and glasses.

Ayesha sits next to Jed with Gibran facing them across the table. As they settle, a waiter arrives and offers refreshments with silent gestures, pouring coffee for Gibran and Jed, and a Libyan version of Pepsi for Ayesha.

Gibran waits for him to leave and close the doors. "Good. Welcome again..."

"Thank you for arranging this - I'm very grateful," Ayesha says.

"No, no, it's nothing. I'm so sorry for your loss. It must have been a terrible shock. Please accept my condolences." He pauses, giving Tom's death a moment of silence, and then nods as if signaling to himself to resume. "Since you called me, I have made some inquiries. The police were a little, let's say, economical in what they would tell me, but I spoke to my contacts at the Foreign Ministry. It's difficult, I'm afraid, because you weren't married..."

Ayesha can feel herself tightening. "Why should that matter?"

"It doesn't to me, of course, but the government is under pressure. They have been told by Tom's father you aren't to be allowed to see..."

"He knows I'm here?"

"It seems so, yes. Tom's father arrived yesterday with someone from the British Foreign Office, a man called Chamberlain. When I phoned the ministry this morning, they already knew you were coming."

"How?"

"I don't know. Not from me. That was the first time I had spoken to them."

"So, Ayesha can't see Tom," Jed interjects.

"I'm sorry, it seems so. I did my best to persuade them she should, on humanitarian grounds, but I have no authority in the matter. I am a university professor, not a government official. I know Ayesha's family, and I met Tom at the peace conference, and I want to help, but, to be frank, the Foreign Ministry is worried about the diplomatic consequences of this. The head of protocol is doing everything by the book, as you would say. He is not concerned so much about relations with Britain – they could not be any worse – but about how the British could make trouble for us internationally... if we make a mistake."

Ayesha watches Gibran sipping his coffee. She remembers his visits to her parents' home in Beirut. She'd liked him because he was so intelligent and mild-mannered. But she's now finding him infuriating. She doesn't want a lecture on international relations. She needs a fighter, someone who will kick bureaucratic doors down for her. She looks at Jed to prompt him to continue.

"Have they told you the cause of death?" he says.

"Drowning. He drowned. The police confirmed that when I phoned them. It was the only thing they would tell me."

"And no sign of anything else?"

Gibran shrugs and shakes his head slowly. "It would appear not."

"But they *have* explored the possibility of him being mugged or attacked?"

"I would imagine so. It is something that occurred to me because, as you will understand, some Libyans dislike Westerners, and they don't make any distinction between those who are our friends and those who aren't. But that option seems to have been ruled out."

Ayesha's frustration with him is reaching boiling point. But she also knows he's her only hope, the only possible route she has through this situation. And it's not his fault that the Libyan Foreign Ministry is bowing to pressure from Tom's father. She tries not to sound as annoyed as she feels.

"Did they say anything about alcohol?" she asks.

"It wasn't mentioned, Ayesha. Why would it be?"

"Another delegate said he'd been drinking."

"Alcohol's banned, as you know. I would be surprised if there was any on the premises, but it's possible the delegates brought some in. I will ask if any was found in his blood."

Gibran takes his glasses off and rubs his eyes. Ayesha looks at her watch – it's eleven in London, one in the morning in Tripoli. She is exhausted and feels the bleakness of the dead hour arriving early.

"It's late – we're all tired," she says.

Gibran looks relieved to be offered an opportunity to leave. "I have arranged for the car to come back in the morning at ten. They will take you to the beach, so that you can see for yourself where Tom was found. If I have any news, any information at all, I will leave a message for you at the reception. And you can call me at any time. Ayesha has my home number and this is my work."

He gives Jed a business card, in English on one side and Arabic the other, describing him as Dean of Civil Engineering at the University of Tripoli.

The three of them stand, and Ayesha shakes hands with Gibran. But she senses Jed isn't finished and steps to one side so that the two men are face to face.

"As Ayesha's lawyer, I'd like to request, formally, a meeting with the police, with whoever is actually heading the investigation."

"But they've concluded it was an accident."

"And we'd like to know how they reached that conclusion."

"I'll see what I can do. But, as I say, the authorities are concerned to minimise diplomatic damage, and they won't want to go against the wishes of the family."

"But you said they wanted to do everything by the book. And failing to meet someone who knew the deceased well, who might have some insight into his state of mind, would be negligent. The family might have rights in relation to what happens to Tom's body, but they can't be allowed to interfere in a police investigation. Can they?"

Ayesha's spirits are lifted by Jed's assertive tone – a side of him she hasn't seen – and she nods vigorously to show Gibran that he is speaking for her.

"I'll pass on your request, but I can't make any promises."

Gibran shuffles a few half-steps backwards, looking like the end of the meeting can't, for him, come too soon.

But Jed isn't finished. "Please point out to them how bad it would look if they compromised an investigation under pressure from Britain."

Gibran's demeanor has visibly changed. The avuncular bedside manner has gone. His back is straighter, his expression tighter.

"I am sure you don't mean to make threats, Mr McIntosh. And I would strongly urge you not to..."

"It's not a threat. I'd just be grateful if you would remind the Foreign Ministry that there is already media interest in this, and that they are bound to ask Ayesha if she's happy with how it's been handled. I'm sure they would want her to be able to say 'yes', without hesitation. That's all."

They fall silent for a moment. Ayesha is mindful that Gibran is a family friend, but she doesn't want him to let the authorities think that a room in their best hotel and his soothing tones will be enough to placate her.

He turns to her, saying in Arabic that she can rest assured he will do everything he can to help. And, with a cursory nod to Jed, he leaves.

Ayesha watches him striding across the lobby and shakes her head.

"He's furious," she says, as they leave the room.

"Did I go too far?"

She smiles. "Not at all. I wanted to give him a shake. I was glad you stepped in. On the phone, he gave me the impression he had influence. He said he had good contacts and to leave it to him, he'd get to the bottom of it. But this evening his tone was completely different."

"I think they're using him to fob us off."

At reception, an elderly man gives them their keys and points to the lift. On reaching the third floor, Ayesha checks her key number against the sign.

"I'm this way. Let's meet downstairs for breakfast at nine. And, Jed, again, thank you, so much. I mean it."

She kisses him on the cheek and makes her way along a dimly-lit corridor, sensing he's still watching. Her room is at the far end. As she goes in, she gives him a wave. She's touched to see him standing there like a chaperone waiting to be dismissed, but her thoughts are turning to the room she's about to enter – the emptiness of it matching how she feels, the luxury of a king-sized bed no comfort when she knows how long and lonely the night ahead will be.

CHAPTER SEVEN

Jed finds the silence awkward as he and Ayesha wait outside the hotel for Ali to arrive. She is wearing a black trouser suit with a crimson head scarf and dark glasses. Jed's glad he chose to put his jacket on, rather than anything resembling beachwear. He appreciates that this is a solemn occasion and he understands why the prospect of going to the beach where Tom died is weighing so heavily on Ayesha's mood – why over breakfast she had shunned small talk – but it doesn't lessen his discomfort.

He had been woken abruptly by a ship's horn bellowing at the same time as the nearby Mosques were broadcasting their calls to prayer. For a moment the sounds and his surroundings – the vast room with marble and dark wood and a faint smell of drains – had disorientated him. He'd jumped out of bed and opened the red satin curtains only to be taken aback by the strength of the sun, which was casting sharp shadows across the terrace and oval swimming pool below.

As his eyes adjusted, he'd looked beyond the walls of the hotel to the cranes of Tripoli's harbour dotting the horizon, ships of all sizes rocking gently in their moorings. A cargo vessel – the likely source of his early morning call – was battling slowly towards a gap in the breakwater. He'd stood there watching until it reached the open sea, struck by the feeling that he was witnessing a scene which must have been replayed thousands of times over many centuries.

As they wait for Ali now, Jed is still eager to get his bearings in a city about which he knows almost nothing.

But the shaded backstreet they are in tells him very little. It's lined with four-storey, whitewashed office buildings and busy with traffic negotiating the narrow gap between cars parked chaotically on either side. Peering into the distance, he's surprised to see a statue of a naked woman stroking what looks to him like a deer. The bronze figure seems incongruous in a Muslim country, but any thoughts of asking Ayesha about it are banished by the grim look on her face and the sudden arrival of Ali in the Mercedes that brought them from the airport.

Ali jumps out of the car, looking slick in a black leather jacket. Ayesha greets him in Arabic but ignores his gesture to sit in the back and helps herself instead to the front passenger seat. Jed is happy to sit alone and enjoy the chance to take stock of Tripoli as they negotiate the city's modern central district, finding their way onto a dual carriageway heading along the coast to the west.

After a few minutes, the road narrows to two lanes, and Ali has to slow down behind a pick-up truck weighed down by wooden crates crammed with chickens. Along the roadside, clusters of busy market stalls alternate with rows of cafés and shops. To the right, undulating unpaved lanes lead to whitewashed houses overlooking the Mediterranean. After a few minutes, the truck veers off to the left, giving Jed a better view of the steely-blue sea dotted with shadows where fluffy clouds are blocking the sun.

They reach the edge of the city and turn right through open gates into a resort complex of three and four-storey buildings strung along a stretch of beach. Ali parks the car in one of the many empty spaces in front of what appears to be the main building. Fifty metres away, a solitary police officer is standing next to a gap in the low wall separating the car park from the beach.

Ali opens the driver's window and calls to him in Arabic as Jed and Ayesha climb out of the car. The policeman jerks his head backwards, indicating towards the beach behind him and shouting something in reply.

"This is it, the place where your friend was found," Ali says

Ayesha doesn't need the English version. She is already walking briskly towards the beach, her head slightly bowed. Jed and Ali follow her, a few steps behind.

The beach is flat and narrow. Tiny waves lap gently onto wet sand barely twenty metres away. To the left, just above the high tide mark, there are a dozen waist-high metal poles in a large circle with red plastic ribbon strung between them.

As they pass through the gap in the wall, the guard says something in Arabic. "Not in there," Ali translates for Jed, pointing to the taped-off area. Jed nods and leaves them chatting.

Ayesha has come to a halt overlooking where Tom's body must have lain. The only sound is the rhythmic slushing of the waves and the distant hum of the traffic on the coast road.

Jed does a lap of the poles, avoiding eye contact with Ayesha. He would readily admit to not being an expert, but he'd expected more effort to protect the site of an unexplained death. Without any cover, the sand inside the ribbon is much the same as across the rest of the beach after five days of exposure. And there is nothing to indicate the exact position of Tom's body.

He decides to leave Ayesha to her thoughts and explore a little further along the beach. Following the irregular high-water mark, he bends down a couple of times to scoop up a handful of surf to see how cold the sea is. It's not icy – not in the wintry North Sea sense – but it isn't remotely inviting either.

After a few minutes, Jed turns to look back at Ayesha. She's sitting on the sand next to the ribbon, her head on her knees, hair loose now and hanging down over her legs. He can't tell if she's crying, but he decides to give her more time and walks over to the wall behind the beach and looks along it in both directions. There isn't a lamppost to be seen, and the nearest building is too far away to have offered any light. He wonders if there was much of a moon that night to take the edge off the darkness and makes a mental note to check.

Beyond the wall, the grounds of the resort are bare, an expanse of dusty gravel peppered with potholes and weeds, shaded here and there by neglected palm trees. There is no outdoor furniture, no obvious place where people would gather at night. It is hard to imagine why Tom would have ventured here on his own in the dark for a walk, never mind a swim. The place is desolate in the morning sun, never mind at midnight.

"Why would he even come down here?" Ayesha makes Jed jump. He turns to find her only a few feet away, her eyes bloodshot from crying, her face drained of its usual colour.

Jed hesitates and then decides there's no point in him being here if he isn't honest.

"Ayesha, you have to accept the possibility that he acted out of character because he'd had too much to drink, maybe inadvertently, not realising how strong the local brew is."

Ayesha nods and looks back at the cordoned off area and then out to sea. "Drunk or not though, I can't see him drowning on a beach like this."

"I know. If there was a cliff, or some rocks, I could imagine him tripping and banging his head. That would explain it. But the sand is soft..."

"And the sea looks so calm."

"But the waves could have been bigger that night. We don't know what it was like. In fact, we know next to nothing. Which is why I'm trying to keep an open mind. It could have been an accident, or he could have been mugged. It would be easy for someone to follow him down here and surprise him. No one around. No witnesses. Drown him and make it look like an accident. The Libyan authorities would have a big incentive to cover something like that up. They've got enough problems with Britain without..."

"I know, I know. You're right..."

In his office, Ayesha had bristled at his suggestion that a Libyan could have killed Tom. He understands her reluctance to think the worst of the people Tom came here to show solidarity with, but he's relieved now to be able to talk frankly. Visiting the beach has only multiplied the questions crowding his mind.

"Has anyone told you what he was wearing?"

Ayesha looks surprised. "You mean when they found him? No, they haven't."

"I'm just trying to get all this clear in my head. If he intended to go for a swim, even if he was drunk, he'd probably have taken his shoes and some of his clothes off. But if he didn't, if he came out for some fresh air and tripped and fell into the sea or was attacked by someone, and then drowned, he'd still be fully dressed."

Jed pulls a notebook and a pen from a jacket pocket, rests it on the wall and starts writing some notes, ending with a list headed 'four options' and below: *mugging, revenge attack, freak accident, foolish swim*. All seem plausible. But what is he missing?

"He could swim, couldn't he?" Jed says the words before consciously formulating the thought. He can't imagine why he didn't ask it earlier.

But Ayesha is nodding vigorously. "Yes, of course."

"Was he a good swimmer?"

"I'm not sure, I only saw him swim once, in a small pool at a hotel."

"Okay, well, that's another thing to check." Jed writes 'swimmer?' in his pad and puts it back in his pocket. "Shall we ask if we can see the bar?"

They follow the wall towards Ali and the guard. When Ayesha pauses for a moment at the spot where Tom was found, Jed carries on.

"We'd like to see the bar," he says on reaching the two men.

Ali seems to have anticipated the question and points towards an open door at the back of the main building. Once Ayesha arrives, they leave the guard at his post and walk across the car park to the bar in silence.

As Gavin had said, the room is not really a bar in the British sense. It stretches the length of the beach side of the main building with tall windows overlooking the sea and about twenty tables, each with half a dozen hard-backed chairs. At the far end there's some soft furniture in L shapes with coffee tables, and along the rear wall is a counter with a vast stainless-steel coffee machine and an empty glass rack that could display snacks. Jed could imagine the room packed with young Western activists like a students' union refectory, some groups enjoying illicit alcohol disguised with Coke.

"And this is the door Tom would have used?"

Ayesha's question prompts a nod from Ali confirming that the way they had come in is the quickest way out to the beach and they stand there for a moment staring through the open door as if it held the secret to what had happened that night.

When they arrive back at the hotel, the lobby is bustling with people talking a noisy medley of languages – French speakers who could be from Algeria or Tunisia, Africans mainly using English, and a good number talking in Spanish. They are all wearing name badges bearing a logo with a dove's head popping out of the globe.

Ali spots Jed peering at a man's lapel. "The non-aligned movement."

"Libya does have some friends," Ayesha tells Jed pointedly.

He sees that she's teasing and returns her smile. But they both jump on hearing a crisp English public school voice English say: "And a lot of them not at all desirable."

They turn to see a smirking man leaning against the reception desk. He bows to Ayesha and holds a hand out to Jed.

"Chamberlain – Edward."

The man looks about forty and is short, dark, and dapper. He's wearing a flannel suit with a white shirt and a red and gold tie that Jed instantly recognises – from his father's cricketing connections – as the mark of an MCC member.

Jed shakes his hand in a perfunctory way.

"You must be Miss Khoury and Mr McIntosh. Shall we go somewhere a little quieter?"

Chamberlain gives Ali a dismissive look, but the Libyan stands his ground and speaks in animated Arabic to Ayesha who laughs.

"Ali was explaining to me that Mr Chamberlain is from the Foreign Office. He says he'll go now and see us in the morning."

Jed senses Ayesha isn't saying in English everything that Ali said, but he guesses it's not flattering about Chamberlain.

As Ali leaves, with a parting smirk for Jed's benefit, Chamberlain leads them through the mingling delegates to the room they had used the previous evening. Sitting at the table is a grim-faced man who avoids eye contact, even with Chamberlain.

Jed sees Ayesha bracing herself. He realises instantly that it must be Tom's father. He looks younger than Jed had expected, with neatly trimmed grey hair and a leathery tan. Like the photographs Jed's seen of Tom, the father is lean-faced with high cheek bones and a strong brow. But, whereas Tom wore those features in an earnest way, the father is severe, almost ferocious, as he rises slowly and buttons the navy blazer he's wearing.

"This is Mr Carver, Major Carver," Chamberlain says in a deferential way.

Tom's father is rigid as if on guard duty. Jed feels a surge of protective anger at his icy attitude towards Ayesha, but he reminds himself he's a man who's lost his son in circumstances about as alien to him as they could be.

Jed looks sideways at Ayesha, expecting her to say something, but she is as unyielding as Carver, their loss hanging between them like a deadweight neither wants to attempt to move.

"Please," Chamberlain says, taking command and pointing to the chairs.

He walks around to the other side of the table and sits next to Carver, facing Ayesha and Jed.

"Terrible business. As your Libyan friend said, I'm with the Foreign Office, I'm here on behalf of Her Majesty's Government to ensure Gaddafi plays ball with the Carver family. Major Carver wanted to be with me today to meet you face to face, and to make it clear that – to put it frankly – he doesn't welcome any outside interference."

Ayesha laughs in an anguished way. "I'm an outsider, am I? Tom would love that."

Chamberlain straightens his back. "That's as may be Miss Khoury, but Major Carver is Tom's father and has every right to insist the authorities here deal only with him."

Jed squeezes Ayesha's hand to signal he wants to take over. "And that includes seeing Tom's body?"

Chamberlain looks sideways at Carver, who shakes his head and blows his cheeks out as if he is about to erupt.

"It does indeed. And I must say that the Foreign Office would not welcome *any* activity that could be used by the Libyans to exploit the situation for their own ends – frankly, for propaganda. Tom was misguided in coming here in the first place, and his family are suffering the tragic consequences..."

"Yes, a very heavy price," Carver growls, staring at Ayesha. "My wife and I and all the family are at one in laying responsibility for this at your door. Tom was infatuated with you. You knew it and exploited it for your own political ends." Carver stands, his hands playing with the buttons on his jacket. "I'm never one to shirk responsibility. That's why I came here to tell you myself, face to face, that you should go. Go back to London – or to

Beirut, or wherever you come from, I don't care – but don't meddle. You've done enough damage, just leave us in peace."

Ayesha is on her feet now as well, but Tom's father's striding to the door as she begins to reply.

"So even in death you deny your son his wishes. Shame on you... shame on you."

As Carver slams the door, Ayesha slumps back into her chair, her hands on the table shaking with anger. Jed puts his hand on her shoulder, trying to calm her, but she shakes it off. Across the table, Chamberlain looks smug, satisfied – Jed assumes – that the encounter has gone exactly as he had intended.

"I think Major Carver has made himself clear. I would strongly advise you not to defy him – or me, for that matter. If you choose to stay in Tripoli, you do so at your own risk. You will not have the protection of the Foreign Office. Is that understood?"

Ayesha laughs derisively, throwing her head back in contempt.

"Understood, yes. But do you really think I care about you or your Foreign Office? Do you know how ridiculous you sound? *Great* Britain. You try to bully a bereaved woman like me after you rolled over pathetically for the Americans and helped them bomb innocent civilians. You are pathetic. Shame on all of you."

"Quite so. But, please, save the rhetoric for your student friends. I have better things to do."

Chamberlain starts to push his chair back, then pauses. "And Mr McIntosh, you're a solicitor, I understand. I believe immigration is your normal remit. You are surely somewhat off-piste here, aren't you? I should be careful, if I were you."

"I'm always careful..."

Jed's remark lands on Chamberlain's back as he leaves the room, and he sits there watching him picking a path through the lobby, avoiding eye contact with any of the groups like they might be contaminated.

Jed gives Ayesha some time. Chamberlain's arrogance would not surprise or hurt her, but he imagines she's wounded by Carver's guilt-tripping nastiness. However unfair the blame he dumped on her, she's bound to wish Tom hadn't come to the conference, to want to rewind the clock.

And Jed is himself unsettled by Chamberlain's threat, and wounded by his dig about being outside his normal remit. Ayesha wants to know what happened. He's here to help her. But they are frozen out of the official channels and working with precious few facts – no post mortem results, no details of who found him or how long he'd been dead, and no witnesses apart from Gavin saying he'd left the bar the worse for wear. Jed is acutely aware he has no experience to draw on – he does feel like a novice skier careering off a mountain top.

The hotel lobby is empty by the time they emerge from the meeting. As they walk across to the reception to collect their keys, the only sound is their footsteps on the marble floor.

Ayesha's subdued. Abruptly, she announces she's going for a swim in the hotel pool and heads off, without asking Jed if he wants to join her. He's not sorry – he feels desperate for a break, something to eat and a siesta.

Back upstairs, he phones room service to order the quickest thing on their menu – a Kebab and some flatbread – and watches Ayesha through the window while he waits for it to be delivered.

She's no doggy paddler. Wearing a conservative black costume, cut like the kind men used to wear in Victorian times, she powers through the water like a torpedo. He soon loses count of the lengths and lies down on the bed, still brooding about Chamberlain as he slides slowly into a warm sea where waves are buffeting him against a rock to a steady ringing sound.

As he rolls onto his side, intending to sleep properly, he's jolted by the realisation that the phone on the bedside table is vibrating and actually ringing. He grabs for the receiver so clumsily it falls to the floor and he has to shout 'hello' as he's picking it up.

"Mr McIntosh," a woman says. "It's reception. A lady called Polly Brittan is here. She would like to speak with you."

"Polly who?"

"Shall I give the phone to her, Mr McIntosh?"

"Yes, I suppose you'd better had."

After some jumbled sound effects, a home counties voice says: "So sorry to bother you Mr McIntosh, but I'd like to speak to you about Tom Carver. I'm a journalist. It will only take a couple of minutes."

Jed's silent for a moment, grogginess from the nap is hampering his ability to process anything. He'd much prefer to go back to sleep, but snubbing a journalist could lead to a bad story. Besides, she might know something they don't, and some media coverage might help put pressure on the Foreign Office.

"I'll be down in a minute."

He splashes his face with cold water and buries it in a soft white towel until he's confident his brain is coming to life. On his way out of the room, he discovers the meal he ordered by nearly stepping on it. Kicking the tray to one side, he locks the door.

By the time he arrives at reception, the journalist has made herself comfortable in one of the deep armchairs in the lobby and is flicking through the pages of a notebook. She's jolly-looking with ruddy cheeks, animated blue eyes and a blond bob that bounces with the slightest head movement. As he approaches, she stands up and straightens her navy business suit like she wants to make a good impression.

"Mr McIntosh, thank you so much for coming down."

"What can I do for you?" Jed asks, as they sit.

"I gather you're a friend of Tom Carver's…"

"Not exactly – a friend of a friend."

"Oh right, but you're here with his girlfriend, partner, I understand. I tried to speak to her but she wasn't in her room, but perhaps you can help me?"

"Who's this for?"

"*The Independent*. You know it? We launched last year…"

She pauses as if waiting for confirmation he's heard of the paper, which he has, though only because it's a by-product of bitter union battles at Wapping, covered nightly on the news only a few months earlier.

"Yes, of course, you're the new competition for the *Times*, taking on Murdoch after the pickets failed. So, what do you want to know?"

"Well, let's start with what you've learned so far from coming here."

She opens her notebook eagerly, and Jed gives her a brief and bland account of what little he knows, including their visit to the beach, but leaving out the meeting with Gibran and the threats from Chamberlain and Carver. As she scribbles furiously, he realises that she's even younger than he is and wonders why her bosses would send someone so inexperienced to cover a mysterious British death in the homeland of the hated Gaddafi.

"Poor Ayesha must be devastated," she says, resting her pen for a moment.

"Yes, really upset, of course."

"She must find it doubly upsetting, given the way she's been cold-shouldered by the family."

Jed's instantly alarmed. "Where did you hear that?"

"I've spoken to the father, and a chap from the Foreign Office, Chamberlain. They weren't giving much away. What's your theory about how Tom died?"

"I don't really have one. What's theirs?"

"There's talk of a rogue wave."

"A what?"

"It's a known thing – not that unusual, according to Chamberlain. He says there've been several cases of people – and ships – being caught unawares by them. He also mentioned drink, that Tom had been drinking. It sounds like he was caught by a wave and didn't have his wits about him."

Jed nods and makes a mental note to ask Gibran about Chamberlain's rogue wave theory. If there had been something like that, he imagines the Libyan authorities would have had other reports of it.

"It sounds like you know more than we do."

"You know about the drinking though? I understand there was some bootleg booze knocking around."

Jed hesitates, the nap still dulling his senses.

"Tom didn't drink," he says. "But it's possible he tried some of the Bokha. I've been told by one delegate that he looked a bit the worse for wear when he went out onto the beach."

He regrets the phrase 'the worse for wear' instantly. She has picked up her pen and is scribbling something in shorthand. Jed cringes inwardly at his amateur error. She was fishing, and he's given her a second source for a version of events that Ayesha doesn't believe, and he isn't completely sure about himself.

"Ah right, what's this other delegate's name?" she asks.

"Look, the drinking thing isn't confirmed, the post mortem will determine that, and I can't give you the delegate's name, not without his permission."

"No worries – that's super, really helpful, thanks. I'm going back in the morning, and I have to file something before my flight and, to be honest, just about everyone has given me the run-around. How have you found the Libyans, by the way?"

Jed looks at his watch. He's annoyed with himself and wants this to end without any further mishaps.

"Hospitable," he says. "They arranged the hotel and took us to the beach..."

"They seem to be willing to do just about everything except provide definite information. You do wonder if they're covering something up, that maybe this *is* a suspicious death. Do you think they're hiding something?"

Jed does wonder. He's sceptical about Chamberlain's rogue wave theory and still finds a mugging more plausible. But what he thinks and what he's going to say to her are different matters.

"I honestly don't know," he says, standing up.

"No, well, I suppose if there was a possibility of foul play Chamberlain would know and would be making waves, so to speak, but he was adamant it was accidental."

Penny Brittan is on her feet now too. She picks up a large brown leather handbag and puts her pen and notebook in it.

"Well, thanks, and please say 'Hi' to Ayesha for me," she says, as if they're old friends. "I'll phone something through to the paper now, but I'm hoping we'll get some kind of statement from the Foreign Office in the next few days, and I may need to contact you for a comment. Is there a number I could have?"

"You can try me at the office – O'Brien's in Islington. But don't say what it's about. This isn't work business."

She raises her eyebrows, and he regrets saying something else that begs yet another question, but she doesn't pursue it and turns her attention to ferreting for something in her bag.

"Here you are," she says, handing Jed a business card. "Do please call me if there are any developments."

As Jed watches her cross the marble floor, heels clipping and hair bobbing, he wishes he'd ignored the phone. He has dealt with journalists before – O'Brien encourages it when client cases needed publicity – but always in situations where he has more knowledge than they do, when he knows where the trip wires are. This time, he was floundering.

With his nap scuppered and his self-esteem dented, he decides to go for a walk. Outside, the late afternoon sun is reaching only half the street. People are on the move, on foot and in vehicles of every shape, size and vintage.

He turns and follows the street towards the statue he'd seen earlier and finds he's soon being followed by a posse of young children who, plainly, are fascinated by the rare sight of a white European wandering alone through Tripoli. He's seen some Western tourists but only in large groups, being ferried around in coaches and minibuses or walking with a guide.

The children are friendly but boisterous. They are smartly dressed and carrying satchels on their backs, apparently on their way home from school. One girl starts talking to him in Arabic, appearing to be asking him something. Jed shrugs and rolls his eyes to signal he has no idea what she's talking about. They find this hilarious.

"American?" a second girl asks.

"No, no, British."

"Ah, Margaret Thatcher," a boy shouts, and they all think that's even funnier and chant the name, adding a few words in Arabic that, Jed's certain, wouldn't go down at all well in Downing Street.

Jed stops at the statue and realises, on closer examination, that it must be a relic left by the Italians. The children – having had their fun – wave goodbye, still laughing and shouting something else about Thatcher. He waits as they snake along the street – a slow-moving peloton, feet kicking dust into the air – and is moved by the thought that what he's watching is so universal he could be anywhere.

The cool air of the hotel is refreshing as Jed pushes through the entrance doors. He spots Ayesha sitting in the meeting room they've been using. She's drinking a tall glass of some icy yellow liquid, her hair wilder than ever from the pool water.

"Where did you get to?" she says as he appears in the doorway, her voice sounding like she thought he'd gone AWOL.

"I've been out. I needed some fresh air after being grilled by a journalist."

"A journalist?" Ayesha screws her face up, looking horrified.

"She came here asking for both of us, but you were having a swim, and I thought I may as well find out what

101

she wanted." Jed can hear himself garbling like a guilty kid. "There didn't seem any reason not to. She said she was from *The Independent*. It was fine."

"And she showed you some ID, a press card or something?"

It hadn't even occurred to him to ask. "Well, no, not ID as such, but she did give me this."

Jed pulls Polly Brittan's business card from his pocket and hands it to her.

Ayesha looks at it disdainfully. "It doesn't even say *The Independent*. She's freelance. She could be working for anyone, for Chamberlain maybe."

"Chamberlain?" Jed is beginning to feel she's becoming paranoid. "Why would he send someone to see us masquerading as a journalist?"

"Who knows? Because he wants to know what we've been doing. Because he wants to find out what we've found out…"

"Which is nothing," Jed says tersely, annoyed at her distrust.

"That's not the point. Chamberlain will be keeping an eye on us. He'll want to know if we've discovered anything that could be a problem for him."

"Listen to yourself, Ayesha, you're sounding…"

"Crazy?"

Jed is tempted to say 'deranged', but he sees how grey and tired she looks and stops himself. The journalist had used the words 'doubly upsetting' and sometimes he has to remind himself how raw Ayesha's loss is and how hurtful it must be to be shunned by the very people she should be sharing it with.

"Don't worry," he says. "I didn't tell her anything that she didn't already know."

Ayesha sneers sceptically and raises her voice. "The trouble with you, Jed, is you're too nice. You're..."

"Yep, naïve. But I am certain she was a journalist. Positive."

"Yes, and I bet she even had a notebook, and wrote things down..."

"Well, now you mention it..."

Jed stops himself, knowing the argument is spiralling beyond all reason. And he sees Ayesha's face changing, mutating from grim to a grin that makes her look unhinged. She starts laughing, stands up and walks round the table to him, her eyes becoming watery.

"Oh Jed," she says, throwing both arms around him and burying her head in his shoulder. "Fuck the lot of them. Fuck Chamberlain, fuck the Major, fuck this journalist. Why am I shouting at the only person who's helping me? I'm sorry. Let's get something to eat."

Jed doesn't need any persuading. His last sighting of food was the cold kebab outside his room. He hasn't actually eaten anything since breakfast.

They make their way across the lobby, stop off at the reception desk to check their messages – still no word from Gibran – and then find a table in a quiet corner of the hotel's restaurant overlooking the harbour, where scores of lights on cranes and ships are glowing through the misty evening gloom.

As Jed studies the menu, Ayesha stares through the window as if hynotised by the scene. When the waitress arrives, she orders a salad while Jed decides to give the kebabs another chance.

"God, Tom's father..." Ayesha's shaking her head like a parent despairing at the behaviour of a wayward child.

"Chamberlain's not much better," Jed says.

"No, but that's to be expected. It's his job to keep me on the side-lines – and to check you out like he has – but I thought Tom's father might at least have shown some respect for what his own son would have wanted, whatever he thinks of me. Tom had told him we were going to get married. Stopping me saying goodbye to him. It's... barbaric."

"It is. I'm sorry, Ayesha, I wish I could offer some hope. But I can't see a way round it. If the Libyans aren't prepared to over-ride Carver and Chamberlain, there's not much we can do."

Jed is conscious of how lame his words sound, but he's not sure what else to say. He can't pretend he has any levers to pull. He's never felt as powerless. But he can see it hardly matters because Ayesha isn't really listening.

When their meals arrive, they eat mostly in silence, Jed's occasional comments on the food meeting with a faint smile or nod. By coffee, served thick and sweet in a silver pot, Jed's own thoughts have wandered to Ali. There is something about him – his fluency in English, a confidence bordering arrogance – that doesn't tally with being simply a driver.

Sipping her coffee, Ayesha senses that Jed's fidgeting towards a question. "What is it?"

"Ali, he's not a driver, is he?"

She smiles. "No, of course not. The guy driving when we arrived was, but Ali's a diplomat. Gibran told me on the phone that he'd be our chaperone. I took it for granted you'd realise he was an official."

"To keep an eye on us."

"In a way. I'm sure any country would assign someone to look after foreigners visiting in these circumstances, partly to help them, partly to keep an eye on them. We should be flattered. Ali is quite senior – he was based in New York at the United Nations, and then they sent him to Dublin."

"Dublin?"

"As trade attaché – mainly responsible for cattle imports."

Jed raises his eyebrows nearly an inch above their normal level and looks down at the scraps of kebab left on the plate he's pushed to one side.

"Seriously, I'm not kidding, it's probably where your kebab came from – Libya is Ireland's biggest customer for meat."

Jed takes a sip of his coffee, struggling to picture Ali on a farm in Donegal counting livestock.

"So, Ali is their answer to Chamberlain."

"Exactly. Diplomacy and spying are bedfellows. Chamberlain won't be here just to hold Carver's hand. He's probably doing a few other things on the side – gathering information, making contacts, anything that might be useful to the British state. Ali and Chamberlain are cut from the same cloth, operating in a grey space where there are no rules, but serving different masters and with a big imbalance of power."

"I suppose Chamberlain would argue that his master is Parliament."

Jed says this knowing it will wind Ayesha up, and is amused to see it does.

"He probably would," she says dismissively. "But do you think MPs have any control over – or even *know* – what people like him do?"

"But is it any better to be under Gaddafi's control?"

"If the alternative is to be a colony... of course, why not? Freedom has to start somewhere."

Jed laughs. "Like Khomeini coming to power when the Iranians overthrew the Shah."

"Exactly. The Shah was just an American puppet."

Jed smiles. He's familiar with the argument. He's heard it from Hannah, and he takes it more readily from Ayesha. After all, who's he to decide what's best for people in her shoes, with the limited choices they have? He's long since decided to concentrate on things he actually understands.

CHAPTER EIGHT

Ayesha sips the steaming mint tea she's ordered and leans back with her eyes closed and head tilted upwards to allow the early north African sun to drench her face.

She's waiting for Jed to arrive for breakfast and has chosen a table on the terrace because she wants to savour the views of Tripoli before flying back to London. Resting next to her tea cup is a small piece of paper bearing a message Gibran had left the night before. Tripoli's police chief has agreed to meet them. Finally, they have an opening, a breach in the closed ranks they've been facing.

Restless, just after midnight, she'd gone down to the pool terrace and stretched out on one of the sunbeds, staring up at the clear sky. Watching the stars, trying to make out the patterns, had been so absorbing she'd begun to slide into sleep until a sudden swirl of wind jolted her and brought Tom to mind again. He would have been walking just a few miles along the coast, at almost exactly the same time, five nights earlier. Perhaps an unexpected gust had thrown him off balance. It was possible. But she still found it doubtful.

On her way back to her room, as she stood waiting for the lift, the receptionist had waved and called out to her. Gibran had only just phoned. The message – which she'd written in an odd mix of Arabic and English – said the meeting would be at the hotel at eleven-thirty, after they had been to Gaddafi's former compound – Bab al-Azizia – to see the bomb damage, as she had requested. Ali would pick them up at nine.

Ayesha's relief had been palpable. She was hardly able to speak when the receptionist – a weary-looking middle-aged woman – asked her if everything was okay. With a mumbled 'yes, thanks', she'd hurried to her room, thinking of calling Jed but then deciding to let him sleep. She wanted him to have a clear head for the meeting, in case she had another sleepless night.

She had been finding her hotel room unbearable in a different way to being at home. In the flat, she could hardly move without something triggering a memory of Tom: a comb with his blond hairs threaded through it; finding she had to separate her clothes from his in the laundry basket; the smell of him still lingering on a pillow in their bed; the notes he'd made on a piece of paper tucked inside Edward Said's *Orientalism,* the book he had been absorbed in for weeks.

But, on the first night in Tripoli, it wasn't only Tom who had haunted her room. The feeling of nostalgia for the Beirut of her childhood that she'd had on arriving in Libya had soon given way to the ugliest of memories. It was as if a sluice gate had suddenly opened, drowning her in dark waters.

Ayesha had, over the years, found a way to normalise the story of her Shatila class debating the probability of being bombed. She had gradually come to be able to tell it to friends and at meetings in a detached way, without breaking down. But that was in London, which seemed so remote from what she'd witness. In her room at the Al Waddan, the girls she'd taught in Beirut came marching back. She couldn't stop herself re-living the last time she'd seen them and feeling again the alternating surges of grief and anger that had driven her from her home city.

It was a Wednesday in September. The heat was unrelenting. The scarf Ayesha was wearing to keep the dust out of her hair was soaked with sweat by the time she arrived at Shatila. She'd been delayed at an Israeli checkpoint and was very late.

Samira was waiting outside the classroom, beside herself with excitement. Ayesha had known what it was as soon as she saw her jumping up and down, her plaits bouncing on her shoulders.

"You must come after school to see my baby sister", she'd said.

Ayesha had calmed her down and let her tell the class all about the arrival of her first female sibling. No twist or turn in a long labour was left out, and there wasn't much maths done that afternoon.

After the class, Samira pleaded again with Ayesha to come with her to see the baby. But Ayesha, worried about getting home safely, said she would visit them on another day, very soon. And she'd intended to go two days later until she woke to dreadful rumours of events at the camp. Her instinct was to rush there immediately, to see for herself what had happened, but her mother - frantic that she might lose another family member – begged her not to.

So, she waited. And the stories grew more horrific. Nothing was impossible in Beirut that summer, but she hoped and prayed they were exaggerated.

Eventually, by the Saturday afternoon, she couldn't bear it any longer and set out with a friend to try to get to Shatila. When they reached the camp, the reality was far beyond the worst she'd thought possible. Much of it was rubble. Aid workers and a few reporters were the only living people in the once-bustling streets and alleys. Bodies were everywhere, some still lying where they were killed, others piled up in a pit with insects already invading them

Ayesha was sick into an oil drum and had to sit in the shade of a tree to let the dizziness pass before beginning a frantic search through the devastation for the house of her pupil. When she got there, she found Samira's mother slumped in what was left of the doorway, the baby still on her breast. A single Phalangist bullet had blown a hole through them both.

Samira herself was nowhere to be seen. Ayesha hunted for her for hours, hoping – with ever greater desperation – that she would find her huddled behind a wall or still breathing among the decomposing corpses. Eventually, she'd had to give up. She was warned it was too dangerous to stay into the evening. The killers could return.

Ayesha had been too shocked and distressed to go back to Shatila the next day, or any day after that. She was told later that the bodies of eleven of her girls had been identified. But Samira – the twelfth – was never found. She remained, as far as Ayesha knew, one of many deemed 'missing'.

On that first night in Tripoli, Ayesha had hardly slept at all. Whether her eyes were closed or open, Samira was always there, chastising Ayesha silently for not protecting her.

On the second night, on returning to her room – her morale lifted by the message from Gibran – she'd resolved to make a renewed effort to find out if the refugee agencies had any news of Samira. And, feeling completely exhausted from her grief and insomnia, she'd fallen asleep and not woken until sunrise – and only then because she'd forgotten to close the curtains.

Now, as she pours herself another cup of mint tea, sleep has sharpened her senses and rekindled her normal determination. She's impatient for Jed to arrive for breakfast so that they can talk tactics for the meeting with the police chief before Ali arrives. After looking over her shoulder several times, she's about to go to reception to phone his room when he appears, striding purposefully across the terrace, wearing his jacket and sandy-coloured Dockers with a notebook under his arm.

"Sorry, sorry," he says, looking at his watch as he sits down opposite her.

"It's okay, we have half an hour. Ali will be here at nine to take us to see Gaddafi's compound... and then we have this."

Ayesha pushes Gibran's note across the table. Jed squints, struggling to decipher it.

"Jed, we have a meeting with the police chief. At eleven-thirty. I hope you have all the questions ready in that notebook of yours."

Jed beams in a smug way and shows Ayesha a page listing everything he thinks they need to find out.

"I brain-dumped that lot this morning. That's why I lost track of time."

"You'd better order your breakfast – I'm having pastries," Ayesha says, taking the notebook.

Jed waves in a reserved English way at a waitress who's hovering nearby and orders fried eggs and coffee.

"Spot any omissions?" he asks Ayesha, sounding eager to please.

"I like it, Jed. I might think of one or two more, but that's a good list to work from. The way we should play it is, let's see what the police chief has to say, and then – if he's still not giving much away – we should really grill him, because this is the only chance we'll get. I'll ask some

111

questions to start with, but don't hesitate to jump in. I'm relying on you to make sure we cover everything. I don't want to leave Libya thinking we should have pushed harder."

"Message received," Jed says.

But Ayesha wonders if 'pushing hard' means the same to him as it does to her. She's only known him for five days. She knows he's kind, and she's seen him quiz Gibran, but she finds it difficult to imagine him being a match for the hardened official the police chief is likely to be. And, if he isn't, she'll have to find the strength somehow.

"Have the notebook open where I can see it," she says, handing it back to him.

As their food arrives, so does Ali, looking cheery and asking how are *we* all today, like a guide greeting a party of tourists.

"Has Gibran contacted you?" he says, sitting down.

Ayesha holds the note up. "Yes. You're taking us to Bab al-Azizia now, and then coming back here for the police chief."

"And I have made fresh travel plans. You mentioned the trouble you had in Paris. So, we have arranged for you to fly to Tunis and from there direct to London."

"We?" Jed says.

"The Foreign Ministry."

"Won't that route take just as long?"

"No, it will be much quicker. It eliminates the Paris problems – changing airports, the possibility of being detained. We have already notified the Tunisian authorities. And the plane to take you to Tunis is on standby at the airport, ready to go as soon as you've finished with the police chief."

Ayesha smiles. "It sounds like you're in a hurry to get us out of the country."

Ali shifts in his seat and sips the coffee he's poured for himself. "Please, if you'd rather go via Paris, you still have that option."

"No, no. Tunis is better. We accept your offer – but strictly on the understanding that the meeting with the police chief won't be cut short."

"Of course."

"And that he provides the information we need, the results of the post mortem, the tests and so on."

"Ayesha, as you know, I am with the Foreign Ministry. I am not involved in the police investigation and I can't make promises, but I can assure you no stone is being left unturned. I have been told they have completed their tests, and I am confident Omar Nasser will be able to answer your questions. Shall we go?"

Ali stands up abruptly and starts striding across the terrace, leaving Ayesha and Jed scrambling to catch up.

Outside, Sabran, the older man who had come onto the plane with Ali when they first arrived, is leaning against the Mercedes reading a paper. He straightens up and opens the two nearside doors.

"Sabran will drive us today," Ali says, sliding into the front passenger seat and leaving Ayesha and Jed to climb into the back.

As the car pulls away, Ayesha ties her hair back and covers it with a black scarf she's pulled from her bag. She closes her eyes, trying to separate herself from Ali and Jed and banish all the questions that have been exhausting her for days. She wants to take a moment to reflect, to remember standing with Tom on the beach at Aldeburgh 12 months earlier looking up at the sky and seeing the planes high above them heading for Africa to drop their deadly cargo on the places she's now about to see.

The Mercedes heads inland towards the south of Tripoli. Ayesha winds her window down and feels the backdraft cool her face and send stray wisps of hair dancing across her forehead.

Four and five storey whitewashed apartment buildings are flashing past, their balconies decorated with laundry swaying in a light breeze. After a few minutes, the road widens as they reach an affluent neighbourhood of vine-covered villas surrounded by hedges and palm trees.

"We call this Garden City," Ali says, turning to face Ayesha and Jed. "The Americans bombed this area. The residence of the Japanese ambassador was hit. And the French embassy."

Ayesha looks down one of the side streets. It's cluttered with cars parked irregularly. Two men are unloading breeze blocks from the back of a lorry. A woman in an olive Abaya is pushing a pram, a small boy dancing along behind. The area seems so tranquil, but she doesn't find it difficult to visualise the explosions and the panic they created. She knows war. She knows what it's like to be breathless with fear and blown off your feet by the force of a blast. She knows that, while flats and houses can be rebuilt in months, the human destruction – of lives, limbs and nerves – is impossible to restore.

"Where were you at the time?" Jed asks Ali.

"Not far from here. In bed. It was two in the morning, did you know that? My wife, my children, me – everyone was sleeping. We were woken up by the noise. We live about one hundred metres from the Swiss embassy. That was hit too. Our apartment shook. It was like an earthquake. Everyone was going crazy. Some people went out onto the streets. We took our children downstairs, into the cellar, until it was over."

Ayesha looks at him afresh. She's seen him only as a diplomat, a government functionary, until now. "How old are they?"

"They're five and eight now, two boys. They were terrified."

Ali grimaces and turns back to face the front. The car falls silent. They pass an elegant old hospital building, with neatly-kept grass on either side of the path to the main entrance. A few blocks later, they reach a roundabout and turn left onto a road Ayesha recognises as the one they'd taken from the airport.

"Bab al-Azizia is here," Ali says, waving to the right.

The car pulls up alongside a high concrete wall. Sabran jumps out and opens Ayesha's door, giving her a respectful nod. He tells Ali in Arabic that he'll wait by the car. Jed and Ayesha are already walking towards the open gates leading into the compound. Waiting for them is a young woman wearing a brown, shin-length skirt and black sweat-shirt. Her dark brown hair is pulled back from her face into a plait that curls around her neck and hangs down in front of her like a scarf. She's patting her hair into place with one hand and fiddling nervously with the strap of a black shoulder bag with the other.

Ali speaks to her in Arabic, thanking her for coming at short notice, and introducing Ayesha, who greets her warmly with a kiss on each cheek. The woman turns to Jed and gives him a demure smile. Ayesha can tell he's instantly charmed.

"Welcome, my name is Rashida, I work as an interpreter for the Department of Tourism and I also study medicine at the university."

She gestures for them to follow her into a walled courtyard where chairs for a hundred or more people are set out in rows facing away from them. To their right is the bombed-out structure of a large house, the exposed interior strewn with broken furniture and rubble. Ahead of them, beyond the chairs, is a twenty-foot high steel sculpture, an arm reaching sky-ward with the fist clenched around what looks like a missile.

They walk over to the building and stop where they can see a staircase in what must have been the entrance hall. Rashida turns to face them.

"This was the home of the Leader of the Libyan Revolution, Colonel Muammar Gaddafi, and his family," she says solemnly, her English even better than Ali's. "There was also a Bedouin tent in the compound, which the Leader used as his headquarters. It was destroyed completely, but the Leader was not here at the time. Only his family were present that night. His wife and two youngest sons were injured. His adopted baby daughter, Hana, was killed."

"Can we go inside?" Ayesha asks, echoing Rashida's tone.

"Yes, of course. But you must follow the marked route, for safety."

Ayesha and Jed step over the threshold, leaving Ali talking with Rashida.

They walk silently into what must have been the dining room. The metal frames of the table and chairs are twisted in the rubble. A painting of a desert scene lies on the floor. Pipes and cables dangle from the ceiling like the innards of a dead animal.

Ayesha nods towards the stairs, and they climb them cautiously. In the upstairs rooms, rubble has crushed the beds and smashed the mirrors. A framed photograph of two children – a boy and a girl – is hanging at an angle from a pillar.

Ayesha can feel herself welling up. Jed touches her arm sympathetically, but she turns away, wanting to hide her tears and have a moment alone. She leaves him standing near the top of the stairs and goes into one of the bedrooms, stepping over some lumps of concrete. There are charred and dusty remnants of clothing and bedding and a dressing table that's barely scratched, but the bed itself is mostly under collapsed concrete. She goes into another bedroom through a blown-out gap in the wall between them and stands shaking her head at the sight of some children's toys.

Ayesha imagines Tom seeing all this and making notes for a passionate piece about how America dropped bombs at night and without warning on a densely populated city, killing dozens of civilians while trying to assassinate the leader of another country.

"Let's go," she says, rejoining Jed on the rubble-strewn landing.

"You okay?" he asks.

She's too sad to speak, but she puts her arm through his and they walk down the stairs together.

Rashida is waiting for them outside, standing alone next to the sculpture. She indicates with a comical imitation of someone smoking that Ali has disappeared for a cigarette.

"Please feel free to see the other exhibits," she says, pointing towards some metal objects on a row of tables on the far side of the compound.

Ayesha and Jed walk over to look more closely. The signs are in Arabic but the exhibits don't need any explanation. Mangled military hardware is spread out along the tables like some strange archaeological discovery: a severed bomb casing the size of a coffin, detonators laid out like large dolls, a missile wing as menacing as a shark's fin. On the table at the end, lying flat, is a thick piece of steel onto which a cylindrical component has been screwed. It's barely ten centimetres in diameter, but the flat surface has enough space for the details of the object's purpose and origins.

TRANSMITTER
ANGLE OF ATTACK
TYPE OR50 SC2
MADE IN U.S.A.
TELEDYNE, INC.
AUTOMATED SPECIALTIES DIV,
CHARLOTTESVILLE, VA

"So, this must be what guided the missile," Ayesha says. "I wonder if the people of Charlottesville know their city's name is on the murder weapon."

Jed laughs. "They're probably glad of a job and believe Gaddafi had it coming. A lot of Americans think foreign policy is like a movie where it's okay for the cop to break the rules to get the bad guy."

"But they didn't even get the bad guy – Gaddafi's still alive."

Ali arrives, catching Ayesha's comment. "Would it have been okay if they had?"

"No, of course not. It would be chaos if every country thought they could kill the foreign leaders they don't like. This is like Nicaragua bombing the White House because Reagan's arming the Contras. Where does it end if states act like terrorists?"

Ali manages to nod and shrug at the same time, and Ayesha suspects her question – rhetorical though it is – is sensitive for him. She doubts he'd want to get into the subject of Reagan claiming the attack was retaliation for the Berlin nightclub bombing that Libya denies being involved in. And she doesn't see much point in going there either, because he'd be too junior to know the truth, and – for her – it still wouldn't justify what the Americans did.

Ayesha doesn't see these issues as academic. Like Ali, her life has been shaped by them. And, normally, witnessing such things again, she would be angry and roused to action. But today – aching with the loss of Tom – she feels too sad and weary even to continue the discussion.

Rashida is fumbling in her bag, awkwardly trying to find something. She pulls a photograph out and hands it to Ayesha.

"Is this your Tom?" she asks, tentatively.

Ayesha takes the photograph and, shaking slightly, holds it with both hands. As the image comes into focus, she sees that it is Tom. He's standing in the compound, only a few feet from where they are, Rashida to his left and a man and a woman to his right, all four of them smiling at the camera.

Ayesha straightens her back and looks into Rashida's eyes, in a distant way, not really seeing her. Her lips are pursed tightly. A tear traces a path across her right cheek. She wipes it away with the back of a hand.

"It is. Yes, it is. Of him, here." She looks around, trying to work out the exact spot.

Rashida steps forward and touches Ayesha's arm. "I'm so sorry. When Ali told me yesterday that you were coming here, I remembered Tom. I was one of the interpreters, and my colleague took that picture."

"Who are the other two?" Jed asks.

"The woman is another British delegate, and the man's from Canada, but I can't remember their names. It was

119

Tom who stood out because he did so much of the talking. So many questions. He made me dizzy."

That makes Ayesha smile, her moist eyes glistening. "He made me dizzy sometimes too. Could I have a copy of this?"

Rashida nods vigorously. "Yes, of course. You must keep it. Please."

"But I'll get a copy made, when I get back, and send it to you."

Ali has started walking towards the gates to the compound. He holds his arm up and taps his watch. "We have to go."

They walk briskly across the courtyard and find Sabran leaning against the car drawing on a Marlboro like it's the last cigarette in Tripoli.

Ayesha embraces Rashida and speaks to her softly in Arabic, asking her to write and saying Gibran or Ali can give her the address.

In the car, travelling back to the hotel, Ayesha feels relieved to have found a person who met Tom here and who – if only in a small way – shares her grief. That thought is comforting as she nods politely to Ali's intermittent commentary – pointing out a Roman arch, the now-repaired Swiss embassy, another hospital.

Near the hotel, market traders are packing up their stalls, and men are gathering in shaded cafes. After what they've been seeing, Ayesha is once again struck by the normality of a city carrying on, the scars of the past mostly hidden.

When they arrive at the hotel, Gibran and the police chief are in the usual meeting room, huddled together and talking intensely in hushed tones. Ali waits, and then, when there's a pause, introduces Ayesha and Jed to him with a deference that suggests – to Ayesha's relief – they are meeting someone important who can probably answer their questions, should he want to.

Omar Nasser is an over-weight middle-aged man wearing – like Ali – a black leather jacket. His hair looks like it's been coloured to match, and his dark brown eyes appear small in the hollows created by his fleshy cheeks.

He greets them warmly – shaking Jed's hand and bowing to Ayesha with a few words of sympathy in Arabic – and gestures for everyone to sit down.

Facing Ayesha and Jed across the table, and flanked by Gibran and Ali, the police chief begins tentatively with a few welcoming words. His English isn't fluent and polished like Ali's or Gibran's, but it's good enough for him not to rely on them for translation, and he's come prepared with notes typed in English, which are placed precisely in front of him.

"Please understand that this is an unofficial meeting," he continues, looking from Ayesha to Jed to confirm from their nods that they do understand this. "I would normally only meet family and officials of the country concerned in a case like this. And I have to respect the wishes of the family. That is why we cannot allow you to visit the mortuary, but I think Gibran has explained that to you. Nevertheless, I understand that you were Mr Carver's fiancé and, of course, I will try to answer your questions."

Having waited a week for this moment, Ayesha finds herself not knowing where to start. She looks down at the notebook Jed has opened in front of them, but the long list of questions is just a blur.

"You asked about alcohol," Gibran interjects.

"Yes," says Omar. "I can tell you the post mortem found only a small amount of alcohol. As you know, alcohol is banned here. But it is not unusual for some tourists to bring it in or to buy it illegally. We have been told there was some drinking going on at the hotel. But your friend had not had much."

Ayesha looks at Jed as if to say 'I told you so'. "That doesn't surprise me," she says.

"But how much is not much?" Jed asks. "Not enough to explain why he drowned?"

Omar checks his notes. "Just under thirty milligrams."

Jed writes the number down. "Okay, so that's the alcohol. I'd like to confirm the basics. Could you run through exactly what happened on Monday morning - what time he was found, who by, how long he'd been dead?"

"The police were called at 7.32am by a member of the hotel staff. He said he had gone onto the beach to smoke a cigarette and saw Mr Carver's body. Our forensics team estimated he had been dead for some time – probably six or seven hours."

"And what was the weather like?"

Omar looks momentarily thrown. "When I arrived, it was sunny."

"But how had it been overnight?"

"It can be cold at night here at this time of year, and windy sometimes. That night was not very bad – there was no storm. But he might have been unlucky. The wind can suddenly be strong. It can come unexpectedly, and disturb the sea. A big wave could have knocked him over."

"A rogue wave?"

Omar whispers something in Ali's ear. Ayesha can't quite hear what he says but thinks he is confused by the word 'rogue'.

"We are not sure what you mean," Ali says. "But the sea can do strange things, and there is no doubt that he drowned."

"But you didn't have any reports of anything unusual happening along the coast, any small boats in distress, for example?"

"That would not be reported to me," Omar replies. "That would be dealt with by the Libyan coast guard – but I am not aware of anything out of the ordinary."

"And what about the moon? Was there a moon that night?"

Omar frowns and shifts in his seat. "I'm not sure."

"What difference would that make?" Ali says.

Ayesha is beginning to feel exasperated. She straightens up, readying herself to say something, but Jed puts a restraining hand on her arm.

"How dark it was is clearly important," he says in a bewildered tone. "He wasn't drunk. The weather wasn't especially bad. But maybe it was so dark he lost his bearings, somehow. Otherwise, how did he drown? It doesn't make sense."

"These matters often do not make sense," Omar replies. "Why was he on the beach in the dark? Why did he go into the sea? What was his state of mind? Perhaps he didn't care about the risks..."

"His *state of mind* – what do you mean?" Ayesha speaks in Arabic, her fury at what Omar seems to be implying giving her no time to think in English.

Omar holds both his hands up and replies apologetically in Arabic, stressing he was only speculating and hasn't jumped to conclusions.

"What are you saying?" Jed asks Omar.

"I was merely clarifying that we are treating it as a tragic accident, because there is little evidence of it being anything else. But I will check whether there was a moon."

Ayesha feels like telling him he's useless, that he hasn't conducted a proper investigation, but she sees that Jed has ticked off fewer than half the questions on his list and decides to let him do the talking.

"But you seem to have decided it was an accident before fully considering other possibilities," Jed says. "Who did you question? Did you question any of the other delegates?"

"Yes, of course." Omar pulls a sheet of paper from the bottom of his small pile. "We spoke to the British delegation leader, Alison Parker."

"Just her?"

"And a man called Gavin Mirren."

"Gavin?" Ayesha gasps.

"And what did they say?" Jed asks.

"They knew only that he left the bar and went onto the beach, late in the evening. Mr Mirren saw him leave."

"And that's it. They didn't say why, or mention anything about Tom having had a lot to drink?"

"No."

Ayesha looks incredulously at Jed. She's baffled by what she's hearing. Why didn't Gavin mention he'd been interviewed? She could understand him being wrong about the alcohol – Tom wasn't a drinker – the small amount of Bokha he'd had might have gone to his head and made him seem drunk. But why did he tell them that Tom was the worse for wear and not say that to the police?

Jed presses on. "And you've completely ruled out the possibility that he was attacked?"

"There is no evidence of that."

"No injuries, no signs of a fight?"

"Only a few scratches and bruises. It was as you would expect. His body had been in the sea, and there are rocks and stones on the seabed in that area. Scratches and bruises are normal when a body has been in the sea."

"And he was fully clothed?"

Omar nods.

"What was he wearing?"

"Jeans, a T-shirt, and socks."

"But not shoes? To be clear."

"Some running shoes were a few feet from where he was found."

"And his clothes were wet and torn, obviously."

Omar nods again, and the room falls silent as everyone watches Jed ticking several questions off his list and writing some notes.

He puts his pen down. "Doesn't it strike you as odd, that he would go to the trouble of taking his trainers off but not anything else, not even his socks?"

"I have seen stranger things, believe me, Mr McIntosh." Omar picks up his papers, shuffles them into a neat rectangle and pushes his chair back, his patience obviously running low. "Have you finished with your questions?"

"Just one more thing, did you find his wallet or any money on him?"

"Yes, there was a wallet near the body. There was no money in it – just two credit cards – but there were some coins in his pocket, some British and some Libyan."

"So, there could have been some notes taken from it. We don't know."

"True, the wallet on its own is inconclusive," says Ali, coming to the police chief's aid. "But – alongside the lack of evidence of a fight – the mugging theory lacks credibility."

"But the scratches and bruises could have come from a struggle," Jed replies. "You wouldn't expect much evidence of a fight because he wasn't a big guy and – in the dark, taken by surprise – he'd be fairly easy to over-power, especially if there were two of them."

"But why kill him?"

"Maybe because he was a Westerner..."

Ali smiles. "This is not a Hollywood movie, Jed. We have to stick to the facts... Is there anything else on your list?"

Ayesha leans across Jed and runs a finger down the list to see if there's anything he's overlooked.

"That's everything on the list," she says. "But I was wondering when you will fly Tom home?"

This is Ali's territory. "We have agreed with Mr Chamberlain that he will be flown back to London – RAF Northolt – from Okba ibn Nafi this evening."

"By the British?"

"Yes, of course, it's normal."

Ayesha laughs grimly. For her, the way Tom is being transported home is anything but normal. He had come to Tripoli to protest against an attack that Britain had assisted, and now the Libyans are allowing the RAF to use the airfield the Americans had actually bombed to take his body back to Britain. She finds this hard to take, but she wonders if Tom would have found it amusing. He liked irony.

"If there's nothing else..." Gibran stands up and looks at his watch. "You need to be in Tunis by four for your flight to Heathrow. The car's outside. I will come with you to the airport."

Ali and Omar are also on their feet, and Jed and Ayesha join them at the doorway for a farewell dance of handshakes and bows. Ayesha makes an effort to be gracious. She knows Tom's death has put the Libyans in a difficult position. But the meeting has been disappointing. Her excitement after receiving the message from Gibran had proved misplaced. She has a few more scraps of information, but none of it makes her feel any nearer to understanding why Tom went on the beach, or what really happened there.

CHAPTER NINE

"Omar was only going through the motions."

Ayesha's verdict on the police chief jolts Jed from staring out of the window at the French countryside below. He was daydreaming about what he might do with the rest of the weekend, feeling relieved to be nearly home, having done his duty, even if the results were inconclusive.

They had been sitting largely in silence since boarding the plane in Tunis. On settling into her seat, Ayesha had pulled a research paper from her bag and proceeded to plough through its dense data. Jed had asked a few questions, enough to establish that it was about the industrialisation of Sub-Saharan Africa and that it was a subject on which he had nothing useful to say. But it was obvious she was in no mood for conversation anyway. And, glad of a break himself, he'd turned to enjoying everything the Tunisair stewards were offering for free, including enough wine to make him drowsy.

The first flight from Tripoli to Tunis had been a bone shaker. They were the only passengers on a six-seater turbo-prop that had flown so low they could see people moving about on the fishing boats below. The compensation had been that, on landing, they were spared the usual queues and checks. The pilot had delivered them to within a few yards of their Heathrow flight to which they were briskly escorted. It was impossible to tell if they were viewed by the other passengers as VIPs or as troublemakers being expelled.

"They were certainly keen to get us out of there," Jed replies.

"We're a diplomatic embarrassment."

Ayesha sips from a can of Coke and starts tapping the top in an agitated way. The tactic of distracting herself with work has evidently worn off after a couple of hours like a pain-killer.

"At least we met him face to face – Omar, I mean."

"But are we any the wiser?"

"Not much," Jed replies, preferring to hear what Ayesha thinks before committing himself.

"Perhaps I should let the whole thing go," she says. "I expect you think I'm mad – it's not going to bring Tom back – but I just can't accept that it was an accident. It doesn't add up. None of it. I mean every new detail makes it odder. They said he was found with his clothes and socks on but not his shoes. But, if he'd tripped, stumbled into the water and then been knocked over by a freak wave, he would still have had his shoes on. On the other hand, if he'd taken a conscious decision to have a swim and gone to the trouble of taking his shoes off, surely, he would also have taken his socks off, and probably his shirt and trousers too? And why would he go for a midnight dip on his own anyway? I really can't imagine it, especially now we know for sure that he was sober."

"But there was *some* alcohol in his blood. And if he wasn't used to drinking, one drink might have gone to his head, on an empty stomach, after a hot day."

Jed can see Ayesha is unpersuaded. She takes a long swig of Coke and resumes tapping the can.

"And you don't think it's more likely that someone else was on that beach, and they over-powered him?"

"It's possible. But why would a mugger leave the cards and the change? Having gone to the extreme of killing him,

129

they'd take everything. And why would the police rule out foul play if there was any real evidence of it?"

Ayesha laughs dismissively. "Because it's bad enough that it happened on Libyan soil, without it being a murder case. Tom's death is a huge embarrassment for them. As you said on the beach, their relations with Britain are already bad enough. So, if the family has accepted it was an accident, why would they want to dig any deeper? It lets them off the hook. And I understand that. In the great scheme of things, one dead Brit on a beach is nothing…"

"For them, maybe — but I don't think you're mad to want to know the truth. Why should you settle for anything less?" Jed only means to empathise but, as he hears his words out loud, he realises that they imply that his job is unfinished, his duty isn't done.

Ayesha contorts herself into a position where she can reach under the seat in front for her bag. She wrestles it onto her lap and pulls a diary out with the photograph Rashida gave her tucked inside.

"I'm going to try to contact her." Ayesha is pointing at the woman standing next to Tom who Rashida said was from Britain.

"Maybe she's Alison Parker, the delegation leader?"

"No, that's definitely not Alison. I don't know her personally, but I've seen her speak. I'll contact her as well. She might be able to tell me who this woman is."

Jed takes the photo and looks closely at the woman. She's small and slender – much the same as Hannah -- and has shoulder-length black hair and light brown skin. She might be Asian or mixed race, and she looks very young – maybe university age, though he finds it harder to tell as he gets older. He isn't convinced that tracking her down will achieve much, but he's not going to discourage Ayesha from following a thread to Tom's final hours.

He hands the photograph back to Ayesha. "We should also ask Gavin about his interview with the police. It's odd he didn't mention to them that he thought Tom was drunk – unless he *did* and it didn't make it into Omar's notes."

Ayesha raises her eyebrows sceptically. "Listen, I've been certain all along that Gavin's been lying about Tom."

"Lying? That's a bit strong. Tom did have some alcohol in his blood."

"Thirty milligrams – that's nothing."

"It's about a pint of lager, and if he wasn't used to drinking."

Ayesha slumps back in her seat, her head tilted back as if she's looking for inspiration from the cabin ceiling. A steward collecting rubbish ready for landing leans over and takes the Coke can from Ayesha's hand. When she moves on, Ayesha turns to Jed and looks into his eyes for an uncomfortable length of time.

"There's something I haven't told you." She pauses and lifts her head above the tops of the seats. The steward's gone to the back of the plane. Ayesha scans the cabin in both directions, like a prairie dog checking for danger, and then ducks back so that she's speaking only inches from Jed's ear. "I had a phone call from Tom that evening. He left a message on my answerphone at just after ten. I was out when he called and listened to it about an hour later when I got back to the flat."

Jed's stunned. He replays the words, first, to himself to be sure he's heard correctly, and then back to Ayesha.

"Let me get this straight. You had a call from Tom that evening, about two hours before he died, and he left a message. And you're telling me this now."

"I know. I should have told you before the meeting with the police chief."

"You should have told me when you came to my office."

Jed's rebuke is so terse it makes Ayesha flinch and fall silent for a long moment.

"I couldn't – it's complicated," she says softly.

"Why?"

"Because the message mentioned Gavin, and I didn't want to talk about it in front of Hannah."

"So, what did Tom actually say?"

"That Gavin was planning something he disagreed with. He called it a stunt. But he didn't say what it was. He said he'd tell me when he got back. God, I wish now I'd tried to phone him back, but I didn't have a number for the hotel and I thought it could wait... I'd be seeing him the next day."

Jed turns to look out of the window again and sees London coming into view, the West End glowing in the evening gloom. He picks out Regents Park and the canal threading its way through Camden and Islington. Somewhere in the greyness is an office where not so long ago he was in his comfort zone. Now he feels a fool, floundering while trying to help someone who's story omitted a vital chapter. He understands why a problem between Tom and Gavin would be difficult to discuss in front of Hannah, but Ayesha could have told him at any time while they were in Libya, and not let him conduct a cross-examination of Omar without knowing this crucial fact.

He wants to let rip – tell her she's on her own – but, turning towards her again and seeing her watery eyes, he realises that his irritation doesn't compare with her agony, that she may never forgive herself for not calling Tom back.

"How did Tom sound?" He tries to sound sympathetic, but that doesn't compensate for the insensitive implication of the question.

"You mean, had the Bokha gone to his head? Did he sound unhinged, as if he was about to jump in the sea? No, not at all. He sounded a bit agitated. But he was coherent, not like someone who'd been drinking."

The PA system crackles. It's the captain saying the plane is beginning its descent into Heathrow and asking everyone to fasten their seatbelts. Jed and Ayesha straighten themselves out and sit there staring in silence at the backs of the seats in front.

"So, what do you think it was? Do you have any idea?" Jed whispers.

"I honestly don't know. I really don't."

"So, let's ask Gavin. See what he says. What have you got to lose?

"Only my friendship with Hannah. And that means a lot to me. So please don't say anything to either of them yet, Jed. I'd like to talk to Hannah myself first."

Jed nods, but his thoughts are drifting to the meeting with the police chief. Replaying the questions that he asked and the replies Omar gave, he realises that knowing about Tom's message would not have made any difference. The Libyans had settled on a version of events. Chamberlain and Carver had accepted it. Ayesha is the only person who wants to know the truth, and she's more likely to find it in London than Tripoli, because it's Gavin who has questions to answer.

Heathrow is as chaotic as ever. The passport hall is heaving with people, many with enough luggage to last a lifetime. Jed suggests they both go in the queue for aliens, so that they'll be together if Ayesha has any trouble. This is home turf for him – he's confident he can help her here.

When they reach the front, the passport official takes a long look at Ayesha's student visa and their boarding cards from Tunis and makes a show of checking something on his computer.

"Everything okay in Tripoli?" he says with a smirk.

"Yes, thanks," Jed replies hurriedly, to pre-empt Ayesha saying something.

As they walk away, she laughs and shakes her head. "I assumed they'd have us on their system, but he didn't need to make it so obvious."

Once through customs, Ayesha sees a Menzies and heads directly for it. By the time Jed's caught up with her, she's already flicking through a copy of *The Independent*. Polly Brittan's report is buried deep inside.

Jed feels a surge of relief when he first spots her name over Ayesha's shoulder – at least she is a journalist and not a sidekick of Chamberlain's. But his throat dries in anticipation of an Ayesha rant when he sees the headline: '*Student drowns after Tripoli bootleg binge*'.

Ayesha looks furious and is shaking her head with each sentence. When she's finished, she hands it disdainfully to Jed and begins prowling around the shop as he reads it properly.

> *A British journalist who died while attending a conference in Tripoli is understood to have been severely intoxicated when he drowned last weekend.*
>
> *Sources close to the Libyan police inquiry say that Tom Carver, who was found dead on a beach in the early hours of Monday morning, had been drinking illegal alcohol with other delegates before he went missing.*

The 27-year-old from Hertfordshire was attending an event held to mark the anniversary of the US bombing of Tripoli with other left-wing activists from Britain and north America.

The results of a post mortem have not been made public, but a Foreign Office source said Carver was partying at a hotel where delegates were staying and seen leaving on his own.

It is thought he may have stumbled into the water after going to the beach to "sober up".

A solicitor who went to Tripoli last week with Carver's partner, Ayesha Khoury, said a fellow delegate had confirmed that the journalist was intoxicated.

"I've been told by one of the other delegates that Tom was the worse for wear when he went out onto the beach," said Gerald McIntosh, an associate with law firm O'Brien's in London. "Ayesha is devastated. The Libyans have been hospitable and arranged everything, but I honestly don't know if they're hiding something."

It is understood that Carver's family had been against him going to Tripoli and have vetoed any information being given to Khoury by the Libyan authorities.

Jed skims the final paragraphs giving some background on *Third World Voice* and the bombing of Libya and then re-reads the part attributed to him. His comment about Tom being the worse for wear is bad enough, but he wasn't expecting the reference to O'Brien's – implying the firm is acting for Ayesha – and he can't remember saying anything about the Libyans hiding something. One paragraph – three things he could have done without.

Ayesha stops prowling and stands directly in front of him.

"You see what I mean," she says, swiping the paper with the back of her hand and nearly sending it flying. "You can't trust these people. That just makes Tom look bad, and it's not true anyway."

"I didn't know that at the time, and I wouldn't have said it if you'd told me about Tom's call. Maybe if you were more open with me, I'd be able to make a better job of helping you."

Ayesha shakes her head as if trying to unscramble it. Jed sees that she's as exhausted as he's exasperated. And being buffeted by people in a hurry wanting to get at the newspapers and magazines isn't helping.

He goes to pay for the paper and meets Ayesha outside. It's nearly nine and the crowds in the arrivals area are gradually thinning. Ayesha's looking forlorn, staring vacantly into the distance, their two bags at her fleet.

"The trouble is, I don't know what I think myself," she says so softly that Jed has to step closer. "I just can't get my head round any of it, I feel like I'm going mad with doubts and suspicions, and I haven't had anyone to talk to. I used to tell Hannah everything, but I don't even see her on her own these days. She's always with Gavin... But one thing I do know is I can't mourn Tom properly until I understand what really happened on that beach, so soon after he'd left that message."

Jed grips her arms and looks firmly into her eyes. "But you do have me to talk to now, and you must tell me everything – otherwise I can't be of any use."

Jed supresses his frustrations and tries to keep his tone calm. He pulls Ayesha towards him, and she nestles her head on his shoulder. When she finally straightens up, tears have left a moist sheen across her cheeks. She pulls a tissue from her coat pocket and dabs her face.

"Yes, you're right, I'm sorry, I know I should have told you about Tom's call earlier."

"Okay, so, we're back now. Once you've spoken to Hannah, we can see what Gavin's got to say for himself."

"I'll let you know when the time's right," Ayesha says, picking up her bag and starting for the Tube.

As Jed follows, he can't help smiling to himself at the firmness in Ayesha's voice. Even in moments of fragility, she's still very much in charge.

Jed and Ayesha take the Piccadilly Line into central London, managing to grab seats opposite each other. By Acton, the carriage is so packed with people heading for the West End that Jed can't even see Ayesha. He decides to read Polly Brittan's report again, but it's no better on further examination. He wonders if it is worth calling her to set the record straight, to explain that Tom wasn't actually drunk that night, but dismisses the idea in seconds as too risky. And he decides not to phone O'Brien either – why alert him to the article when there's a chance he won't have seen it?

At Leicester Square, the crush eases and a sound asleep Ayesha comes into view, her head slumped and bobbing like a doll with a broken neck. Jed moves into the seat to her left that's now empty and gives her a gentle nudge, whispering "nearly at King's Cross" in her ear.

She is still bleary-eyed when they get off, and Jed has to make sure she's going in the right direction for trains to Kentish Town before taking the escalator for the walk home. It's a long, mostly-uphill hike from King's Cross, and he's tempted to stop for a pint at The Sutton Arms on the off-chance Frank McClintock is pulling the pints, but the prospect of a bath followed by watching some present-day footballers on *Match Of The Day* is even more appealing.

Until Ayesha and Tripoli, Arsenal's mixed form was one of the bigger issues in Jed's life. In early April he'd seen them beat Liverpool in the League Cup final at Wembley, which gave him hope they could still win the First Division title, until a defeat at West Ham a few days later put paid to that. And now it all seems a lifetime ago.

Jed's struggling to remember the score in the West Ham game when his house comes into view and he sees light from the living room window glowing above the hedge. He's sure he switched everything off. Doubting himself, he stops to check if it is actually his. They're all very similar, owners aren't allowed to mess about with a Georgian terrace. He counts – six houses from where he's standing. There is no doubt about it.

Fuelled by Ayesha-instilled paranoia, Jed decides to sneak down a side alley so that he can approach the house through the garden. On reaching the back gate, he puts his bag down and eases it open slowly, knowing the hinges can creak. He has cover from a solitary bush and squats behind it. His caution was justified. He can just about see enough through the kitchen window and the open doorway into the living room to know the place has been trashed. Bookshelves are empty, pictures on the wall are askew, but there is no sign of anyone moving around.

He waits, keeping out of view. His eyes are fixed on the window. His breath is alarmingly foggy in the cold night air. He mulls the options. He has a fleeting image of himself rushing in and overcoming the intruder like in a movie. But he knows he's no Gene Hackman. The adrenalin pumping in his chest is strictly for flight rather than fight. He decides his best hope – if someone *is* inside – is to get a good look at them.

Jed continues to stare through the window for ten minutes or more, not daring to move, not even to check his watch. Eventually, sure no one is in the house, he steps back cautiously through the open gate to pick up his bag and then starts to inch forward in a crouched position, like a child imitating a chicken, his clicking knees providing appropriate sound effects.

Jed's efforts are actually absurd because, once away from the bush, he has no cover – he's in full view whether crouching or not. After a few shuffles, he's near enough to touch the backdoor. A prod with the tip of his finger sends it swinging open.

The kitchen has hardly been touched, but books, files and photographs are strewn across the carpet in the living room. Virtually everything from the shelves, desk and filing cabinet is on the floor.

Jed walks through to see properly. The TV is still in place, but the video unit underneath is empty. None of the framed prints and posters on the walls have been taken, but a burglar wouldn't need to work for Sotheby's to know they are worthless.

Jed goes upstairs and finds more mess in both bedrooms. It's mainly clothes thrown on the floor, on top of the dirty ones that were there when he left. He's wearing the gold watch his parents gave him for his 21st birthday, and the cufflinks untouched on his bedside table are of no great value. It was a poor haul for whoever had gone to so much trouble.

But that isn't much comfort as he walks through the house one more time to take it all in. Back in the kitchen, he robotically puts the kettle on and picks up the phone. When he gets through to the police, their disinterest is obvious. Another Saturday, another burglary. The woman takes his address and the bare details and gives him a crime number.

"You'll need that for the insurance," she says.

"How soon will you be here?"

"How soon?"

He waits assuming she hasn't finished.

"I mean, roughly," he says, when the silence continues.

"It's Saturday night. We don't have anyone available. You'll have to bear with us. It might be two or three hours. Can you secure the house?"

Jed hasn't thought of that and looks across at the backdoor. The lock has been forced, ripping a slice of wood from the door frame, but there are bolts at the top and bottom that would secure it. He'll just have to hope the next intruder doesn't have an axe or a crowbar.

"Yeah, sort of," he replies.

"In that case, your best bet is to lock up and go to bed. We'll send someone out in the morning. To take the details. But don't touch anything in the meantime…"

Jed wants to say "that wouldn't be easy with so much on the floor", but she's gone. Feeling needy, he thinks about calling someone, but it's late, too late. He opts instead for pouring a whisky and turning the TV on. He's just in time for Barry McGuigan chatting to Harry Carpenter about an Irish guy losing to a Columbian in an "epic" fight. The Irish accent reminds him of Ali, and he imagines him again inspecting livestock in Donegal, and then he thinks of him in a basement, shielding terrified children, explosions shaking the building, planes roaring overhead.

CHAPTER TEN

Sunlight is squeezing through a narrow gap in the curtains. The flat faces east and day break over the villas on Haverstock Hill can be dazzling. But the curtains are thick, and there isn't enough light for Hannah to find her watch. It's somewhere on the shelves near the bed, but she doesn't want to turn the bedside lamp on because Gavin is still asleep. She lies there trying to guess the time, listening to his even breathing, feeling the warmth of his body. She decides it must be about seven, far too early to get up on a Sunday. The essays she has to mark can wait.

Gavin is facing away from her. He always sleeps like that. Hannah would prefer him not to, but she's grown used to it, and she enjoys seeing his bare back twist and twitch as he sleeps. She's staring at him now as the gap in the curtain sends a shaft of light across his shoulders, making them look even more muscular than usual.

They'd made love twice the night before. He had come round to the flat after being away in Kent for several days with his parents, and they'd gone to bed straight away. She'd missed him and wanted him inside her. With the five nights in Tripoli, it was the longest they'd been apart in the four months they'd been seeing each other. But the strength of her desire was out of all proportion to that; and she feels a twinge of shame now as she thinks of Gavin's face when they were kissing and her hand reached down to touch him as soon as he walked through the door, how surprised he looked and how desperate she must have seemed.

She finds the thought of her emotions being out of control unsettling. She's normally better at keeping them in check. But nothing's normal at the moment. Nothing at all.

Poor Tom. She dreams about him all the time. He appears incongruously in jumbled images drawn from random parts of her life. Like most dreams, they're quickly forgotten; but the one that lingers and recurs is of him appearing in Bristol when she was a student. She's in the students' union bar, and Tom and Jed arrive, but it's Tom who kisses her and then they leave together. She's had the dream every night since finding out Tom was dead. The thought of it when she wakes up makes her squirm. It seems so disloyal to Ayesha, and it's weird she would have the two of them in a dream when they had never even met.

She puts it down to latent guilt because she'd been so attracted to Tom when she first saw him speaking at LSE. He had phoned her a few days later to ask her to go out for a drink. She wasn't seeing Jed at the time, and she was thrilled.

They met at a pub in Covent Garden and he was charming, so interested in everything and so eloquent about politics. But, as they talked, she realised he kept steering the conversation towards Ayesha. He wanted to know all about her: where she was from, what she was studying, how she'd come to be in London. He knew a lot himself about the Middle East. He'd visited Egypt and Iraq. His magazine had sent him to a Palestinian refugee camp in Jordan to write a feature about it. He hadn't been to Beirut but he knew all about what happened in 1982 and understood the enormity of it.

As the evening went on, Hannah began to realise it was Ayesha he was interested in, and she asked him outright if that was the case.

He was embarrassed. "Am I being that obvious?"

"Obvious is an understatement. Do you want me to sound her out?"

Hannah remembers his hesitation. He said he thought she would see him as too young, and Hannah laughed, finding it hilarious that blokes can never get their heads around dating a woman who's older than them.

The thought of that awkward moment and Tom's naïve face makes Hannah smile wistfully. She still can't believe she won't see him again, and she lets out a long sigh as she swings her legs off the bed, picks up her dressing gown from the floor and puts it on. She doesn't share Gavin's liking for walking around the flat naked. When he does, she feels almost as uncomfortable as she did as a child when her mother's boyfriends would turn up in the kitchen wearing next to nothing. She's torn between admiring his lack of inhibition and thinking he's a show off.

As she opens the bedroom door now, she looks back at him lying on top of the duvet and stands for a moment, feeling pleased to have him back with her and thinking she shouldn't be so intolerant of a handful of habits that annoy her. There's far more she likes about him than she doesn't. And maybe that's as good as it gets. She had expected too much from Jed. She'd been too intense. But she doesn't want to spoil things with Gavin by trying to change him or make demands of him.

In the living room, she finds the remnants of their meal the night before – a pizza carton dotted with discarded crusts and two greasy plates lying on the floor. After they'd made love and slept for a while, Gavin went out to get a takeaway. He came back with the biggest pizza she'd ever seen, and they'd eaten it cuddled together on her two-seater settee watching *Bergerac*.

Gavin had been quiet all evening. There was none of his usual banter, nor any of the not-very-funny jokes. Hannah put it down to his father being so ill and asked him how the chemotherapy was going.

"Not very well," he'd said without taking his eyes off the television.

"I suppose they won't really know until afterwards, will they?"

"I suppose not. But it's not looking good."

"There are secondaries, are there?"

"Secondaries?"

"I mean it's spread, from his bowel."

"Yeah, that's what I meant by 'it's not looking good'."

"Where's he being treated?"

"He's an outpatient."

"Yes, but for which hospital?"

Gavin turned his head. He looked angry and pointed at the television. "Hannah, give me a break, I'm trying to take my mind off it."

Hannah squeezed his hand, feeling guilty, and they watched the rest of *Bergerac* in silence. When it was over Gavin pulled her onto his lap, facing away from him, and they'd had sex again like that, mechanically. The passion she'd felt earlier had gone, and Gavin came quickly.

Afterwards, they started watching *Lady Sings The Blues*, which Hannah had loved when she'd seen it at the cinema with her mother, but Gavin fell asleep, and Hannah nudged him to say she was going to bed. He'd looked at her blankly, completely disorientated, and she'd left him there.

Now, picking up the pizza box and plates, she tries to remember him coming to bed. But she can't. She must have gone straight to sleep. Sometimes, these days, tiredness overwhelms her.

Hannah goes into the kitchen, puts the plates in the sink and leans the pizza box next to her waste bin. She's been meaning to ask one of the neighbours about recycling in the area but rarely sees anyone coming or going.

She'd bought the flat only a month earlier in a rash moment after her job at LSE was made permanent. She still can't quite believe she's grown up enough to own her own place in London, but she's loving it. She's glad she no longer has to clean up other people's messes or listen to housemates who knew each other before she came along gossiping about people she's never met. She's enjoying being near Camden Market and Primrose Hill and the ease of her commute from Chalk Farm to work. And, when Gavin's not there, she makes the most of the solitude to do marking and prepare lecture notes.

The only problem is the mortgage. It's stretched her finances and left her without much spare cash for furniture. Apart from the new double bed, everything's from her mother who drove up from Brighton in a rented van loaded with a small Formica breakfast table, three hardback chairs, the settee, a single mattress for the spare room, two shelf units, a dozen or so boxes of books, and a suitcase full of old clothes Hannah had forgotten she had and will probably never wear. She was so grateful she made Ally a meal with fresh salmon and a bottle of Chablis and even listened attentively when the alcohol sent her mother into a repetitive ramble about her unhappy marriage and how Hannah had 'saved her life'.

Waiting for the kettle to boil now, Hannah remembers her seven-year-old self finding her mother standing in the kitchen one morning holding a piece of paper, her tears

145

landing on the red ink. Ally had instantly folded it up and tucked it with other post between the cookery books, but Hannah had caught sight of the words in capital letters and read well enough to know that 'FINAL DEMAND' wasn't good news. For years afterwards, she would keep an eye out for brown envelopes arriving through the letterbox and watch her mother closely for clues as to how demanding they were.

That memory has always made her slightly uneasy, but her anxiety is heightened of late. For a start, she doesn't know for sure how much the flat will cost to run. When she writes all her estimates down and adds them up, the total leaves enough for the mortgage and food and not much else. She should just about manage. But she's decided to delay decorating and buying living room curtains for now, to be on the safe side.

She's determined not to be dependent on Gavin, but she can't help feeling that it would be nice to know what he's thinking about them living together. He stays with her most nights, when he's not visiting his parents. Moving in would save him a lot of money. It seems to her like a no brainer. But, so far, he hasn't shown any sign of it being a possibility, and she'd like to know where she stands. She hates not having a plan.

She pours the hot water on a tea bag in the big Free Nelson Mandela mug she always uses. While she waits for it to brew, she watches the early risers passing on Haverstock Hill, most of them with thick Sunday newspapers under their arms, reminding her of the report on Tom's death in the previous day's *Independent*. It seemed to confirm that it was an accident, but – despite what Gavin said – she couldn't imagine Tom touching alcohol while he was in Tripoli. She'd only seen him drunk once, and that was on New Year's Eve. If he was in a country where drinking was banned, it would be out of character for him to be disrespectful. It was odd, but Gavin was insistent, and maybe she didn't know Tom as well as she thought she did.

Hannah takes her tea into the living room and sets it down on the table next to the pile of essays she has to mark. She does a course for first year's on developing economies. She's had to make some compromises on the syllabus to get it past the Academic Board, but she has some latitude when it comes to essay questions and has asked the students to discuss: *"If Live Aid was the answer, are we asking the right question?"*

As she flicks through them, the answers seem promising. She picks out the one written by her best student as a benchmark and then reads a couple more for comparison. That gives her a sense of the quality and views. They are only first years, and it doesn't count towards their final degree, but she prides herself on being fair, and she's been warned by other left-wing lecturers that she has to watch her back. "It won't be long before Thatcher comes for us," one had told her the other day.

The marking is absorbing, and the students surprise her with the power of their feelings and arguments. Half the group are overseas students. Most of them are polite about Live Aid, but Gloria, an older student from Ghana, says scathingly she doesn't recognise the Africa portrayed by Bob Geldof and thinks the real question is how Africa can be compensated for wealth that's been stolen. Hannah hasn't seen some of the data she uses before and makes a note to look it up. Must keep one step ahead of the students, she tells herself.

Hannah's still reading Gloria's paper when Gavin bursts through the bedroom door. She jumps to her feet, taken aback. She'd momentarily forgotten he was there. And now he's standing a yard away, completely naked.

"Shit, what time is it, babe?"

Hannah looks at her watch. "It's ten."

"Ten. Okay, that's not so bad. I thought it was later."

"What's the rush? I thought we could…"

"What?"

"I thought we might spend some time together. Go for a walk or something."

"Sorry, Han, I can't. I've got to go to see my parents." He gives a regretful shrug.

"Your parents? Again? But you only came back yesterday."

Gavin looks thrown now, and Hannah raises her eyebrows.

"You did come back yesterday, didn't you?" she asks.

"Yeah, yeah, of course. I'm losing track of the days. I came straight here."

That doesn't sound convincing to Hannah, but she lets it go and then feels a pang of guilt. Why would he lie? His father's seriously ill. I'm being selfish.

"So, what's the situation, with your father I mean, you having to go back so soon?"

"It's only that he's having more chemo tomorrow morning, early. That's why I need to get down there today. And I've got to nip back to the flat to get some things before I catch the train."

"Have you got time for breakfast?" Hannah is trying to sound supportive, but her stomach is churning. She feels nauseous and close to tears. She would really rather he just left now, and she flinches as he steps forward and puts his arms around her.

"I'm sorry Han. But my father needs me."

He tightens his embrace, and she feels him hardening.

"I don't want that Gavin," she says, pushing him away and stepping back.

He looks hurt and holds his hands up in a gesture of surrender.

"Okay, okay. I thought you might want a quickie."

"Well, you thought wrong."

Gavin turns away and goes back into the bedroom, and Hannah slumps back onto the chair and starts flicking through Gloria's essay. But she's not reading the words now, and she's struggling to hold herself in check, but she can't – the nausea is worse – and she has to rush to the toilet, getting there just in time to throw up.

As she re-emerges, dabbing her lips with a tissue, Gavin is in the living room ready to leave, his coat on, a sports bag over his shoulder.

"I'm off then," he says.

Hannah nods. She feels angry and guilty all at once, and she can taste the vomit on her lips. She doesn't want them to part like this, but she can't find the energy to move towards him.

"What about Tom's funeral?" she says finally.

"I've checked where it is. No stations nearby. We'll have to go in my car. I'll pick you up at eleven."

His tone is clipped, like he's anxious about his father or angry with her. She's not sure which.

"Thanks."

Gavin steps over, kisses her forehead and leaves, the door thudding closed.

Hannah goes over to the window, just in time to see him striding down the path and turn towards Camden Market. She assumes he'll walk back to his flat and imagines him on the canal path. And now she feels she should have walked with him.

Why didn't she suggest that? More to the point, why didn't he?

CHAPTER ELEVEN

Waking up to a fuzzy TV screen and the sound of banging, Jed finds himself stretched out on the settee, fully clothed, an empty glass in his lap, a damp, brown stain running from it down his left trouser leg. His new Dockers are ruined. The whisky smells more like medicine than malt now.

"Can I come in?" a voice is shouting.

Before he can answer, he senses the presence of someone in the house and jumps to his feet in momentary panic, the glass falling to the floor. He is facing the silhouette of a tall, willowy man who's stooping slightly in the doorway from the kitchen. They both watch the glass roll across the carpet, and Jed wonders if it looks like he was having a shot for breakfast.

"Mr McIntosh?" the man says. "The door was unlocked."

Jed has him in focus now. He's young, uniformed, and holding a helmet in one hand. Jed remembers his call to the police and feels a stab of panic at the thought of watching his own house from behind a bush and wondering if someone was inside.

"Right, yes," he says, picturing the damaged back door and the bolt he had intended to lock.

The man scans the wreckage on the floor. "I see you've left everything as you found it. I'm PC Swinburne. Do you mind if I have a look round?"

Without waiting for an answer, he brushes past Jed to go into the hallway and climb the stairs. Jed heads in the opposite direction, needing coffee to help him process what's happened. His black MFI wall clock has survived the break-in. It's nearly eight. Too desperate for caffeine to mess around with the filter machine, he puts the kettle on, spoons Nescafe and Marvel into two mugs and wets the mixture to produce a steaming dark liquid peppered with puss-like globules.

When PC Swinburne returns, it's obvious he isn't impressed. He leaves his mug on the counter and pulls a notebook and pencil from the breast pocket of his jacket.

"The toerags have left no stone unturned by the look of it. I'll need to take a statement."

They sit at the kitchen table for half an hour as Jed describes what he found the previous evening and the officer laboriously turns it into police-speak for him to sign. He manages to avoid saying why he'd been away. With a few embellishments, he makes the story of his stake-out and re-capture of the house sound plucky.

"And did they take anything of value apart from the video recorder?" Swinburne says, nodding at the shelf where it was once housed.

"I haven't checked my law notes yet."

"Let me know if there are any missing."

Jed sees he's written 'possibly law notes'. "It's okay, you can leave that out," he says.

Once on his own, Jed starts gathering the detritus off the floor – putting his eclectic selection of books randomly on the shelves and the law notes and files into piles on the settee and table. With most of the floor cleared, he finds the three framed photographs from the mantelpiece. The ones of a family holiday and of him with Jonathan in Managua are intact, and he sets them back in place. But, when he tries to pick the third one up, it disintegrates, sending shards of glass flying in all directions and the photograph falling back onto the carpet.

Jed picks it up and slumps onto the settee, staring wistfully at the image of Hannah propped against him. He's wearing a black academic gown and an over-sized grey suit his father had lent him. She's in a purple cotton dress, looking achingly attractive, despite the inane grin that a few glasses of wine had induced. The broken glass has torn the photograph. He lays it carefully on his lap and surveys the room. It's not much to show for 27 years. Even if all of it had gone, it wouldn't be worth more than the excess on his insurance. And, yet, its value to him is incalculable, and it's been sullied by intruders.

"Bastards," he shouts, banging his fist on the arm of the settee. "Bastards."

He decides he has to tell someone. He goes across to the phone on the table and picks up the handset, but his hand is shaking so badly he struggles to get his forefinger into the dial. He holds it up and stares at it, bewildered by this out-of-control, delayed reaction to the intrusion.

Trying the phone again, he starts to dial Adam — his drinking buddy at O'Brien's — but changes his mind. For some reason, it's Ayesha he wants to share this with. He hunts — with close to manic urgency — for his address book and finds it lying on one of the shelves open at the page where he'd neatly written her phone number six days earlier.

His finger steadier, he dials the number as quickly as his old rotary phone will allow. As it rings, he realises Hannah or Simon or even Gavin could answer, and he isn't in the mood for any of them. But it's Ayesha who picks up with a 'hello' that sounds distant and vague, like he's woken her.

"Some bastard's trashed my house," Jed says without preamble.

"Someone's what?"

Ayesha's squawk is so piercing Jed pulls the handset from his ear.

"I've been burgled," he replies, more calmly.

"Overnight?"

"No, yesterday, before I got home. They'd broken in and wrecked the place, stuff everywhere."

He can hear Ayesha breathing evenly, digesting the headline. She doesn't need to ask another question. Jed is like a pan boiling over. Gone is the relative calm of his interview with PC Swinburne. This time his account is garbled and littered with profanities. He lurches from raving anger to choking up at the mention of anything of the slightest sentimental value. He is so upset that he can't finish his explanation of what the culprits had done to his graduation photograph.

"I'll come over," Ayesha says, hanging up abruptly.

Ayesha's taxi ride from Kentish Town to Islington gives Jed enough time to change into a tracksuit and jog down to the corner shop for milk, eggs and bread. By the time she crosses his front doorstep, he's calmer and the comforting smell of real coffee, freshly-brewed, has filled the house. She's wearing jeans, a grey LSE sweat shirt and a Palestinian-style embroidered scarf long enough to wrap around her neck. They hug and she follows him into the living room.

"What a mess," she says, looking at the piles of files on the settee and the broken glass he hasn't yet cleared up.

"You should have seen it an hour ago."

"What's that smell, whiskey?"

"That was me – drowning my sorrows, last night."

Jed goes into the kitchen and starts breaking eggs into a bowl and scrambling them with a fork.

"Breakfast? This is unexpected," Ayesha says, leaning against the doorway.

Jed pours two coffees and hands her one.

"So, did they go upstairs?"

"Yep, turned the whole place over."

"Do you mind if I have a look around?"

Jed hesitates, then shrugs his assent. He is even less comfortable about Ayesha seeing the dirty clothes strewn across his bedroom floor than he was the police officer and cringes with each creak of the floorboards above.

As she arrives back in the living room, Ayesha spares him any comment and goes straight over to the TV cabinet where she squats down to take a look at the space where the video player would have been.

"And all they took was the video?"

"Yep, but it was only an old Betamax."

Ayesha stands up and gives Jed a look of disbelief.

"A Betamax – you're kidding me? Jed, nobody steals Betas. They're worthless. I can't even believe you still had one."

Jed blushes. Ayesha discovering that he lives like a slob is bad enough, but being the owner of a Betamax is worse. It's so uncool, and no amount of explaining how he's recorded a lot of good films on Beta tapes and doesn't have time to copy them all onto VHS is going to alter the instant impression that he's in a home entertainment time-warp.

He's relieved to see that her attention has been caught by his address book, which is still lying open on the shelves.

"And where was this when you got back?" she says, running a finger over her own name.

Jed closes his eyes and tries to visualise finding it to phone her only an hour earlier.

"I don't know, I mean when I called you earlier, I found it there, like that. So, I suppose that's how it was when I got back."

"Open, on this page?"

"I'm not sure... yes, I think so. But what's your point?"

Ayesha gives Jed an incredulous look as if her point is obvious.

"Well, they were either very stupid burglars, who can't tell a Beta from a VHS, or it was someone with a different agenda."

Jed has to think about that. They fall silent, both of them staring at the notebook, Ayesha's long elegant forefinger still resting on her own name. She lifts her hand and puts it on Jed's shoulder.

"Oh Jed, you're so naïve sometimes. Do you think they wouldn't send someone round to check you out? They've tried to make it look like a burglary, of course they have. But if they were burglars, why didn't they take anything apart from a worthless old Betamax?"

"Because there wasn't anything much else?" Jed replies, feeling irritated by her patronising tone.

"A burglar would clear you out, Jed. Really. They'd take the coffee machine, the kettle, the wall clock... Anything that can easily be sold in a pub. Once they're inside, they wouldn't walk off just with an old Betamax...This is probably someone sent by Chamberlain."

"Come on, you've been watching too many spy films."

As the words fall out of Jed's mouth, he realises they're worse than patronising. He's talking to someone who's been traumatised by war. She doesn't base her opinions on spy films. Before he can row back, she's pacing the room, looking furious.

156

"You think I know this from movies, from watching too much James Bond?"

Shaking her head, she slumps onto the settee, knocking some files onto the floor in the process.

"Sorry, that was a daft thing to say. But it just seems a bit far-fetched, that's all. I haven't done anything much politically since I was a student. Why would they be so interested in me?"

"Because you've gone off-piste. You heard what Chamberlain said. When people like him make threats, they mean business, and they have an army of people to back them up. You've just been to Libya – a country they consider an enemy – to look into a death that's highly sensitive, with a Palestinian woman who they're bound to see as a troublemaker. Photographing your address book is the least they would do."

Jed falls silent. He knows she could be right. He's always seen these things as something that happens to someone else, picketing miners or the Greenham Common women – activists like Ayesha. His trouble-making days were brief, and he thought he'd left them behind. But he's been reading *Spycatcher*, and he picks it up from the shelf now to show Ayesha he's not completely out of touch.

"Wright says in here somewhere that they had two million personal files when he joined MI5 in the fifties, and the number rose dramatically in the seventies."

Jed offers Ayesha the book, but she waves him away.

"I know. I've read it, and I remember that bit. I worked out that two million means they had a file on one in twenty adults when he started. If that rose dramatically, it's probably more like one in ten now. Do you think you wouldn't be one of them? If you weren't before you went

157

to Tripoli, you definitely are now. And that's my fault. I'm sorry for causing you all this trouble."

Jed's grinning. "I might have guessed you'd be on top of the maths. So, do you reckon this place is bugged?"

He's joking, but Ayesha takes him seriously.

"I definitely won't be discussing what happened to Tom in this house." Ayesha stands up and nods in the direction of the kitchen. "How about cooking those eggs now?"

"Eggs? Yes, of course."

Jed had completely forgotten his plan to make breakfast, but he's glad of the chance to turn his attention to something practical. In no time, he's brewed more coffee and is setting two plates of steaming scrambled eggs and toast down on the table.

They eat in silence. It's the nearest either of them have had to a proper meal since breakfast the previous day in Tripoli. Jed is surprised by how comfortable he feels with a woman he's known for only a week. It reminds him of the easy, slow-moving Sundays with Hannah in their better spells, but, as he glances at Ayesha surreptitiously every so often, he could not envisage ever seeing her in a romantic way. He wonders, though, if she will always be so difficult to fathom, shaped as she is by events she doesn't readily talk about and he finds impossible to imagine. Her obvious resilience sometimes makes her seem cold, yet she had the kindness to arrive on his doorstep within half an hour of his call and help him deal with this invasion of his privacy – whoever it was by.

When Jed suddenly remembers that his mother is expecting him for lunch, they set off on foot immediately for King's Cross and travel together on the Tube as far as

Camden Town. In the nearly-empty carriage, Ayesha speaks freely about how she's going to talk to Hannah on her own and call Alison Parker to try to find out who the woman in the photograph is. As she steps off the train, leaving Jed to go on to Golders Green, she tells him – with no time for a reply before the doors close – to meet her in The Camden Head the following evening at seven.

Jed's mother greets him on the doorstep like he's been away for four months rather than four days. His father, who's watching the *Maltese Falcon*, gives him an unusually cheery wave with his good hand.

"Welcome aboard," he says.

"How's Sam Spade?"

"Terrific, as ever. Great lines. Forget Chandler, Dashiell Hammett invented hard-boiled. How was the trip?"

"It was fine. I came back in one piece."

"Tell me about it when we eat."

Jed leaves him to join his mother who's basting a sizzling leg of lamb in the kitchen, the smell of rosemary filling the room.

"Are you hungry?" she says.

"You know me." He tries to sound convincing, despite over-indulging on eggs and toast.

"It'll be an hour. Be a love, in the meantime, make a start on the boxes in the attic."

She hands him the torch she had ready on the kitchen table and, without another word, he's on his way, pleased to delay his mother's inevitable questions about Libya or the possibility he'll blurt something out about the burglary, never mind Ayesha's theories.

In the attic bedroom that was once his own, he has to crawl into a cramped loft space in the eaves, a torch in one hand and with a back aching from a night on the settee. The boxes are lined up, covered in black dust and stretching further than the torch can throw light in the triangular tunnel. He pulls the nearest one out into the bedroom and kneels next to it staring at the bulging manila files inside.

He lifts the top file out. Black and white photographs spew everywhere – a collage of images of California in the 1940s, judging by the look of the cars and clothes. He picks one up of a man looking deep into the lens, leathery skin etched by squinting in the sun, a weariness in his eyes. On the back, stamped in fading black ink are the words 'Farm Security Administration'.

As he rifles through the other photographs, many have the same label. Others bear the names of newspapers and magazines. Some have no marking at all. Mostly they are of people – children and women as well as men – in bleak and barren rural settings. But there are also bustling street scenes and parades, American football and baseball games, and film stars he vaguely recognises arriving at the Fairmont and other stylish hotels he's seen while on holiday in San Francisco.

Jed pushes the photographs to one side and pulls another manila file from the box, this time packed with letters, newspaper cuttings and a few random receipts and invoices. This is the world of Charles McIntosh Photographer of 1105 Sansome Street, San Francisco. The dates span a decade from the early 1940s to 1953, the year before he came to London. Jed sifts through the file, page by page, looking for things that might be significant, hoping he'll know them if he sees them.

By half way through the pile, he has the troubling feeling he's entered the life of a complete stranger. Uncle Jack had always been the glamorous sibling, the successful Californian architect. His father had been, as he sometimes himself put it, an Average Joe. Now, here he is, sought after and praised by editors, profiled in magazines, invited to speak at colleges and schools, a man seemingly at the peak of his profession – and only in his twenties.

It's a life he had never spoken about, not in Jed's presence, though maybe that was because he'd never asked. He'd always found other people's parents more interesting when he was a teenager.

The boxes had always been there, only a few feet from the bed he'd slept in as a teenager, but they'd never aroused his curiosity. And now his father can hardly speak.

Jed picks up a cutting so fragile the yellow newsprint paper is crumbling at the edges. A faded picture shows a young Charlie standing next to a display of photographs of assorted dilapidated houses and apartment buildings.

Photographs Expose Blight In San Francisco

City master plan earmarks districts for redevelopment and sets standards for population density

In a hall better known for rowdy labor gatherings, a young photographer is playing his part in shaping the future of San Francisco.

The City Planning Commission gave Charlie McIntosh the task of capturing the slum conditions in Western Addition, Mission, Chinatown and other districts, and now his work is on display at Albion Hall, a venue once renowned for meetings of striking longshoremen.

McIntosh, who hails from Seattle and started his career with the Farm Security Administration, thinks the venue well-chosen since it is in the heart of one of the areas considered blighted.

"The exhibition tells the story of areas where the housing is decaying and substandard and there is a lack of open space for playgrounds and gardens," he declared.

"I spent weeks walking the streets in these districts taking photographs that I thought would capture the conditions and show why the Commission's proposals for redevelopment are so necessary."

Jed puts the cutting on one side to show his father. It seems a good enough way to try to get him talking. He badly needs a steer from him. His mother may be eager to clear stuff out, but he has no idea what to keep and what to dump. And to estimate the scale of the task, he needs to sample all the boxes.

Jed crawls back into the eaves and pulls another one out. It's mostly filled with books from the same era. Jed knows the names of some of the authors – Hellman, Dubois, Steinbeck, Trumbo – but others are new to him – Gurley Flynn, Bridges, Debs. His father had brought them half way across the world but, like the photographs and papers, he has no idea why or how to value them. As he digs through the books, taking some out and piling them on the floor, he finds a manila file underneath them.

He sits down on the bed and leafs through the sheets of paper – some airmail blue, others white and wafer-thin bearing smudged carbon copies of letters that his father sent. He picks out one dated December 11, 1954, from Edward Brodsky in Chicago.

'*Things are going from bad to worse here,*' it says. '*The Feds turned up at Walter's house in Brooklyn unannounced and had the low down on everyone he'd ever met. The Photo League is as good as dead. No one dares admit they were ever hooked up with it. That stoolpigeon Calomiris really earned her dough.'*

Jed puts the letter aside and turns to another sent by Charlie's mother, Elizabeth, dated April 3, 1953, asking him if he's found a job in New York. She says she's missing him and is sorry how things have worked out. *'I don't know where it's going to end,'* she writes. *'So many of your old friends are in prison or out of work now. But I do hope you won't allow fear to come into your thoughts, for evil men rely on minds being sickened by fear.'*

Jed is mystified. He knows this must be about McCarthyism – mention of the Feds is a giveaway – but he didn't know his father had moved to New York, or what drove him there that Jed's grandmother would be sorry about. He feels his task is becoming both more difficult and more intriguing with each fresh discovery, and he's only opened two of the nine boxes.

Deciding he has time to sample one more, he drags the next nearest box into the light. It's full of albums, six altogether. Five are from Charlie's childhood – mainly family snaps with his mother, father and Jack on various trips and with other relatives and friends Jed doesn't know. But the photographs in the sixth album come as another complete surprise to Jed. His father is in a naval uniform of some sort, most of them on or next to a ship marked YMS-445. The captions are hard to decipher, but he makes out the names of the places – Apamama, Makin and Guam.

"Lieutenant McIntosh. He wasn't bad looking, was he?"

Margaret's words so surprise Jed he bangs his head on a rafter.

"Sorry, love, I thought you'd have heard me on the stairs."

"I was engrossed."

163

"I can see that. Anyway, food's ready"

"I had no idea he'd been in the navy."

Margaret takes the album and turns a few pages. "No, he doesn't talk about it."

"What does YMS stand for?"

"It was some kind of minesweeper."

Jed notices she's looking at the letters strewn across the bed.

"I was reading some of those," he says. "There's one from a guy called Brodsky who mentions someone else, Walter. What's that all about?"

Margaret looks ashen. "Oh God, Jed, I didn't know he'd kept all that stuff."

"What's the problem?"

Margaret has her brow furrowed and seems to be struggling for words.

"Just take it steady with him, Jed, that's all. Check with me before you talk to him about any of this. I don't want him getting upset."

"I will, of course. But why? Is there something in particular? Because I was going to show him the letters now."

"You'll be lucky," she replies. "He's sound asleep. But if he wakes up, the letters are strictly off limits for now. Take them home with you, and then we can talk."

CHAPTER TWELVE

The four-storey Victorian building that houses the sixteen staff of O'Brien and Partners is slowly decaying. It's had a few improvements — newly-fitted fire doors, a coat of paint in the hallways, a bit of carpet here and there — but all the windows are drafty, the stairs are rickety, and damp is never far away.

But Conor O'Brien isn't someone who worries much about appearances. When he came to London from Derry to study in the 1950s, he wasn't aiming to make a mint as a corporate lawyer. Once qualified, he settled in Willesden where he worked in a Law Centre helping Irish families fight Rachmanite landlords and cowboy contractors. After a few years, he set up on his own from a spare bedroom but, when three daughters came along in quick succession, he was soon ousted and decided to buy this ramshackle building in Islington.

That's not to say money doesn't matter to him. O'Brien is pleased that gentrification has sent the value of the building soaring. It gives him an extra nest egg to maintain his comfortable lifestyle when he sells the family home in Willesden and drags his wife, Mary, back to Derry to retire.

For now, though, he likes his steady life in London. He's respected in his community. He's expanded from housing and industrial injury into immigration and nationality. He knows his field inside out. And he no longer has to work on weekends to keep the business afloat.

His Sundays are, especially, a work-free zone. While Mary goes to church, he's in the habit of taking Cael, his Labrador, for a walk in Roundwood Park, then picking up a pile of newspapers on the way home. By the time he's done that, Mary is back from Mass, and he cooks a big fried breakfast for them both and reads the papers for as long as he can stave off the inevitable nap. It's a ritual he's enjoyed since the girls left home, and he doesn't take kindly to it being ruined.

And now it's Monday. As O'Brien stands in his office looking down at the deserted street where, on any other morning, stallholders would be setting up, he shakes his head at the memory of the previous day — the worst intrusion into his sacrosanct day of rest he can remember. What was Jed thinking, getting himself tied up in all this? He'd phoned Jed's home number a few times to find out, but there was no answer, and he was too annoyed to leave a message. He's still so vexed that he's made himself a larger-than-usual pile of toast with his morning coffee and is about to settle down to eat it when Jed knocks and his sheepish face appears around the door.

"You wanted to see me?"

"You bet I did, son. Come in, grab a pew."

O'Brien has given himself the only room that spans the width of the building. Whereas the associates in the offices below have one window each, he has four, giving him enough space for a large oak desk at one end and three armchairs and a coffee table at the other.

Jed looks relieved when O'Brien directs him to the wooden chair in front his desk. It's well known in the firm that, if you are in really serious trouble, you're given the compensation of hearing the bad news in the comfort of an armchair at the other end of the room. If he's going to give you what he likes to call "a word to the wise", he does it from the desk. But O'Brien knows this is known, and he wants to catch Jed with his guard down.

166

"Good to see you back in one piece," he says, landing his plate of toast on the desk like a pilot with a precious cargo and settling into his own padded leather hair.

As O'Brien munches, Jed decides to make the first move. He was tipped off by Adam as soon as he arrived at the office that the firm's number two, Barry Austen, had told the Friday staff meeting that he'd heard from his Home Office sources that Jed had gone to Tripoli. Adam said that O'Brien had been relaxed about it.

"I hear Austen's been complaining about me."

O'Brien smiles at Jed's boldness. He likes that about him. And, normally, Jed's assumption that he doesn't usually care what staff do in their own time, or give much credence to anything that comes from the Home Office, would be right. But things had changed since Friday.

"Austen is the least of your fucking worries." O'Brien words are muffled by a mouthful of toast, but it doesn't soften their impact. He watches Jed gulp at the realisation that his opening gambit had missed the mark.

"What do you mean?"

"What I mean is, I don't take kindly to having the spooks banging on my door on a Sunday morning."

"Spooks?" Jed says, so surprised he jerks back in his seat and nearly topples over.

"Well, I don't know for sure who the fuck they were. One called himself Chamberlain. And there was another fella with him who didn't give his name. Chamberlain did the talking. He said he was with the Foreign Office and that he wanted a word about your trip to Libya and involvement with Palestinian extremists. He said it was a security matter and wanted to come in. For fuck's sake Jed, what have you got yourself into?"

O'Brien picks up another piece of toast, carefully allowing the butter to drip onto the plate before taking a large bite and then washing it down with some coffee. He is past caring about his weight. As his sixtieth birthday approaches, he may be a bit chubby, but he still has a good head of hair and no health problems he knows about.

"Who exactly is this girl, Jed?"

"What do you mean?"

"Jesus wept, Jed, it's not a complicated question. What's she told you about herself?"

O'Brien stares at Jed, who seems to be having difficulty marshalling an answer.

"Her name's Ayesha Khoury," he begins, hesitantly. "She's Lebanese – I've seen the passport. Her father is Lebanese, her mother's Palestinian. They live in Beirut, and Ayesha was a teacher there until she came here a few years ago."

"What year?"

"Late eighty-two or early eight-three, I'm not sure exactly. She has an aunt here with a flat in Kentish Town who encouraged her to do a masters at LSE. And now she's doing a PhD."

"But that's not why she came here, according to Chamberlain."

"I wasn't saying it was. But you can't blame her for wanting to get out of Beirut."

O'Brien laughs. "That's true," he said. "It's worse than Derry. But, according to Chamberlain, she left in a hurry because she's tied up with the PLO. He says her uncle – I can't remember the name – is – or was – a big cheese in the PLO. He called him 'Arafat's money man'. You do know, do you, who Arafat is?"

O'Brien watches Jed flush. It's obvious all this is news to him.

"Of course I know who Arafat is," he says, in a truculent tone. "But I don't think whatever Ayesha's uncle did is relevant to the fact that her boyfriend died in Tripoli. I was doing her a favour, not her uncle."

"Her uncle's dead anyway – he was killed in the fighting in Beirut, according to Chamberlain – but the point is she left just afterwards, at more or less the same time as Arafat and the PLO were forced to leave Beirut. Arafat set up camp in Tunis, that's where he's based now, and Chamberlain claims Ayesha was sent here by the PLO."

"But, so what? What if she is? The PLO's recognised by the United Nations. Arafat is their leader. Why shouldn't someone in London represent them...?"

"Jed, Jed, you don't have to give me the lecture. They said De Valera was a terrorist. They say Mandela is a terrorist. I know what the British are like – one minute they're calling someone a terrorist, the next they're inviting them for tea with the Queen. But that's not the bloody point. You didn't know what you were getting into, and now I've got MI5 – or whoever they are – on my back. These fuckers don't give up their Sundays for trivial pursuits. There was a threat behind Chamberlain's visit. And I don't need the hassle. I'm trying to run a business here. I've got to keep my nose clean."

O'Brien picks up the last piece of toast and disposes of it in two bites. He's silenced Jed, but he's not sure where this leaves him. O'Brien has always trodden a fine line between battling the authorities and not making outright enemies of them. He's reluctant to get involved in Jed's project – and risk further annoying Chamberlain – but he knows he can't undo what's done, and he decides his best option is damage limitation.

"So, what's the state of play?" he asks, wiping his mouth with a tissue. "What did you find out in Tripoli?"

"To be honest, not a lot. The Libyans were friendly but didn't give much away. They insisted it was accidental, that he went onto the beach and somehow drowned. Chamberlain turned up at our hotel with Tom's father, Major Carver, but he was hostile. He blames Ayesha for Tom being there and seems to have accepted the freak accident theory."

"But Ayesha's still in denial, is she?"

"In denial?"

"She can't accept it was an accident. She wants someone to blame."

"I guess she just wants the truth."

O'Brien laughs in a guttural way and starts coughing so fiercely he has to take a tissue from his drawer and cover his mouth.

"She'll be lucky," he says when he's finished. "Chamberlain's all over this. I'm not sure why the Foreign Office would be so bothered about a dead peace activist on a Libyan beach, but I assume it's either because Carver has some clout or it's to do with Ayesha. I can't work it out, but he's not going to let her rock the boat when drunken misadventure obviously suits him, and he's even got you quoted in the press backing it up."

Jed shifts sheepishly in his chair. "That was before we met the Tripoli police chief. One witness had told me that Tom was the worse for wear, but the post mortem found only thirty milligrams of alcohol in his blood."

"Jesus, that's not enough to make you jump off a cliff."

"There weren't any cliffs."

"And he was of sound mind?"

"Ayesha thinks so."

"So, you're telling me it might be foul play. Did he have any injuries?"

"A few scratches and bruises, but the Libyan police say those probably came from his body being dragged on the sea bed."

"And what was he wearing when they found him?"

"He was fully clothed, except for his trainers, which were lying nearby. And he had a wallet on him, but no cash in it, only two credit cards."

O'Brien gives Jed a puzzled look, his thick wiry eyebrows knotting together. "His clothes were wet, presumably?"

Jed nods.

"And what about the trainers?"

"I don't know, why?"

"You need to find that out, Jed. I presume you're planning to see Ayesha again. She should check with her Libyan contacts whether or not the shoes were wet."

O'Brien ignores Jed's confused look. He can't be bothered explaining his reasoning. He's pondering what ground rules to set – his anger's abated now, but he still needs to ensure that Jed doesn't land the firm in any more trouble.

"Look," he says, finally. "If you want to see her, I can't stop you. But if you couldn't get to the bottom of this in Tripoli, I can't for the life of me see what you can do for her now. But if you feel you must try to help her, for God's sake, be careful. I don't know what Chamberlain's got on Ayesha – or how that ties in with this lad's death – but he means business, that was obvious. So, find out what the story is with her uncle, and keep me in the loop. You clear on that? Report back to me tomorrow."

Jed looks relieved and is on his feet starting for the door the moment it's clear O'Brien has finished.

"Jed, hang on – there's something else." O'Brien waits for Jed to turn around. "Chamberlain said something about your father, and the trouble he'd had when he came here. He's American, isn't he? And, in passing, Chamberlain made a comment about how you wouldn't want to get yourself into trouble like your father did when he came here."

"What's that supposed to mean?"

"I've no idea. But you'd better ask your father about it. Chamberlain meant it as a threat. The man's as subtle as a brick."

CHAPTER THIRTEEN

Back in his own office, Jed starts to browse through the files that have piled up while he was away. Two days off, and there are twenty of them. Most are old ones, now back on his desk after O'Brien or Austen had looked over them and scribbled a few comments. Six are completely new and would need an hour or so of reading each.

He finds it hard to concentrate at first. Chamberlain's threat is unsettling, the words 'when he came here' play on his mind. He'd been too tired to go through his father's file when he got home the night before, but the letters he'd read at his parent's house were about his father's troubles before he left the US. He has no idea what Chamberlain means.

But at least O'Brien wasn't as hard on him as he could have been. He'd looked foolish for failing to grill Ayesha like he would a client, but he isn't surprised her uncle was a PLO official or, for that matter, about the possibility she was sent to London by them. Whether she was on their payroll or not didn't really matter, she hadn't made a secret of her views.

Jed did, though, feel a worry nagging at him, which he hadn't dared mention to O'Brien. Ayesha's failure to tell him about the call from Tom until they were on their way back made him wonder now how many other things she might be keeping to herself.

Jed doesn't have this problem with his clients. The letters, forms and official documents in their files usually cover almost every personal detail of their lives. He picks up the one at the top of the pile. It has a note from O'Brien attached saying 'worth an appeal'. It's a case that came in just before he went to Tripoli of a woman from Bangladesh who wants to join her fiancé in Britain. They're up against a presumption of guilt – the premise being that, unless they can prove otherwise, the primary purpose of an Asian woman marrying a British man must be to gain residency.

The file is thick with supporting evidence, even down to some love letters that are embarrassingly intimate. But, after months of to-ing and fro-ing with the Home Office, while their wedding plans were in limbo and the woman waited in Dakha, their application has been turned down. Now, a Bangladeshi community group in Tower Hamlets has hired the firm to help. Jed makes some notes and adds it to his 'for action' tray.

The next file is another new referral with a similar story and the same note from O'Brien, who seems to be grooming him to be the firm's 'primary purpose' specialist.

As Jed browses wearily through the documents, the buzz of an internal call comes as a welcome interruption.

"Ah, there you are Jed." It's the gravelly voice of O'Brien's personal assistant, Norah, who has a knack of making him feel guilty even when he's where he's supposed to be. "I've got a message from your friend, Ayesha – she says she'll meet you at The Camden Head at seven-thirty, rather than seven."

"When did she phone?" Jed says, thinking it odd she hadn't wanted to talk to him.

"Only about five minutes ago. She seemed in a rush, a bit rude she was. But don't go, I've got a young woman on hold for you. She wouldn't give me her name."

After a few clicks, Jed hears someone on the line breathing softly.

"Hello, Gerald McIntosh speaking," he says, in his work persona.

"I hope you don't mind me calling you," a timid young voice says.

"It's fine, no problem – what can I do for you?"

"I don't want to give you my name," she continues, still sounding wary.

"That's fine," Jed says, having had this a few times from women in trouble and been told in his first week by O'Brien never to sound impatient.

"The thing is, I saw the report in the paper, *The Independent*, about the guy who died in Tripoli."

"Right..." Jed says, jolted out of work mode.

"Tom wasn't drunk like it said. Like you said."

Jed hesitates, wary of admitting how that had come about when he has no idea who he's speaking to. She doesn't sound like a journalist, but that could be a ploy to get him talking.

"Yes, that's been cleared up now," he says. "I gather he hadn't had as much to drink as some people thought. But how do you know about this?"

"I was there, I was with him."

"You were?" Jed replies, wondering if he's talking to the woman in the photograph, but not wanting to rush her.

"I was also a delegate, and I was with him and some Canadians, but he only had a couple of sips of mine. He was drinking tea."

There's a nervous quiver in her voice. Jed picks up his pen and starts to make notes.

"So, what time was that?"

"We got back at about eight, from then on... We went to this bar area they had and sat talking for a while and then he went off to speak to this other guy from Britain who was with another group. And when he came back, he was furious, really upset."

"What about?"

"Something to do with gay rights. He didn't say much at the time, just that they were planning a stupid stunt and he thought it was disrespectful to people who'd died in the air strikes. He kept saying 'there's a time and a place for everything'."

"Do you know what this stunt was?"

"Apparently, they were going to unfurl a gay rights banner in Arabic from one of the hotel windows."

"Really? Okay, so, he came back, and he was agitated about this banner, and what happened then?"

"He went off again. We'd been talking and he'd calmed down a bit, but then he got up and said he was going to make a phone call."

"What time was that?"

The caller doesn't reply immediately. Jed can hear a faint hum of traffic and realises she's in a call-box.

"Just after ten, I think. I'm not sure."

"And was that the last time you saw him?"

"No, he came back. I think it was about half an hour later, maybe more. But he walked straight past me and went over to the guy he'd been talking to. He looked really angry... Tom, I mean."

"Can you describe the other guy?"

The woman falls silent again, and Jed begins to worry she could hang up at any moment.

"I'm trying to picture him, but all I can remember for sure is that he was very tall," she says finally.

"White?"

"Yes."

"Thick brown hair, and very athletic looking?"

"Yes, thin but with broad shoulders."

"Then Tom stormed out, did he?"

"Not exactly."

"What do you mean?"

"He didn't leave on his own. They went out together. It looked like the tall guy wanted to get Tom out of the bar."

"Are you saying he was forcing him?"

The caller pauses again, but this time the traffic noise is much louder and a man's voice abruptly says, "how much longer you going to be?"

"What's your name?" he asks.

But the hum of the line going dead drowns his desperate question.

"Shit," he says, banging his pen down on the desk.

The afternoon passes so slowly Jed feels like he's on a backward-moving conveyor belt. He has decided to forego lunch so that he can make an impression on his pile of files. The cases are, at least, a distraction. For the time being, he's glad of a break from worrying about Chamberlain's threats, Ayesha's possible links with 'extremists' and the inconsistencies in Gavin's accounts of the night Tom died.

Norah delivers more files almost as fast as Jed gets through them, but she does soften the pain by bringing him a mid-afternoon mug of tea with a large chocolate éclair.

He's wiping the cream off his face with a tissue when Adam pokes his head around the door.

"Did O'Brien give you a hard time?"

"Not as bad as it could have been," Jed says, not wanting to give away that Austen bad-mouthing him hadn't been the main problem.

"Austen's a wanker," Adam says, in a hushed voice, checking over his shoulder. "O'Brien knows that. He's not stupid. I don't think he likes the fact that he's in so thick with the Home Office crowd. Who knows what he feeds them?"

Jed nods but doesn't want to get into a discussion with Adam about Austen or the meeting with O'Brien. They've been good friends since starting as articled clerks together, but he knows Adam can be indiscreet, and he isn't someone he'd turn to for advice about anything sensitive.

"Look at this lot," he says, tapping the pile of files. "Twenty cases, and Norah keeps them coming."

"They take the piss sometimes. How about a drink tonight? You can tell me all about Tripoli."

"I can't, sorry, I'm seeing Ayesha."

"I hear she's hot."

"Get lost," Jed says, as Adam's smirking face disappears.

An hour and three files later, Norah is back. This time, she's empty handed.

"I'll take what you've done and anything for typing."

Jed hands her some files with the letters he's drafted replying to clients or lodging appeals.

"And Hannah called – the funeral's on Wednesday at two-thirty."

"Right, was that it?" Jed says, his voice tinged with annoyance that he'd just been to Libya to help her friend and she hadn't asked to speak to him.

"Yes, that was it – she did ask for you, but I said you were catching up on your files."

Jed smiles. So, this, he now realises, is O'Brien's way of punishing him. He's told Norah – who's been keeping the men at O'Brien's in line for two decades – to make him sweat.

After waiting for her to climb the stairs back to her office, and out of earshot, he decides he's earned a break and picks up the phone to call Hannah.

"Hello, Hannah, here," she answers in a brisk, business-like tone.

"It's Jed," he says. "I wasn't sure if you'd be at your own place."

"But here I am! How was Tripoli?"

"A bit of a wild goose chase, to be honest," Jed says, and gives a brief account of the trip that covers the basics but leaves out any mention of alcohol or gay rights. Both are subjects he wants to ask Gavin about face-to-face, whatever Ayesha says, but without giving him advance warning.

"Sorry if I've wasted your time roping you into this, Jed, but I'm sure Ayesha appreciated your support," Hannah says.

"You've seen her, have you?"

"No, she's been busy, but she called."

"Is Gavin there?"

"No, why?"

"Nothing. I was going to arrange to see him. There are a couple of things I want to ask him about."

"He's away. He came back at the weekend, but had to go home again because his father's having chemo today. He'll be back for the funeral on Wednesday. What is it? Can I Help?"

"No, no, it's nothing, just a few details to clear up..."

Jed waits for Hannah to say something, and he's surprised she doesn't. Normally, she'd wheedle whatever she wanted to know out of him – or, at least, muster the energy to try.

"See you at the funeral then," she says.

"Yes, see you..."

The phone clicks before he's finished. For the second time that afternoon, a call has ended abruptly.

Jed sits back in his chair and stares at the phone. He knows Hannah so well he's certain there's something wrong. It was probably the first time they'd had a whole conversation without any banter. And he has a hunch that she cut him off because she was going to cry.

CHAPTER FOURTEEN

Ayesha has decided to walk from her flat to Islington. The days are longer now, and it's summery for April. She only needs a light jacket over her jeans and blouse, and a scarf to stop her hair going wild in the breeze. She'll follow the canal as far as King's Cross and then walk along Copenhagen Street to get to The Camden Head. It's a route that she and Tom had walked many times, often ending with a meal at their favourite Cypriot café on Upper Street.

Each step along the towpath in the sunshine helps to settle her mind. She wants to savour Tom, live and breathe the things they did together. It's the only way to compensate for not seeing his body, not being able to say goodbye.

She hasn't decided yet whether or not to go the funeral. She shudders at the thought of being in the same room as Major Carver again and of being publicly shunned, as seems inevitable. But it's her only chance to see Tom's coffin. Does that matter? Or is it better to do this, to walk where they used to walk and imagine him by her side?

And then there's the memorial event his friends are organising. When she left her flat, another meeting to plan it was still going on. Hannah wasn't there. She'd sent a message saying she didn't feel well. But she'd organised everything in her usual meticulous way. Invitations were ready to go out. The meeting only had to finalise the readings and music.

Ayesha had told them she would read a poem from Mahmoud Darwash's *Ward Aqall* — because Tom had bought it for her birthday – and they should end with *Something Inside So Strong* – because it was 'their' song. And she couldn't speak after saying that. It was all too much. Had she tried to say anything else, she'd have wept, and she didn't want to do that in front of the whole group. She'd left them to it. And now she can't get Labi Siffri's voice out of her mind as she approaches The Camden Head.

She's ten minutes early. The pub is busy for a Monday evening, the fine weather having brought in the after-work drinkers. Ayesha decides to wait for Jed outside and positions herself so she can see along Camden Passage, assuming that's the way he'll come.

When he appears in the distance, she moves into a side street and watches him go into the pub. After a few moments, she follows and taps him on the shoulder, making him jump.

"Shit, where did you come from?"

"I was early, I wanted to see if you were alone." she whispers.

"Alone? Who would I bring?"

"Being followed, I mean. Never mind, let's go."

"Where?"

Jed looks confused, but Ayesha is already on her way out of the door and he tags along as she walks briskly towards Essex Road and stops, ready to cross. As he draws level with her at the kerb, she puts her arm through his.

"We're going to a Greek place on Upper Street," she says without taking her eyes of the passing traffic. "It will be quieter. And more private. Some Cypriot friends run it."

After a hair-raising dash to the pavement opposite, they skirt around Islington Green and along Upper Street until they reach a double fronted café. Across the road, people are queuing to see *Dirty Dancing*. But the area is otherwise quiet, and the café itself is empty apart from a stocky, grey-haired woman, wearing a black skirt and white blouse, who greets Ayesha with an ostentatious embrace.

"I'm so, so sorry for your loss, Ayesha – Tom was such a nice young man," she says, in a thick Greek accent.

"Thank you, Christina," Ayesha replies, softly, swallowing hard and stepping back from her as if the woman's kindness could tip her into tears.

"Now, we have some really good food for you tonight. Where you want to sit?"

Ayesha nods towards a small round table against a rear wall decorated with an Athenian-style mural in garish blues and oranges. Christina ushers them over to it and gives them menus before disappearing into the kitchen.

Ayesha takes the seat facing the entrance and undoes the knot in her head scarf to let her hair fall freely onto her shoulders. Taking her jacket off, she points to her peasant style blouse with a blue pattern on white cotton.

"Christina gave this to me. Tom lived around the corner when we first met. We used to come here a lot."

"It's nice."

Ayesha shrugs, as if to add an 'ish' to his comment. She's only wearing it for Christina.

"Were you seriously worried we might be followed?" Jed asks.

"Only because of the break-in. It was just a precaution. You never know."

"You certainly don't. My boss had a visit from Chamberlain."

"What?" Ayesha gasps, looking horrified.

Jed is about to explain, when Christina returns with a tray of houmous, Taramasalata, and warm flat bread. Ayesha thanks her in Greek and watches her go back into the kitchen. When she turns to face Jed again, he's preoccupied piling houmous and flatbread into his mouth.

"Sorry, all I've had all day is a chocolate éclair," he says, the words barely audible.

She's not impressed by his priorities. This development is not to be taken lightly. She had assumed Chamberlain is senior, and probably using the name of the Foreign Office loosely. And she isn't surprised that Jed is on his radar. But going personally to see O'Brien – that's a surprise and a worry.

"Sorry," Jed says, swallowing. "Okay, so, Chamberlain turned up on O'Brien's doorstep on Sunday morning with a sidekick. He told him your uncle was Arafat's money man and that you were sent to London by the PLO..."

Ayesha laughs out loud. "Seriously. To do what?"

"He said something about you being an extremist and a security threat, and implied that LSE was just a cover."

"And that's it?"

She shakes her head and lifts both hands in the air in a gesture of exasperation.

"They think they can just say these things. Make Arafat out to be a terrorist. Throw words like 'extremist' around. And I'm guilty just because I'm Palestinian, and I oppose an illegal occupation of our land. They make me sick..."

Jed leans forward and takes one of her shaking hands, squeezing it gently. "Look, I know all that," he says, softly. "And so does O'Brien, to be fair. But Chamberlain rattled his cage. He was caught on the hop, and then when he asked me about you, I looked stupid because I knew so little about you."

"So, what do you want to know? Come on, ask me anything."

Jed suddenly looks uncomfortable and embarrassed.

"Look, I'm sorry - forget it. You don't owe me any explanations."

Ayesha sits in silence for a moment. She picks up a piece of flatbread and holds it in front of her, completely still, as if any movement would disturb her thought process.

"No, you're wrong, Jed. Actually, I *do* owe you an explanation. You've been very kind. And I really do appreciate it. Not many people would have done what you've done. And there are many things I haven't told you about myself, partly because they are not things I talk about much – they're too painful – and also because they aren't relevant to what happened to Tom, or I didn't think they were. But maybe they are. Chamberlain's behaviour makes me wonder."

"Like what? Why is Chamberlain gunning for you in such a big way?"

"That's a good question, because – if his spies are doing their job – he must know I wasn't sent to London by the PLO. *Of course* I support the PLO. Why wouldn't I? Palestinians have to have a voice. The PLO is far from perfect, but who would speak for us otherwise? But I have no role in it. I came to London because things were so bad in Beirut. And I stayed because my aunt offered to sponsor my studies, like I told you. And, yes, I do hope that, one day, maybe I can be of some use to a free Palestine. What's so bad about that?"

Ayesha looks down at the flatbread, her shoulders dropping as she sighs wearily, feeling that too often she finds herself on the defensive, justifying what to her is obvious.

"So, forget Chamberlain," Jed says. "Tell me more about yourself because *I* would very much like to know."

Ayesha smiles, wanting him to see that she accepts the sincerity of his question.

"But what, exactly, do you want to know?"

"Tell me about your family for a start."

"You may regret this. There are a lot of us. I have four siblings. I'm the eldest. But, okay, I'll start with my mother. She's from Galilee, a village called Eilabun near Nazareth. I've never been there. It's part of Israel now, but it was supposed to be in the Arab State when Palestine was partitioned. My mother was nineteen when she left with her mother and younger brother – the uncle that Chamberlain was talking about. That was in 1948, of course."

Ayesha dips a small piece of flatbread into the Taramasalata and eats it slowly, taking a few moments to think about how to sum up a horror story about which her mother would – or could – herself only rarely speak.

"Eilabun was one of the last villages to hold out," she says, finally. "My grandfather died in the fighting. When it was captured, the Israelis executed most of the young men and told everyone else to leave. They had to go on foot to the Lebanese border, twenty kilometres away. Then, for some reason, the Israelis changed their minds and said the Christian villagers could come back. But my grandmother was Muslim, and she decided the three of them should go on to Beirut with the other refugees pouring into Lebanon. There were thousands of them. The Red Cross had to set up camps, and they ended up in Shatila..."

"Shatila?"

"One of the camps in Beirut. My mother and uncle were luckier than most. They were only in Shatila for a couple of years."

"But what happened to your grandmother?"

"She died. In the camp. My mother says she was exhausted and heartbroken. She'd lost her husband, her home, everything. Once she got my mother and her brother to safety, she just gave up."

Ayesha falls silent as Christina arrives to clear away the empty starter plates and take their order.

"We have a nice moussaka, and the fish today is mullet fried with lemon and oil."

"Mullet for me," Jed says, and Ayesha's nods to signal she'll have the same.

Once Christina's gone, Ayesha continues. "So, a year or two after that, after my grandmother had died, they left Shatila. My mother had met my father. He's Lebanese, from an affluent family. He was studying law at the American University in Beirut. After he graduated, they got married. That was 1953. And I was born later that year. So, I was lucky too. I wasn't born in a refugee camp, and I grew up in a nice part of Beirut."

"And what happened to your uncle?"

"My father was very kind to him – he lived with us when I was a small child, and my father treated him like a brother and paid for him to study."

Ayesha pauses and looks at Jed as if inviting a question. But she answers it herself.

"To be an accountant. So, yes, you could say he was 'Arafat's money man' or one of them," she says, with sarcastic emphasis on Chamberlain's words. "But he was actually more like a civil servant. The PLO represents millions of Palestinians, and it has to have offices all over the world... Someone has to do the books."

Ayesha enjoys her own joke – until Jed brings them abruptly back to reality.

"So how did he die?"

The word 'die' is drowned by a sudden burst of noise as the café door opens and a large group pours in, everyone talking at once in loud, inebriated voices about what they want to eat and where they're going to sit.

"Killed," Ayesha says, as they both watch the newcomers jockeying for position at a long table.

"Killed, did you say?"

"Yes, to be accurate about it. My uncle didn't die in an accident or of natural causes. But let's not continue this here. Not with, you know, all this..."

Ayesha jerks her head sideways towards the other customers who are now seated and shouting their drink orders to Christina.

"So, are you in trouble with O'Brien?" she says.

"He wasn't best pleased about Chamberlain, to put it mildly. But once he'd calmed down, he wanted to know what had happened. And, for some reason, he seemed to think it was important to find out if Tom's trainers were wet."

"Wet?"

Jed shrugs. "I didn't get a chance to ask him why, but could you find out from Gibran? If only to show O'Brien that I was paying attention."

"I'll phone him tonight. And I've already phoned Alison, from CND, to ask about the woman in the photograph with Tom. But she wasn't sure who it could be from my description. So tomorrow I'll get a copy made and send it to her. She lives in Manchester."

"I may have spoken to whoever it was," Jed says, looking sheepish.

"What do you mean?"

"I had a call today from a woman who was with Tom that evening. She didn't give me her name."

Ayesha drops the flatbread she's been nibbling, completely astonished. They've been together for more than an hour. She'd felt guilty about not telling him more about herself or about Tom's call, and he's been keeping this to himself.

She doesn't need to say anything – Jed's discomfort is visible as he hurriedly recounts what the caller said about being in the bar with Tom, who wasn't drunk but who was wound up about a stunt being planned by someone who, judging by her description, was almost certainly Gavin.

"What stunt?"

"Gavin and some other delegates were planning to unfurl a gay rights banner – in Arabic – from one of the hotel windows."

"They were *what*?" Ayesha tilts her head back and closes her eyes, thinking of the voice message Tom had left, the garbled words she'd re-played over and over again. "So, that's what Tom was agitated about."

She's brought back into the present by Christina arriving with two plates that are barely big enough for the mullet, fries and salad on them.

"Sorry about, you know," Christina says, rolling her eyes in the direction of the other group as she sets their meals down.

Ayesha forks a small piece of fish into her mouth and chews it slowly. She imagines Tom confronting Gavin in that bar, accusing him of gesture politics, of pulling a stunt that would detract from the barbarity of killing innocent civilians in an air strike. She can hear him saying it – and would have agreed – but she would also have calmed him down and helped him work out what to do.

As she takes another mouthful of the mullet, she watches Jed clearing his plate like a dog that hasn't been fed for a week.

"I suppose Gavin had a point, about gay rights," he says, putting his knife and fork down on the plate. "I mean, Libya does treat homosexuality as a crime, doesn't it?"

"Yes, and so did Britain until not so long ago. Tom was right – it was a childish stunt. A nice photograph for the Western liberal press. But a distraction from America's crimes."

"Okay, but regardless of who was right or wrong, we now know they had a row."

"And if I'd phoned Tom back, maybe…"

"Maybe he wouldn't have carried on arguing with Gavin and gone onto the beach with him."

"*With him*… you mean they went out there together?"

"That's what she said. Tom told her he was going to make a phone call and, when he came back, he looked angry and went straight over to Gavin, and they left together. She said it looked like Gavin wanted to get him out of the bar. I'm not sure how she could tell. I tried to ask her, but she was in a phone box and hung up."

Ayesha tries to keep her composure, but her lips are quivering. "I'll be back in a minute," she says, standing abruptly and heading into a passage at the back of the café.

Ayesha pushes the door open into the women's toilet, a tiny windowless room, and locks it behind her. She slumps down onto the lid of the toilet and stares into the mirror above a wash basin opposite, watching tears meandering across her cheeks and dropping into her lap.

The room smells – an acerbic mix of bleach and lavender air freshener that stings the back of her throat. She wants to think through what she's just heard, but she can hardly breathe. She decides she needs space and air.

When she comes out, dabbing her face with tissue, Christina is hovering near their table with a plate of Baklava.

"Have a few of these, my dear, they're lovely and fresh," she says, putting the plate down and squeezing Ayesha's arm.

Ayesha smiles and mouths a silent 'thanks' as Christina leaves. Still standing, she turns to Jed. "I'm sorry, you must be sick of me crying, but this new information is...." She's not actually sure what it is, what it means.

"We need to talk to Gavin, see what he's got to say about it."

"No, no. Not yet. I need to think. I'm going to go. I need some fresh air. Let's meet tomorrow, what time can you get away from work?"

"I'm going to see my parents in the afternoon, but I could see you after that, at four. Shall we meet at Golders Green. You know Bar Linda?"

Ayesha nods. "Tell Christina 'thanks' from me," she says, picking up her jacket and scarf and heading for the door.

Outside, the cool air and a fine drizzle instantly sharpen her senses. She crosses Upper Street and walks briskly towards the Angel, passing the *Screen On The Green*, where people are emerging and fanning out towards the pubs for last orders.

At first, she intends to hail a cab – to get back to the flat as quickly as possible – but she sees the telephone boxes and decides to act on her instincts. She'll make the call straight away. It's clear to her now what she has to do.

Chapter Fifteen

Jed's mother puts a finger to her lips as she opens the front door. "Your father's asleep," she says, nodding towards the closed door of the dining room.

Jed follows her into the garden where two thickly-padded recliners are side by side on the small patio, shaded by an umbrella. Between them is a small circular table with newspapers piled high on one side and a copy of *The Handmaid's Tale*, open and face down, on the other.

"I don't know what's come over him, he's been out here with me reading all morning," says Margaret, nodding at the papers. "He even did a lap of the lawn with his frame. It's worn him out."

"Blimey, I wish I'd been here to see that."

"He went for a lie down half an hour ago. Do you want a tea?"

"Just a Coke or something."

Jed settles into one of the recliners. He's so tired he dosed off on the Tube coming from work and nearly ended up in Edgware, waking in time only because the sun was so dazzling as the train emerged from the tunnel just before Golders Green.

After Ayesha's abrupt departure the previous night, Christina had insisted he stay for a glass or two of Retsina and a little chat. By the time he left, the bottle was empty, and she'd drained every detail of the trip to Tripoli from him. He was hoping the alcohol would knock him out but, when he got home, he found the conversation with

Christina had only made him more unsettled by all the loose ends.

Christina had made it plain she didn't like Gavin in the least, and she'd suggested that he must have made up the story about Tom being drunk because he didn't want people to blame him for what happened.

"That's the kind of man he is," she'd said. "If he was a true friend and thought Tom was really far gone, he'd have stopped him going onto that beach, if you ask me."

Jed hadn't asked her – he'd soon discovered Christina didn't need to be asked – but he found the theory plausible. What he couldn't understand was why Ayesha kept delaying the inevitable confrontation with Gavin about it. Hannah would surely be understanding now that so many questions have piled up.

In the hope of taking his mind off Tripoli, Jed had chosen his father's file for his bedtime reading. It proved to be the last thing he needed to help him sleep. Each letter tempted him to start another. He'd read until nearly three and found his confusion growing at about the same pace as his curiosity. Only two things were clear: someone called Doreen Stevens didn't like Charlie at all, and he'd been sacked not long after coming to London. But Jed wasn't sure if or how the two things were connected.

Jed's beginning to dose off again when his mother arrives with a can of Coke and hands it to him. She sits down on the other recliner and lets out a contented sigh. She's wearing what she usually does once there is a hint of summer – sandals, light blue slacks and a short-sleeved white blouse.

"I see he's been doing some serious reading – I haven't seen so many newspapers in the house for years," Jed says, flicking through a pile that includes not only the *Guardian* and *Times*, but also the *Times of India*, *Le Monde* and the *Washington Post.* "It reminds me of how his study upstairs used to be. You couldn't move for newspapers and magazines from all over the world. It used to fascinate me."

"I didn't find it so fascinating. What with his smoking and the dust, that room was filthy, and I couldn't get in to clean."

Jed smiles, seeing that his mother is saying this with a fondness, as if she'd give anything to have that Charlie back.

They sit in silence for a long moment. In the early afternoon, the Tube trains are few and far between, and it's quiet enough to hear the migrant birds who've arrived back in abundance to enjoy the unusually fine weather.

"So, you were in the paper then," Margaret says, pulling Saturday's *Independent* from the pile, and holding it up with the report of Tom's death displayed. "You're a dark horse. You didn't tell me when you came on Sunday."

"It's just one report, I doubt there'll be any more," he says, defensively.

"So, it looks like this Tom had had too much to drink and the sea got the better of him."

"Something like that." Jed decides not to admit that his moment of glory in the newspaper is hopelessly flawed.

"Is that it then? You've done this girl a favour and you're off the hook now?"

"More or less. I'm going to the funeral tomorrow. But there's not much else I can do after that."

"Good. I'm glad to hear it."

They fall silent again. Jed's not sure how to approach the subject of what Chamberlain said about Charlie. Because she's usually so reluctant to talk about the past, he opts for shock tactics.

"There is one thing, though," he says. "There was a Foreign Office guy in Tripoli, accompanying Tom's father, and he'd obviously checked me out, somehow, because he said Dad had had some kind of trouble when he first came to London…"

Margaret looks stunned and stares at Jed for a long moment, her lips pursed.

"He said what?"

"That was it, just that he'd had trouble."

"And why didn't you simply ask him?"

"He mentioned it to someone else. I wasn't there when he said it."

Margaret lets out a long, exasperated sigh and turns towards the lawn. Jed isn't sure for a moment if she's going to speak at all.

"There's nothing they don't know, these people, is there?" she says, finally. "Why would he bring that up? It was thirty years ago."

"I've no idea. He was trying to put me off, I suppose."

"Threaten you, more like."

"I wouldn't put it that way." Jed tries to sound casual, realising the blunt approach has backfired.

"Why else would he bring it up? I'm not daft, Jed."

"Okay, but what exactly was he talking about?"

Margaret shakes her head. "I really don't want to talk about this."

"But Mum, you wanted me to sort the files out, and there's a letter in the one I took home from someone saying Dad had deceived everyone and should be ashamed of himself…"

"Oh no, not that letter," Margaret says, breathlessly. "That's Doreen. I didn't know your father had kept it. She was vicious."

"But what had Dad done?"

"Nothing. He'd actually done nothing at all. But she blamed him for her husband not being allowed into the States to take a job he'd been offered."

Jed waits, watching his mother's eyes darting in all directions as if she's worried someone's going to leap out of a bush. She looks closer to tears than he can remember ever seeing her. She had always been the calm and stoic parent, in complete contrast to Charlie who could be demonstrative and get emotional at the slightest thing.

"I really don't want you bringing this up in front of your father. If he wakes up, we drop it. Understood?" she says.

Jed nods and edges his recliner closer so that she can talk softly.

"Doreen's husband, Graham Stevens, was Charlie's boss when he first came here, in 1954. He was British but he ran *Life* magazine's London office and, when the job of chief photographer came up, Charlie was recommended for it by someone in New York, a mutual friend."

"So, in what way did he deceive him?"

"He didn't. Graham knew Charlie had been blacklisted in the States. Charlie was a top photographer. He was well known. But once the witch-hunt got going, he couldn't get work anywhere in California. So, he went to New York to try his luck there, but it was just as bad. And then, naturally, he leapt at the chance of a job in London."

"And if he hadn't, you would never have met, and I wouldn't be sitting here."

Margaret smiles. "Funnily enough, we met through Doreen. She was very high-powered. Another journalist. An American who'd come to London at the end of the war and stayed here writing for various women's magazines. Doreen and I worked for the same publisher – I was in the finance department – and we'd become friendly, and I met your dad at a party they had at their house in Finchley."

Jed takes a sip of his Coke. He's amazed that he's never heard any of this before, and he's eager to get to the crux of the story, but he doesn't want his mother to get upset again. "So, everything was fine, to begin with."

"It was. It was great. Charlie settled into the job. We started courting – dating to you – and we saw a lot of Graham and Doreen. They had two daughters, toddlers, and because they lived up the road, we saw a lot of them. And, when we got engaged, Graham was going to be Charlie's best man. But then it all turned sour…" Margaret gets to her feet, her lips quivering. "You'll have to bear with me – I haven't talked about this for years."

Margaret steps onto the grass and walks slowly along the borders of the lawn as if she's inspecting the flower beds for weeds. As she turns back towards the patio, Jed can see that she's composing herself.

"Take your time, Mum," he says. "I'm sorry to dredge all this up, but I didn't want to just chuck letters away without knowing what might be important. And I can't remember this couple ever being mentioned."

Margaret shakes her head as she settles into the recliner again. "Oh God, no, Jed. Your father would spit blood any time Doreen's name came up. It all went wrong when Graham was offered a job with *Life* in New York. Doreen was thrilled. She was from Connecticut herself and she was excited about going back to the States, living closer to her parents and her daughters going to school there. They sold their house. Doreen gave up her job. We even had a leaving-do for her. And then came the bombshell that Graham had been denied a visa. It was completely unexpected; we were all baffled. But, when he went to see the US Consul, he was told it was because he was a threat to national security. *A threat to national security*. It was laughable. Graham wouldn't harm a fly,

197

and he was practically apolitical. But Doreen instantly blamed your father. And it turned out she was right. Her family was well connected and an uncle of hers spoke to someone in the State Department who said it was to do with Graham giving Charlie a job. Because of that, they assumed he had communist sympathies, and they wouldn't budge."

"Wow, so they ended up staying here. Relations must have been pretty strained after that. No more parties."

"No more anything, Jed. Graham sacked your father, and we had to postpone our wedding. We had no money. I didn't earn much, and Charlie hardly knew anyone in London. He was starting from scratch, trying to get bits of freelance work. It was a real struggle for a long time, for years in fact. Odd jobs for peanuts. Continual insecurity. One minute he'd have too much work, the next it would dry up completely for weeks at a time. It nearly broke him."

Jed tries to recall this but his early memories of his father are sketchy. Only fragments come to mind, fleeting images of walking to school with him or of the back of his head while he was driving. He has little sense of what he was going on beyond his infant world.

"Sounds like this Graham Stevens was a shit," he says.

Margaret frowns at that, as if she doesn't entirely agree. "You have to understand the times, Jed. Your father didn't see it that way. He'd say Graham was a victim too. That's how it was. Charlie had experienced it in California and New York, people he thought were his friends turning against him because they were scared of losing everything. And that's what happened with Graham. Doreen had gone back to the States with the two girls and Graham couldn't even get a visa to see them at first. Eventually, they gave him one for fourteen days, but he had to report to the FBI while he was there. He was treated like a criminal. And we think Doreen must have given him an ultimatum – either sack Charlie or she'd leave him. So, a few months after he got back, he sacked your father, and the next thing we heard he'd got a visa and was off to the States for good."

"But what reason did he give for sacking him?"

"He didn't need much of one, not in those days. But someone tipped him off that Charlie had given one of the print unions some photographs for their journal. It was completely unpaid, but it was considered moonlighting, and Charlie was out."

"And does he know who snitched on him?"

Margaret laughs. "No, but I bet your Foreign Office man does."

"And it looks like I've prodded the beast."

"Yes, it does, but there's nothing they can do to Charlie now. It's you I worry about."

The remark is pointed, and Jed takes it as a rebuke. His mother had always disapproved of him getting into trouble with authority. If he had an issue with his teachers at school, she would say "what did you do?" Even if he was plainly in the right, she'd say "don't fight battles you can't win". And now it made sense. While he knew she had similar views to his father, she usually kept quiet about them. She had seen how risky being a rebel could be and must have feared for her children if they went down a similar path.

Jed decides to lighten things up. "So, that's how Dad ended up doing sports photography. And paying for your wedding with the money from the Laker photographs."

"Charlie has embellished that story over the years but, yes, that was a stroke of luck. He'd hardly earned anything for nearly a year when a photographer friend who was double booked asked if he'd cover for him at Old Trafford. And that got him established. From then on, no one questioned his cricket credentials, although it was a while before he…"

"…knew a leg break from a googly," Jed finishes the sentence for her, and they laugh together at the punchline Charlie had used so many times for his Laker story that it's become a family joke.

Margaret stands up abruptly. For a moment, Jed thinks she's upset or cross about Chamberlain again, but then he hears what she's much more attuned to hearing than him – the sound of Charlie calling.

"I'm coming," she shouts.

"Do you need a hand?"

"I'll see to him. You can put the gas on under the potatoes. I've got steaks, and there's some salad made up in the fridge. We'll eat out here."

Jed goes into the kitchen where some new potatoes are scrubbed and ready to cook in a pan on the hob. He lights the gas and listens to his mother gently urging Charlie to use his frame rather than the wheelchair. Jed knows how touchy his father can be about people watching him struggle and doesn't go out until he hears him settling into one of the recliners.

As he appears at the kitchen door, Charlie throws him a smile with the good side of his face. Jed's surprised to see how much better than usual he looks. His eyes have some sparkle, his skin has caught the sun, and his hair looks freshly washed. Margaret is standing over him, with a comb in one hand as she uses the other to tuck some stray hairs behind his ear.

"Welcome aboard," Charlie says, his drawl more animated than usual.

"I'll go fix the lunch, no arguing while I'm gone boys," Margaret says, looking intently at Jed to signal that she's telling him not to continue the previous discussion.

"Great to see you back from Gaddafi-land in one piece. How's Reagan's favourite bogeyman?" Charlie says, once she's gone.

"I didn't actually have the pleasure, Dad, but it was a good trip. Interesting."

"Gaddafi fascinates me. He always has, ever since he threw us out in the sixties. You know we had a base there? Wheelus. It was enormous, the biggest outside the States. The Pentagon must've been really pissed." He grins and shakes his head, like it's a satisfying memory. "So, what's Tripoli like?"

Jed hesitates, suspecting his father knows far more about Libya than he's learned in three days.

"We didn't see a lot. It was busier and more prosperous than I expected. Some of it looks Italian. Some's very African. We weren't there long..."

"And the boy's death..." He taps the pile of papers with his right index finger. "I guess it's misadventure while under the influence."

"Probably," Jed says, sticking to the vagueness he'd used with his mother.

"So, how's the girl taking it?"

"Ayesha. She's very upset and angry..."

"It's tough, the boy's family's giving her a hard time, I see — blaming her for him being there. She's Lebanese, Mags was saying."

"And Palestinian."

"Really? Born in Palestine?"

"No, her mother was. She was from a village in Galilee. Under Partition, it should have gone to Palestine but the Israelis took it over and the family had to leave."

Charlie nods, but with a distant look like he's trying to remember something.

"I was there," he says, finally.

Jed throws him an incredulous look, thinking his father must either have misheard or is mixing memories up.

"I said *Galilee*, Dad."

"Yes, I know, but I'm talking about Lake Success, where they took the decision. I was sent to cover it by the *San Francisco Chronicle*."

Charlie leans forward, his eyes fixed intently on the pile of papers on the table between them. Jed senses that he isn't finished, that his damaged brain is still rummaging for the memory and trying to shape it into the words he needs.

"Lake Success, Long Island, the UN was based there. It was forty-eight. I did a heck of lot of work for the *Chronicle* in those days. They sent me for the debate. I was hanging around for days, great pictures. It was very tense. The US pushing the creation of the state of Israel. The Soviets supporting it. But India and the Arabs against. And Britain – it was their colony but they abstained, wanted to wash their hands of it and keep in with the Arabs."

Charlie sits back, looking exhausted but pleased he's managed to string the story together.

"Wow. That must have been quite something – to be there, I mean."

Jed's amazed that – like the Stevens story – he's never heard any of this before. His father would have been twenty-six at the time, not that much older than Ayesha's mother was when – on the other side of the world – she'd had to leave Eilabun, her fate decided by a vote he'd witnessed.

Jed's mother returns with Charlie's meal on a tray. It has clips underneath, which she attaches to the arms of his chair. She's cut his steak and potatoes into small squares so that he can eat one-handed with a fork. Jed watches him prod the pieces of steak, as if trying to decide which one to eat first.

His mother goes into the kitchen and comes back with two more plates, handing one to Jed and leaving the other on the table while she pulls another garden chair over. They eat, mostly in silence – Jed's father lost in his memories and his mother on edge, watching to ensure the food is making it into his mouth.

Jed arrives at Bar Linda to meet Ayesha ten minutes early. He's left his parents sitting in the garden reading and is glad of a moment to himself to mull over his father's story and the fresh light it casts on his childhood.

As a teenager, he'd treated Bar Linda as a second home. He probably spent more waking hours there than in his own bedroom – and definitely more than in Maths lessons. It was way too convenient, that was the trouble. Being in the bus station made it the obvious place to meet or hang-out. And the coffee was reckoned to be the best in north London, although the truth was that there was hardly any competition in those days.

Jed buys a Cappuccino and sits at the counter along the window facing the buses. He's onto his second by the time Ayesha arrives, abruptly and in a flurry of agitation. She slides onto the stool beside him and lets a large leather shoulder bag drop to the floor. Her cheeks are red and beads of perspiration are gathering on her upper lip. Just below the crew neck of an immaculate yellow top, a sweat mark is forming.

"I'm sorry I'm so late." With both hands, she clasps her hair, which is wild from rushing, and ties it back sufficiently for Jed to see fully the anguish on her face.

"What's up?" he says.

She turns away and looks down the narrow café. It's empty apart from an elderly couple at one table, two women at another, and a man hidden in a shroud of tobacco smoke at the far end.

"I need a drink," she says.

"The coffee's good."

"No, just water. That will be fine."

The woman behind the counter seems slightly grudging as she fills a glass from the tap. It reminds Jed of when he and his friends would sit there sharing one can of coke until the owner threw them out, and he orders a shot of Espresso to keep the woman sweet.

Jed gives Ayesha the water and watches her empty the glass in three long gulps. Jed smiles to himself, thinking she drinks as she lives – taking everything that comes her way in deep gulps, not wanting to leave a drop behind. In their week together, he'd found she could be gentle and tender, but the moments of calm were rare, just a pause in the restless forward movement of her life.

As if to demonstrate this, she puts the glass down decisively.

"Let's go Jed, we can't talk here."

This is definitely not up for debate. She's already on her feet. As Jed stands up, he downs his Espresso, sensing he'll need it. They turn right out of the door and cut through to Finchley Road, walking towards Temple Fortune. Ayesha strides at a rapid pace, and Jed is permanently a foot or more behind her.

"Where are we going?" he says to a bouncing bundle of hair as they turn into Rotherwick Road.

"The Heath Extension," she shouts over her shoulder.

"So, seriously, Ayesha, what's wrong?"

"I'll tell you in a minute, I need to think."

Jed would like to point his house out to her, but the pace is relentless. They reach Hampstead Way faster than his teenage self would ever have imagined possible and, cross over to the Heath Extension where Ayesha finally slows like a racehorse easing to a canter.

Jed draws level. "Ayesha, what the hell is this all about?"

She stops but doesn't look Jed in the eye. Schoolkids are dawdling home across the Heath, staring as they pass. Jed steers Ayesha along a path away from their route and circles around so that they're face to face. Tears are streaming down her cheeks.

"I'm furious with myself," she says, lifting her head. "I should have phoned Tom back. I knew he was suspicious of Gavin. He didn't like him at all. He thought he was pushy and insincere. But I didn't take it seriously. I come from a place where politics is life or death. But in London everything felt like a game, playing at it, nothing on the line. But I was wrong. *This* is where the power actually is."

"Ayesha, I really have no idea what you're talking about."

"I'm certain now that Gavin has lied to us."

"Lied is a bit strong. Not mentioning the gay rights banner or that he'd left the bar with Tom is omission, not lying. And the drink thing could just be exaggeration. We haven't heard what he's got to say for himself yet."

"I don't really care what he's got to say. And I'm not talking about those lies or omissions or whatever you want to call them."

"So, what are you talking about?"

"He said he had a history degree from UCL, that he'd graduated in 1985 and then taken a year off. But I phoned a friend last night who works there, and she checked for me. I was waiting to hear back. That's why I was late. She says there is no record of a Gavin Mirren graduating in any subject. None at all. He wasn't a student there."

"Are you sure? I mean, are you sure you got the year right?"

"Absolutely sure. I asked her to check the lists for the year before and the year after to be certain."

"And he definitely said UCL?"

Ayesha nods as she takes a tissue from her bag and dabs her tears away. She starts walking — at a steadier pace this time — across the grass towards the woods further up the extension.

"But people do bullshit about these things. There could be an explanation. It might be that he was trying to impress everyone."

Ayesha gives Jed a benign smile that in other circumstances he'd find patronising. This time he knows as he speaks that his words don't sound convincing. It's clear that Gavin has a problem with the truth. The question is why?

"Okay, so we need to confront him, have this out, once and for all," he says. "But let's wait until after the funeral. It's only tomorrow. And for your own sake, I think we should leave it until after that."

"Shit. The funeral — I've hardly had time to think about that," Ayesha says, slumping down onto the grass and lying flat on her back, eyes fixed on a faint moon above. High wispy clouds have taken the edge off the sun, but it's still warm and the grass is dry and freshly cut.

Jed sits cross-legged next to her, looking over the lower trees towards the elegant homes of the Garden Suburb and the spire of St Jude's church. As a teenager the area had been like a playground where, for him, being dumped by a girlfriend was the worst thing that ever happened.

He looks across at Ayesha. Stray strands of hair are lying across her face, and she reaches up and tucks them behind her ear. He has difficulty imagining how her childhood must have been, and he still has so many questions – about her uncle and so much more – but the latest revelation about Gavin has put all that on hold.

"I don't know if I can face the funeral – I really don't," Ayesha says, as if mainly talking to herself. "I want to be there. I have every right to be there. And I know Tom would want me to be there, but I don't think he'd want me to suffer the humiliation of being made to sit at the back like someone with a contagious disease."

Jed has no answer to that. He's never been to a funeral, never mind one where the atmosphere would be so fraught. And considering what Tom would think seems strange to him, as someone with zero belief in spirits or an after-life, though maybe he'd feel differently if it was someone he knew.

"Only you can decide that, Ayesha," he says.

"And then there's Gavin and Hannah. They'll be there. Gavin pretending to be sad. I don't know if I can face that."

Ayesha jumps to her feet as suddenly as she'd arrived at Bar Linda.

"I have to go," she says, dusting the grass cuttings off her trousers.

"But what about tomorrow? I mean, do you need a lift?"

Ayesha steps forward and puts her arms around Jed, holding him tight without saying a word. They stand like that, perfectly still, for a long moment, breathing evenly and in rhythm.

"Thank you, Jed, you've been wonderful – I'll never forget what you've done," Ayesha whispers as she releases him. "I'll think about tomorrow and call you if I need a lift."

Before Jed can reply, she's marching across the grass towards the woods and Hampstead beyond, her bag swinging from her left shoulder.

Jed watches her go. When she's about to disappear into the trees, she lifts her right arm and waves – without turning around.

CHAPTER SIXTEEN

Ayesha feels frantic. Her pulse is racing. Time is tight. She wants to be sure she catches Hannah coming home from the funeral. But she can't risk being seen by Gavin if he's with her. Not yet. She needs to speak to Hannah first.

She's looking for a vantage point on Haverstock Hill, high enough to watch both the entrance to the flats and Hannah's living room window.

She finds a spot about fifty yards up the hill. Standing on the other side of the road, the parked cars provide cover. Although there's nowhere to sit – the low garden walls along the pavement are overgrown with bushes – there is a tree to lean against, and the weather's fine. It will do, and she'll phone from the call-box down the hill before she goes in, just to double check Gavin's not there.

It's a few minutes after four. They won't get back until four-thirty at the earliest. She decides to kill some time by walking down to Chalk Farm to buy a takeaway coffee and something sweet to keep her going. She hasn't eaten since leaving the flat to go to Somerset House, and her research there took hours. There was no time for food.

When she gets back to her vantage point, she sips the coffee and chews the last mouthful of a doughnut, trying to look casual, as if she's waiting to meet someone, not spying on the flats opposite. She's never understood how guards on duty manage to stand in one spot. She finds it impossible and has to pace in an arc around the tree, occasionally stepping aside for people passing by.

Every few minutes, she feels in her pocket to see if the folded certificate is still there, as if it might be stolen when someone brushes past her. It's her proof that she's not losing her mind, that her suspicions – which, at first, she'd been ready to dismiss as paranoia – were justified.

As a precaution, she's made three copies of the certificate and left two in the flat and posted one to Eleni with a note telling her to hide it in a safe place. On the way home, she'd changed trains when she didn't need to at Euston. On the way to Hannah's, she'd walked through the backstreets, occasionally stopping to see who was around.

As her watch nudges five, Ayesha begins to worry that Hannah and Gavin aren't behaving as expected. She'd assumed he would bring her home and then go to his flat, but maybe they've gone off somewhere. She walks down the hill to the call-box. As she opens the door, the smell of urine makes her gasp. She has to wedge the door open with her foot while she pushes some ten pence pieces into the slot and dials Hannah's number.

"Hello, Hannah here."

Ayesha feels her anxiety easing. "Thank God," she nearly says out loud.

"Hello, who's this?" Hannah says, sounding irritated by the silence.

"Sorry, it's me. I was thinking of popping in. I just wanted to see if you were there."

"You sound strange, you okay?"

"Is Gavin there?"

"No, he's gone back to his flat."

"I'll come over."

"About twenty minutes then."

"No, I'm across the road."

Ayesha is knocking on Hannah's door barely a minute after hanging up.

"That was quick," Hannah says, as she lets Ayesha in. "What were you doing across the road."

"I was waiting for you to get back."

The two women stand facing each other in the living room, only a few feet apart, neither quite sure what to say. Eventually, Hannah breaks the silence.

"It was just as well you didn't come to the funeral. The person they were talking about wasn't the Tom we knew. And his father gave Jed a hard time. I dread to think what he'd have said to you. Do you want some tea?"

Ayesha shakes her head, sits down at the table and puts her head in her hands.

"God, I'm glad I wasn't there. I wouldn't have been able to contain myself."

"But where have you been? I tried ringing you this morning, but you were out. What's up, Ayesha? You're acting very strangely."

"I know, I'm sorry. I wanted to talk to you on your own, and now I don't know where to begin."

Hannah walks over to the settee and sits in silence like a counsellor giving a client time to offload.

"Come on, Ayesha. You know I'm here for you," she says finally.

"I know, but this is going to come as a terrible shock."

Hannah laughs. "Things are so shit, I'm beyond shocking. You may as well give it to me straight."

Ayesha takes a deep breath and launches into an account of what she and Jed have discovered, watching her friend's reaction closely as she unpeels each layer of the story.

Hannah receives the news that Tom hadn't had much to drink impassively and gives the argument about a gay rights protest a dismissive shrug, as if viewing it as a routine disagreement about tactics. But, when Ayesha mentions the caller who said that Gavin and Tom went onto the beach together, Hannah frowns.

"Really?" she says, taking a moment to digest this. "Are you certain? I mean, it's weird enough that Gavin got it wrong about the alcohol and didn't mention the gay rights thing, but saying Tom went out on the beach on his own when he didn't... That's beyond weird. Are you sure this anonymous woman isn't getting mixed up, or shit-stirring for some reason?"

"I'm not sure, no, I can't be totally sure, and if it was just that..."

Ayesha pauses. She was going to talk about how odd it was that Tom was fully clothed and how unlikely it seemed that he would have fallen into the water on a beach that had no obviously hazardous rocks. But she can see that she needs to get beyond the circumstantial and give Hannah some hard, irrefutable facts.

"Gavin is not who he says he is," she says. "I checked with UCL yesterday, and he's never been a student there. And, today, I got this from Somerset House."

Ayesha pulls the certificate from her pocket and takes it over to Hannah. Sitting back down at the table, she watches Hannah read it line by line, several times over, with growing bewilderment.

Certified copy of an entry – death.

Registration district: London Borough of Lambeth.
Date and place of death: Dead on arrival at King's College Hospital, Denmark Hill on Sixteenth March 1971.
Name and surname: Gavin John Mirren
Sex: Male
Date and place of birth: 9th July, 1958 – London Borough of Lambeth.

Cause of death: Severe head injuries, road traffic accident
Signature of registrar: C R Harris
Date of registration: Twentieth March, 1971

Hannah looks across at Ayesha, her mouth half open as if she wants to say something but can't find the words.

"Gavin is not Gavin," Ayesha says, softly, not sure yet if Hannah has reached the inevitable conclusion.

"But, hang on, just because there's someone else with the same name..."

"And exactly same date of birth? Come on. The chances of that are virtually zero, but, anyway, I've double-checked. There definitely weren't two Gavin Mirren's born that day. Only one. And that's his death certificate. He died in a car crash when he was twelve."

Hannah reads the certificate one more time, her face now drained of colour and her hands shaking.

"I checked his birthday with him only the other day. July ninth. I put it in my diary. I was thinking we'd do something special. Surely, this can't be right?"

"I wish it wasn't, Hannah, believe me."

Hannah doesn't reply. Ayesha wants to talk to her about how they should confront Gavin, but she can see that her friend needs more time to absorb the shock. She's not sure how strong her feelings are for Gavin, and she's braced for her suddenly becoming angry and defensive.

"I must admit, I had begun to have my doubts about him lately," Hannah says softly, without looking at Ayesha, as if reasoning with herself

"What do you mean? Why?"

"I never imagined anything like this, but I think he lied to me about coming back from his parents on Saturday. I think he came back earlier, and – to be honest – it made me wonder if he's been seeing someone else... But this seems incredible?" Hannah waves the certificate. "If he isn't Gavin Mirren, who the hell is he? And what's he hiding?"

Ayesha has already reached a conclusion about that, but she's not sure if Hannah's ready to hear it. They'd once talked about undercover policing. It had come up during the miners' strike when the union complained that the police were always one step ahead of them. But it's one thing to know that undercover police officers exist, quite another to digest the possibility that you've slept with one.

"You never know, there could be an innocent explanation," Ayesha says.

"Or he could be a fucking spy," Hannah replies, taking Ayesha by surprise with her ferocity.

"Well, there's a simple way to find out. And that's by putting that certificate in front of him and seeing what he's got to say for himself."

Hannah looks at her watch. "It's nearly six. Let's go round to his flat now. He's going for a run, but we could catch him before he leaves. Now I've seen this, I want to know."

Ayesha shakes her head firmly. "Being on our own with him is too risky. We don't know what we're dealing with here. We don't know what really happened in Tripoli. We don't know what he's capable of."

"Do you seriously think he...?"

"Did something to Tom? I think anything's possible, yes. Maybe their argument got out of hand. Who knows? But I don't think we should take any chances because we thought we knew him, but we obviously didn't. And he's a big man. I wouldn't want to be in a room with him when he loses his temper. It would be safer to confront him somewhere in the open, where we can easily get away if we have to."

"While he's out for his run?"

"That's what I was thinking. Do you know the route he's taking?"

"It'll be the usual one along the canal as far as the Zoo, and then over Primrose Hill to here."

"And he's definitely coming here."

Hannah lets out an angry, anguished laugh. "Are you kidding? He'll want a shag."

Ayesha cringes at how bitter Hannah sounds and doesn't know what to say. She wants to hug her, squeeze the pain out of her, but she's worried about the time and desperate herself to get this ugly situation to some kind of conclusion. She's been wrestling with her doubts about Gavin for days, but concern for Hannah has held her back. Now, she's certain it's best for both of them to act quickly and act together.

"What time does he go out for his run?"

"He usually gets here at about nine-thirty. Working backwards, I'm guessing he must leave his flat at about eight."

"Okay, so I'll go there and follow him at a good distance along the canal, and you can wait at Camden Lock. When he gets there, just say you fancied a walk. And keep him talking while I catch up."

"What if we miss him, if he goes out earlier than usual?"

"I'll get to his flat as soon as I can, well before eight. And you should be at Camden Lock early enough too. If it goes wrong – if we do miss him or he takes another route or something – come back here. If we haven't been able to confront him, I'll phone you here. If he's with you, just say you're too tired to talk and I'll hang up, and we can try again tomorrow. If you're worried about being with him, say "I've got a headache" and I'll come straight over. But whatever you do, don't bring all this up with him on your own. Okay? It's too risky."

Hannah shrugs in a defeated, placid way that worries Ayesha. This is not like her at all. She expected her to be in denial at first, but then become angry, her usual combative self. She thought she'd have to restrain her. Instead, she seems vulnerable and lost.

Ayesha looks at her watch and leaps to her feet. "I must go or this plan will never get off the ground."

Hannah stands wearily, and Ayesha steps over and pulls her into an embrace. The top of Hannah's head barely reaches Ayesha's nose and is engulfed by Ayesha's dark hair as the two women lean into each other. They stand there like that, rocking gently, Hannah's tears tickling Ayesha's neck.

"I really can't believe this," Hannah mumbles. "Just when I thought everything was slotting into place – my job being confirmed, this flat, a man who actually seemed to care, and…"

Ayesha waits for a moment, not sure if Hannah's finished, then she releases her and steps back, eager to go but wanting to say something before she does.

"You know, don't you, that I couldn't have coped without you when I first came here. I've never really told you properly before, but it meant so much to me. You rescued me from a very bad place. And now, I'm here for you Hannah. I really am. I'd do anything for you."

CHAPTER SEVENTEEN

Jed watches Tom's aunt walk briskly down the drive to re-join her sister. They want to know the truth, she'd said. And he realises how much he does too.

Ayesha not showing up at the funeral has given him every excuse to get in his car, drive away and forget the whole thing. But, somehow, he can't. Partly it's stubbornness, a feeling that the truth is important, that he shouldn't bow to Chamberlain's bullying. Partly it's because he's conditioned, once he's taken on a case, to pursue it to the end. But, mostly, he now feels a loyalty to Ayesha that he can't explain to himself, never mind anyone else.

And he's worried about her. He didn't really expect her to come to the funeral after what she'd said on Hampstead Heath. And Carver's hostility to him showed that her fear of being humiliated was justified. But not attending must be painful in a different way. The thought of Tom being cremated must be so final and devastating. And she's having to bear it alone. He decides he has to find her.

Jed's car is oven hot after more than an hour in the sun. It's a five-year-old, bottom-of-the-range Ford Escort, and he knows its fan will make little impression on the sweltering air. He winds the front windows down before starting the engine. Once he's on the road, the fresh breeze bouncing off the hedgerows soon replaces the smell of baked plastic.

The unseasonably warm and sunny April has brought the best out of the Hertfordshire countryside. The trees are blossoming and fields of rapeseed are already a brilliant yellow.

Jed takes his time negotiating the minor roads, thinking through the best route to take to Kentish Town once he's on the M1. He decides to leave the motorway just before Edgware and cut through Hendon on the Great North Way to Henlys Corner and then on to Archway.

It seems like a good plan until he reaches the painfully slow traffic on Falloden Way. He's tempted to take a detour through Highgate but he knows he'd only hit a different set of bottlenecks. The schools are out, and the evening rush hour is building. He thinks about stopping to call Ayesha's flat – to see if she's even there – but each time a phone box catches his eye it's already too late to stop.

Once he reaches Ayesha's neighbourhood, there are no parking spaces anywhere to be seen. He cruises around the side streets a few times and eventually gets lucky: someone is pulling out just opposite her flat.

When he presses the buzzer at the entrance to her building, a muffled male voice answers.

"Who's that?" Jed says, unsure if he's used the wrong one.

"It's Simon. If you're after Ayesha, she's out."

"Can I come in and wait?"

"Sorry mate, I've got to go out. I'm working tonight."

"But she won't mind me waiting. It's Jed."

"It's not my call mate. I can't just let anybody in."

Jed begins to feel frustrated by Simon's jobsworth attitude.

"I'm not anybody – I went to Tripoli with her for fuck's sake."

"I recognised the voice Jed, but I've got strict instructions. She didn't give me any exceptions."

"Is this a new thing?"

He had to think about that, which convinces Jed that it is.

"Not exactly. But she stressed it when she went out."

Jed senses their conversation is attracting interest and looks over his shoulder. A man has stopped on the other side of the street but moves on hurriedly when he realises he's been noticed. Jed catches only a glimpse of him, but there's something odd about his behaviour. He makes a mental note of what he saw – white, maybe thirties, overweight, black hair, wearing jeans, checked shirt – and wonders if Ayesha's paranoia is contagious.

Simon has gone. Jed presses the buzzer again.

"Look, can we have this conversation face to face," Jed says when he answers.

This time Simon releases the lock. Jed pushes in and jogs up the stairs. Simon's at the door, in boxers and a vest, when he reaches the flat.

"You're okay for a bit, but you'll have to leave when I go out."

Jed nods and follows him in.

"So, what's going on?" Jed asks.

"What do you mean?"

"Why the raised security level?"

"I don't know to be honest. Ayesha went out really early and I've been out myself. I haven't seen her all day. She had something to do, and I think she must have gone straight to the funeral afterwards."

"But she didn't."

"You been there?"

"Yep."

"Well, in that case, I've no idea where she is. All I know is she was very uptight, and she said not to let anyone in. No one." Simon hesitates for a moment as if deciding whether or not to add something. "Especially Gavin, she said."

Jed suspects Simon knows why that might be. And he probably realises that Jed knows why too. But they stand there letting that thought circle between them. Jed doesn't want to make life difficult for Simon – they both seem bound by loyalty to Ayesha.

"Okay," he says. "If she's not back when you go, I can always wait in the car."

Looking relieved, Simon nods and disappears into the bathroom. Jed makes himself comfortable on the settee, but ten minutes later Simon is ready to go and Ayesha isn't back. They leave the flat together, Simon taking his time to double lock the door.

On the street, Simon looks thoughtfully at Jed. "Look, I don't know what's going on but I'm worried about Ayesha. I've never seen her so jumpy. She can be uptight, but not this bad. I don't think she slept at all last night. I heard her pacing around in the kitchen. Something's seriously wrong. And, whatever it is, she shouldn't deal with it alone."

"I agree," Jed says. "That's why I'm here. But I'm not sure what's going on either."

Simon chews his lower lip for a moment, shaking his head and avoiding eye contact as he does. He looks weighed down by worry.

"Okay, well, good luck, I hope she turns up soon so you can talk to her," he says, giving Jed a bro handshake and turning to head down the street at a brisk pace.

Jed checks his watch. It's five forty-five. Hannah would be back from the funeral. He decides to use a phone box he's seen at the end of the street to call her. She might have heard from Ayesha.

She picks up instantly and sounds breathless saying the number.

"You okay?" he says.

"Jed?"

"Yes, it's me."

She falls silent.

"What's up?"

"Nothing. I just got back, and I'm really tired."

"You looked tired at the funeral."

"Thanks."

"Is Gavin there?"

"No, he's gone back to his flat. He doesn't live here, you know."

Jed is taken aback by her terse tone. That afternoon, at the funeral, she'd stepped in to rescue him from the wrath of Tom's father. He has no idea why she would be like this now.

"Have you heard anything from Ayesha?"

Hannah hesitates. "Why?"

"Because she wasn't at the funeral, obviously. And I'm at the flat, and she's not here, and I want to see if she's okay."

"I'm sure she's fine Jed. She doesn't need you stalking her."

"Stalking her? For fuck's sake, Hannah, what's that supposed to mean? It was you that roped me into all this."

"I know, but she probably needs some space now." Hannah pauses and lets out a sigh. "Anyway, I'm tired, Jed. It's been a long day."

When they hang up, Jed stands outside the phone box for a few moments, still reeling from Hannah's attitude. He's tempted to go straight to his car and forget he ever set eyes on Ayesha, but he's not sure Hannah's right that his help would be unwelcome. He assumes she doesn't know that Gavin lied about UCL – things had seemed normal between them at the funeral – or been told by Simon how jumpy Ayesha is.

It's just after six. He'd kept an eye on Ayesha's flat while he was in the phone box, but there had been no sign of her. On the corner opposite the phone box, a small queue has formed at a fish and chip shop. Jed decides he needs sustenance. He joins the queue, orders extra-large chips, douses them with salt and vinegar, and returns to the car.

The chips are long gone by the time Ayesha appears. Jed's surprised to see her looking like someone who's coming home from the office, smartly dressed in a navy suit, pleated plum blouse and high heels.

He lets her reach the path to the front door before getting out of the car, hoping that he's timed it so that she would be opening the door just as he gets there. It's not that he would force his way in, but – after what Simon had said about her mood – he doesn't want to make it easy for her to turn him away.

"Ayesha," he says, as he steps onto the path.

"God, Jed, you made me jump."

And she has, literally, jumped a few inches back through the open doorway, with one hand on her chest in a gesture of shock. She looks flustered, but it isn't obvious to Jed whether the surprise is welcome or not.

"Sorry," he says. "Lucky I wasn't sent by Chamberlain."

"That really isn't funny."

She's still blocking the doorway.

"Are we going in?"

She hesitates and looks over her shoulder as if the answer might be found in the dark passage behind her.

"Yes, but I want to get out for a run while it's still light."

Jed's dumbfounded. Her being keen to go out for a run is the last thing he expected. But he doesn't push his luck by saying anything and follows her up the stairs in silence.

She takes the steps in pairs, moving with surprising ease and speed for someone in high heels. Her bare legs are smooth and tanned. With each upward stride, her muscular calves expand and contract like those of an athlete. Jed's out of breath by the time they reach the top, but Ayesha has no difficulty speaking.

"I mean it, about the run," she says, pulling the key out of her jacket pocket. "It will be dark soon. I don't have much time."

Jed is completely baffled by the casual way she's dismissing him. She hasn't even asked about the funeral. It's as if she's gone through a personality change overnight.

Once in the flat, she leaves him standing in the hallway and goes into her bedroom. He's uneasy, not sure what to do with himself. He goes into the living room and paces from end to end trying to stay calm.

She seems to be taking a long time. A clock on the sideboard says it's nearly seven. It will be dark in less than an hour. The streets are well lit, but she probably wants to run along the canal or to a park. But why was he even thinking about this? Tom had been cremated only a few hours earlier, and he's worrying about encroaching on her leisure time.

Finally, she reappears. She's wearing a grey track suit with a hood. Her hair is firmly tied back, and she's manoeuvring a baseball cap onto her head so that the rear strap is underneath the pony tail. As Jed watches her, he feels he has to break the stifling silence.

"So, what happened to you today?" Jed is trying to sound casual but he's struggling to hide how annoyed he is at her attitude towards him. "I guess it must have been important."

"You guess right," she says, in a tone that's gentler than he expected. "But I'm not going to discuss it now. I had to make a choice, and what I had to do couldn't be delayed. That's all I'm going to say."

"But Ayesha, I thought you wanted my help?"

"I did, and you've helped me, and I'm grateful. But now it's down to me, and I want you to leave. I have to go for a run."

Jed shakes his head in disbelief. One minute he's her indispensable buddy, the next he's being kicked out like a dog who's strayed into the wrong garden.

"It was probably for the best that you weren't at the funeral," he says, feeling he should at least say something about it. "Carver was pretty nasty to me. I'm glad you didn't have to go through that."

"I'm sorry, that must have been difficult – but thank you," she replies. "Knowing you were there was important to me."

Ayesha puts a hand on Jed's shoulder and starts to steer him into the hall. As he's processing her strangely detached words about the funeral, his encounter with Tom's aunt comes to mind.

"It's okay, I'm going now," he says, stopping in the hallway. "But there's one last thing. Tom's aunt, Dorothy. She spoke to me afterwards, gave me a message for you. She said Tom's mother also wants to know the truth, and that I should tell you that. She gave me a card to give you and said to contact her if there was any news."

Jed starts fumbling in his jacket pockets, trying to find the card.

"That's okay. You keep it."

"But she wanted you to have it."

"It's okay. I know how to contact her. I don't need the card. But you might."

As she speaks, she has one hand opening the door. Her other hand is in the middle of his back, and he's not sure if this is a friendly farewell gesture or a readiness to push him out if he doesn't go quickly enough. He decides not to put that to the test.

Back on the street, he goes over to his car. On opening the driver's door, the acrid smell of grease and vinegar hits the back of his throat. He sits down but leaves the door open. He needs a few minutes to think about what has just happened. It was all so abrupt and unexpected. He feels rejected, humiliated in a way. How could he have so completely misread the situation? He'd deluded himself into thinking there was something special between them, a bond forged in battling those trying to stop them finding out the truth about Tom's death. Okay, he sometimes felt she should let it go, but not like this, not by ditching him. He's stunned, and it hurts.

He's still sitting there, gazing blankly through the windscreen when Ayesha comes out. She glances in his direction, looking irritated to see him there. Then she turns and runs in the other direction, towards the chip shop and Kentish Town Road. He watches her head rising and falling evenly with each stride, her bushy pony tail bouncing against those broad shoulders. She reaches the end of the street in no time and disappears from view.

Jed sits shaking his head, wondering what to do with himself. Ayesha and her problems had monopolised his time and thoughts for days. And now he's redundant, surplus to requirements.

He decides to call Adam to arrange to go for a drink. He gets out of the car and walks down to the telephone box again. Adam is his backstop, and he knows his number well enough to dial it from memory.

"Adam Williams," he answers, sounding pompous.

"It's Jed. Do you fancy a pint?"

"Prince Regent?"

"Give me half an hour."

It takes Jed no time to drive back to Islington. He parks near his house and walks the half mile or so to The Prince Regent. Adam is already there with two pints of Stella on the bar when he arrives.

"I've put 20p down on the pool table – we're next," he says, nodding at a young couple using the table, taking their time, more interested in each other than in sinking any balls.

Jed takes his lager and downs half of it at the first time of asking.

"You needed that then," Adam says.

He knows Jed well enough to sense something is wrong, but not well enough to expect to be told what it is. And Jed is seeing him for a drink to avoid thinking about Ayesha, not to discuss her.

"Yep, long day," he says.

"How was the funeral?"

Jed has to think about that. It now seems such a long time ago, and so much had changed.

"I don't have anything to compare it with – and I didn't know Tom – but, put it this way, if it was *my* funeral, I'd be disappointed."

"Not a rip-roaring send off, then?" Adam says.

"No, maybe the wake part was better, but I wouldn't have been welcome at that. You ready for another?"

Adam nods, and Jed waves to the woman serving and orders two more pints and some crisps. The pub is quiet, apart from a group of boisterous regulars playing darts at the back.

Adam and Jed stand there chatting about work and watching the couple slowly finish their game. Once they have, Jed sets the balls up, while Adam gets another round.

Jed can feel the alcohol beginning to numb him. It's a pleasing sensation, but it doesn't do much for his pool playing. Adam wins without him sinking a yellow.

"Another game?" Jed says, preferring to be thrashed at pool than answer any more questions.

Adam nods, and they go through the ritual again, this time with Jed buying the round and Adam setting up. A fourth pint of lager is one more than Jed usually allows himself in the middle of the week, and he's beginning to feel unsteady on his feet. He somehow manages to sink a few balls, but Adam finishes off the rest and lays his cue down as if to signal that he isn't going to prolong the humiliation.

"Another lager?" Jed says, holding his glass up.

Adam hesitates and looks at his watch. It's half past ten. "I've got an early start – I'm seeing a client at eight."

"I'm going to have another one." Jed can hear himself sounding desperate. And he is: the prospect of going back to an empty house to dwell on being dismissed by Ayesha isn't remotely appealing.

"Okay, one for the road, just a half," Adam says.

Jed buys the drinks and takes them over to the table where Adam is waiting. Jed sits down and immediately takes a long gulp of lager.

"Take it steady. That's strong stuff."

Jed puts the glass down, but he's beyond caring how bad his hangover will be.

"Shit day," he says.

"I thought something was up."

"Ayesha didn't turn up at the funeral. She left me in the firing line. I got a verbal flogging from Tom's father, and I didn't even need to be there."

"Bloody hell, that's a bit rich. Where the fuck was she?"

"Good question."

"Have you spoken to her?"

"I went round to her flat after the funeral, but she wouldn't say where she'd been, and she practically threw me out."

"Jesus, what a cow. After all you've done."

"She probably has a good reason, but it doesn't make me feel any better."

"A good reason? What reason could she have for missing her boyfriend's funeral? You've been used, mate. Face facts."

Jed guzzles down his lager with Adam staring at him like he's a loser who's too drunk to even know it. He does feel used, but he could do without a lecture on the subject and regrets mentioning Ayesha's no-show at the funeral.

"I'd be as mad as hell if I was you," Adam continues. "You go to Tripoli with her, get yourself in O'Brien's bad books, and then she leaves you in the lurch. But it doesn't surprise me – anyone who'd give Gaddafi the time of day must be a nutter."

Jed's self-pity is suddenly replaced by an urge to defend Ayesha.

"Shut up, Adam. This hasn't got anything to do with what she thinks about Gaddafi. She needed someone to go with her to Tripoli because that's where Tom died..."

Adam laughs derisively. "But she couldn't even be bothered to go to his funeral. Give me a break. Listen to yourself, Jed."

Listen to himself? Jed's having trouble seeing straight, never mind producing a coherent argument. Besides, he doesn't have one. He still wants to give Ayesha the benefit of the doubt, but he's wounded and confused by her sudden change of mood. His only certainty is that, if he has to listen to Adam trashing Ayesha for much longer, he might do something that would not be good for office relations at O'Brien's. Jed sinks the last of his lager and puts the glass down firmly to signal that he thinks it's time to go.

"I need to sleep on it," he says, standing up.

"You need to sleep it off, more like."

They laugh and tumble out of the pub together into chilly late evening air that's tinged with diesel fumes from the taxis racing up and down Liverpool Road. They stand there for a few moments, Jed swaying slightly and conscious of Adam eyeing him sideways.

"You want me to walk your way?" he asks.

"No, no, I'm fine." Jed pats him on the back and heads down Richmond Avenue, walking briskly and inhaling deeply to try to sober up.

He can feel the chips and lager like a deadweight in his stomach, but the fresh air is helping to clear his head. He's glad not to have fallen out with Adam. Five minutes more, and he might have done, even though he knew he had a point about looking like a mug. Had he too readily agreed to go to Tripoli? Perhaps, and yet – as hurt as he feels – he doesn't really regret it. Eight days with Ayesha had been more eventful and interesting than eight months would normally be. It was fun, worth the risk to his feelings... and maybe more.

Or was it?

On reaching Richmond Crescent, Jed senses eyes on his back. His pulse instantly quickens. He spins round, in a manic way, thinking he could surprise whoever it was. He's certain he glimpsed a figure stepping behind a van and waits for a moment to see if there's any further movement. A car cruises past, the two young lads in it showing no interest in him. The lights are off in most of the nearby houses. Jed starts walking backwards, his eyes scanning the van and the cars parked either side of it.

He begins to wonder if he was imagining things, the alcohol re-activating a feeling of paranoia. But, after the burglary and Chamberlain's threat, he isn't going to take any chances. Probably looking seriously unhinged, he turns and runs the final four hundred metres to his house at the fastest pace he can manage in a suit.

Once inside, with the front door firmly bolted, he's gasping for breath. The oxygen deficit hits him like a punch in the stomach. His legs are suddenly leaden from lactic acid, and he feels the blood draining from his face.

Sensing that he's about to be sick, he sets off across the living room towards the kitchen and downstairs toilet.

But he doesn't make it. About half-way, he throws up spectacularly and finds himself looking down at lumps of potato swimming in a sea of fetid brown liquid. He slumps onto the settee and watches in despair as the vomit soaks into his already-shabby beige carpet.

The whole sorry mess is like a metaphor for his day. He sits there feeling foolish for running from shadows and for thinking that risk-taking is fun. But he's lost the desire and energy to dwell on any of that. He just wants to clear up the vomit as best he can and get some sleep.

For the second time in five days, Jed finds himself waking up on the settee. On Sunday, a police officer and the smell of whiskey greeted him. This time, it's the nauseating stench of vomit. His suit, white shirt and black tie are splattered with it.

He's completely disorientated, uncertain as to why — once again – he'd slept, fully-clothed in the living room. He sits up faster than it takes for the blood to reach his brain. His head rocks with the dizziness, and he has to wait for a few moments for his vision to recover. When it does, he checks the clock. It's nearly seven.

There's a large oval damp mark on the carpet near his feet. Next to it is a bowl with a cloth floating on a repulsive brew of spew and soapy water. He had obviously made an attempt to clean the mess up the night before but must have abandoned it. He couldn't leave for work without giving it another scrub.

As he stands up, the dizziness strikes again, this time accompanied by a painful blow to the forehead. He winces and stands still to let the ache ease. He decides his body will need water and coffee before he can tackle the carpet.

It's a good decision. As he sips cautiously from a glass, he feels the cold water land in his empty stomach and send a refreshing tingle through his torso. Having then made a coffee, he strips down to his underpants, puts his suit into a plastic bag ready to take to the dry cleaner and sets about giving the carpet a scrub with hot soapy water. When he's finished, he can still detect a bad odour, but he realises it's probably mainly his own and goes upstairs for a shower.

A pummelling with hot water works wonders. By eight, his headache is subsiding, and he's ready to set off for work wearing a clean navy suit, white shirt and his most colourful tie.

To the neighbours, he would have looked much the same as he normally did. Inside, he is not only the worse for too much drink, but also emotionally mangled. He feels some relief that Ayesha's troubles will no longer dominate his waking hours. But he also feels sad at the thought of no longer being in her life. She may have turned his upside down, but that was no bad thing. "I was in a rut and needed a good kicking," he tells himself as he walks along Penton Street to Chapel Market.

The market is busy. When he stops at the café to pick up his usual bacon sandwich, there's a long queue of stallholders and early shoppers waiting to be served. He's thinking of giving up, and coming back later, but the smell of bacon keeps him lingering indecisively.

As he stands there, calculating how long the wait will be, he realises someone is calling his name. The voice seems to be coming from the back. He steps out of the queue and peers into the gloom. A man, sitting at a table in the far corner, is waving at him. He makes his way over warily, feeling pangs of paranoia yet again.

As he gets nearer, he recognises him. It's Simon, but he's not someone he would expect to see in the café and his appearance had undergone a transformation from scruffy student to what Jed's mother would call 'well-groomed'. His hair is freshly washed and neatly combed, and he's wearing a checked shirt and a brown suede jacket.

"What are you doing here?" Jed says, as he reaches the table.

Simon scans the tables filling up around them and nods at the seat opposite him. Leaning forward as Jed sits down, he pushes a sealed white envelope towards him.

"It's from, you know who."

Jed feels his throat going dry and his stomach starting to churn. He has just begun to get used to the idea of not being part of Ayesha's life, and now she's playing havoc with his nerves again.

Simon's right hand is holding the strap of a rucksack next to him on the floor. He looks even edgier than Jed feels, as if he's ready to make a run for the door.

"What the hell's happened?" Jed says.

Simon leans forward again and speaks so softly Jed can hardly hear him.

"Listen, I don't fucking know. But something's up, big time. Ayesha came back late last night. I was already back from work, asleep, and she woke me up and told me I had to leave, scarper, first thing. No explanation. She said it was for my own good. And she gave me this for you, and told me I had come here for eight and not leave until I'd given it to you." Simon flicks the envelope with his finger and sends it into Jed's lap. "Sorry, I'm pissed off. I've got nowhere to stay now. But I owe her, so I'm doing this as a final favour."

Jed picks the envelope out of his lap and holds it up, poking a finger into a gap in the seal to start to ease it open. But Simon swipes it from his hands.

"Not here," he says. "She also said to tell you to open it in private and to show what's in it to your boss, O'Brien. She says he'll know what to do."

Jed takes the envelope back and stares at it. He's completely at a loss as to what it could contain. And he doesn't like the idea of Ayesha thinking he'll need O'Brien to tell him what to do with whatever it was. His self-esteem already shredded, that's an insult he could have done without.

"Okay, well, I'd better go and find O'Brien," he says. "Is Ayesha still at the flat if I need to contact her?"

Simon laughs. "Are you kidding? She left at the same time as me, in a rush, with a suitcase…"

As that sinks in, Simon's edginess begins to make more sense. If she's doing a runner, this must be serious. Jed stands up, and Simon is quick to follow. He picks up his rucksack and swings it onto his back.

"Where are you going to go," Jed asks.

"As far away as possible. And, no offence, but I'm not going to tell you."

"Good luck," Jed says, tucking the envelope into his suit pocket.

Once in his office, with the door firmly closed, Jed sits down at his desk and opens the envelope. Inside is what looks like an official document. As he opens it, a scrap of paper falls out with the words 'Tom's trainers were wet' written on it neatly in capital letters.

Jed puts the note to one side and reads what he sees is a death certificate. He's handled dozens like it in the files of clients, but this one sends panic surging through him. Gavin John Mirren was dead on arrival at King's College Hospital. Sixteen years ago, aged 12. Killed in a road accident.

Jed reads the certificate several times over, trying to stay calm. Gavin must be about twenty-eight, but he doesn't know his exact age or his middle name. He assumes, though, that Ayesha isn't sending him the death certificate of a random Gavin for fun, that she's telling him that not only was Gavin not a student at UCL, he isn't even using his real name.

If Ayesha is right about this, then – Jed admits to himself – the message Simon gave him is also right: he does need to talk to O'Brien. Though he's niggled by the implication that he wouldn't know what to do, he's wise enough to realise the death certificate raises the stakes. This is too big to handle on his own.

When Jed knocks on O'Brien's door, he doesn't wait for him to answer. O'Brien is sitting in one of the armchairs. Norah is standing next to him with a notepad in hand.

"We've had a call from the police," she says, without waiting for Jed to speak. "They said it's in connection with a death. A man's body has been found in the canal near Camden Lock. Apparently, there was a press cutting in his pocket. It names you and the firm. The police are on their way here now."

CHAPTER EIGHTEEN

O'Brien watches Jed put a hand on the bookshelf near the door to steady himself. He has a sickly pallor, and he's holding a document in his shaky spare hand.

"What's that you've got there?" O'Brien says.

Jed gives him the death certificate, and O'Brien gives it a cursory glance as if it's just another piece of paper from a client file.

"What's this got to do with anything?" he says, flicking it with the back of a finger, staggered that Jed's bothering him with something trivial at a time like this.

"The only person I can think of who'd be at Camden Lock with that cutting in his pocket calls himself Gavin Mirren – the name on that certificate. He was on the delegation to Tripoli with Tom and was the person who said Tom had had a skinful. I didn't mention his name on Monday because it didn't seem important, then."

O'Brien reads the certificate again with more care. "Sweet Jesus," he says, under his breath. "So, this is why Chamberlain came knocking on a Sunday."

"Ayesha had that delivered to me today. I think she's trying to tell me…"

"I know what she's trying to tell you. Delivered, who by?"

"By her lodger, Simon."

"Have you checked the certificate out – it's legit, is it?"

"I only got it twenty minutes ago."

"Where's Ayesha now?"

"I've no idea."

"But you saw her, yesterday, at the funeral?"

"She didn't go. But I saw her later. At her flat.

"Where's that?"

"Kentish Town. She'd been out – I'm guessing now that she'd been to Somerset House. And she was in a rush to go out again. She sent me away."

O'Brien stares at Jed, not really seeing him but trying to picture these events. Ayesha not going to the funeral doesn't surprise him, given the family's hostility. But what made her so suspicious of this man that she would check out his identity? And does she now believe he killed Tom?

"In a rush to go where, did she say?" he asks.

"She was going for a run."

"Along the canal, no doubt..."

Jed nods sheepishly.

"For the love of God, Jed, I told you that you were out of your depth. How old is this man who calls himself Gavin?"

"Late twenties."

"Norah, tell Adam I want him to go to Somerset House pronto. Tell him to take a taxi. I want him to find out if there were any other Gavin Mirrens born in the late fifties or early sixties. Photocopy this and give it to him. Then, make four more copies. Don't let it out of your sight, and don't say a word to anyone. Tell Adam the same. And tell him to phone in as soon as he has any info."

Norah goes through to her adjoining office. O'Brien stands up wearily and walks over to his desk. He wants to be behind it when he's talking to the police. He gestures for Jed to sit on one of the hard-backed chairs in an arc facing him.

"Let's assume the body in the canal is this Gavin fella," he says.

Jed shrugs. "Like I say, who else would carry that cutting around? Apart from Chamberlain perhaps."

237

Jed sounds flippant, and O'Brien throws him a look as if to say 'don't try to be clever'.

"Tell me everything you know about Gavin," he says. "Don't leave anything out, but make it quick. The police will be here any minute."

Jed squirms in his seat, looking as if he's not sure where to begin and scared of making any more mistakes. But, once he gets going, he rattles through the story as systematically as he would a case summary, and it doesn't sound good: Gavin's been economical with the truth about the alcohol, the argument with Tom, going onto the beach, and studying at UCL.

O'Brien's concerned to hear Gavin's been dating Hannah. "Poor girl's going to be mortified," he mumbles to himself. And he isn't in the slightest surprised when Jed mentions that Ayesha had said that Tom was suspicious of Gavin and she hadn't taken it seriously.

"That must have been before even going to Tripoli," O'Brien says, his pen hovering over the notepad. "Anything else?"

"There's this, Ayesha sent it with the certificate," Jed says, handing him the note about the wet trainers.

O'Brien reads the four words. "That figures. I was thinking it might be a mugging when I asked about that. Obviously, the shoes being wet means they were likely taken off after he'd drowned – or, should I say, someone had drowned him and tried to make it look like an accident."

"But why wouldn't they take some of his clothes off too?"

"Maybe they were disturbed. Who knows? If this body in the canal is the man calling himself Gavin, we'll probably never find out. But, to cut to the chase, if Ayesha thinks Gavin was dodgy and that he killed Tom, that gives *her* a motive for killing him... Which makes you a potential accomplice, doesn't it?"

O'Brien puts his pen down and sits back, taking pleasure in watching Jed turn even more ashen than he was.

"Shit, but I can't believe Ayesha would do something so crazy," Jed says.

"What you believe is immaterial. That's how the police will see it. It's not as if she's some shrinking violet from Surrey. She has motive and is an extremist in their eyes. She'll be in trouble if she can't explain her whereabouts, as will you. Where were you last night?"

"Drinking with Adam."

"That helps."

O'Brien pauses as Norah bustles in and hands the death certificate and four copies to him. He gives Jed one copy, puts the other three on his desk and gives the original back to Norah.

"Put that in the safe, please," he tells her. "It's Jed's life insurance policy."

"What do you mean?" Jed says, once Norah's left.

O'Brien smiles. "What I mean is that the police thinking you're in cahoots with Ayesha – that you may have helped her kill this Gavin – could be the least of your worries. In fact, if Gavin isn't Gavin, if Ayesha's suspicions are right, the police have a problem. But, so do you. And your problem isn't the police, it's Chamberlain."

Jed looks completely baffled now. "Chamberlain? I don't get you," he says.

"Look, let's assume Gavin is Chamberlain's asset. Even if he doesn't think you were involved in Gavin's death, he'll assume you believe Gavin killed Tom, and he'll be worried that you know the truth about his identity. In other words, you know something he won't want known. And I mean,

239

really won't want known. Imagine the embarrassment to Her Majesty's security services if it came out that one of their operatives might have killed a British citizen – the son of a retired army major – on foreign soil. On Libyan soil – of all places."

O'Brien pauses again to allow Jed to process the thought that his life might be in danger.

"What did the guy who was with Chamberlain on Sunday look like?" Jed asks, finally.

"Thick set, black hair. Why?"

"I saw someone in Ayesha's street yesterday who seemed to be watching me. He was a bit overweight and had dark hair. I only saw him for a second, but I'd say he was in his thirties." Jed takes a deep breath. "And there's something else. I had a break-in on Saturday. I got home from Tripoli to find my house had been trashed."

O'Brien shakes his head, not quite believing that Jed has held back another piece of vital information – or doesn't even seem to know when something is vital. Somehow, he must impress on him the gravity of the situation.

"For God sake, Jed. Now you're telling me this."

"It might just have been a burglary."

"Was anything taken?"

"Only an old video player."

"Was there anything else of value in the place?

"Not much. Some cufflinks in my bedroom, a few kitchen appliances. Ayesha thought it was odd, so much mess and some obvious things left behind."

"And Ayesha was right. Did you report it?"

"Yes. They sent someone round, who took a statement, but he was just going through the motions."

O'Brien sits back in his chair, puts his hands on his head and turns towards the window. A light shower is hitting the glass, sounding like the monotonous brushing of a drum. O'Brien rocks gently in rhythm.

"And is there anything else you haven't told me, *anything* at all?" he asks.

Jed shakes his head, but O'Brien isn't looking in his direction and thinks he might be about to reveal something else. "Well, is there?"

"Sorry, no, nothing, that's everything."

"Right, listen to me, Jed. I'm not exaggerating about a life insurance policy. People have been killed for less than you know. For Chamberlain, you're a smoking gun. It would be very convenient for him if you had a nasty accident. Very convenient. So, we need to make sure he knows that the death certificate is in a safe place and that if something happens to you, it will become public..."

O'Brien stops abruptly when Norah's head appears around the door.

"They're here," she says.

"Okay. Have you heard from Adam?"

Norah shakes her head.

"Jed and I need a minute – I'll buzz you when we're ready."

O'Brien stands up, walks around to Jed's side of the desk and, facing him, puts a hand on his shoulder. His fingers are thick, like they've seen plenty of manual work, and dotted with wiry grey hair.

"Listen, son, take it from me, we can't be too careful. I've come across bastards like Chamberlain before. Butter wouldn't melt in their mouths. I want you to take some extra precautions, until we're confident Chamberlain has got the message. You're not to go home. After the police have gone, I want you to find a hotel. I don't need to know which one. Away from here, but not too far. Somewhere fairly busy. Don't walk down any backstreets. On your way, you can buy a change of clothes, toiletries, anything you need. I'll give you some cash. You mustn't use a cashpoint or your credit card. You mustn't contact anyone. No one. Understood?"

Jed nods feebly. He looks overwhelmed by this turn of events, but O'Brien thinks he's got the message and circles back to the other side of the desk.

"Once you've found a hotel, lie low until tomorrow. That will probably allow enough time for word to get back to Chamberlain."

"But how will I know?"

"Tomorrow, after breakfast, give me a call, here. Don't use the phone in your hotel room. Find a payphone. I'll tell you if it's okay to come into the office."

"And how will you get a message to Chamberlain?"

O'Brien pushed one of the buttons on his phone. "This is how. Norah, we're ready for our visitors now."

When Norah ushers the two men into the room, O'Brien stands up and walks over to greet them with vigorous handshakes and the welcoming smile he usually deploys for clients.

"Gentlemen, Conor O'Brien, apologies for keeping you – take the weight off your feet," he says, gesturing to the wooden chairs facing his desk alongside Jed.

The older of the two men introduces himself as detective inspector Walcott. He's in his mid-forties and grey in every way – suit, hair, complexion, manner. His side-kick, a detective constable called Smith, who looks about Jed's age, has ginger hair and an impressively freckly face. He wears a snappy black suit and a grey tie of the skinny kind that's just come back into fashion.

"This is Gerald, who I think you're here to see," O'Brien says. "He's asked me to sit in. I take it that this is informal?"

"Yes, we just wanted a little chat at this stage," Walcott replies, with an unsubtle emphasis on 'at this stage'. "As we told your secretary, we're investigating the death of a man found last night in the canal at Camden Lock. We haven't had a full autopsy report yet but we're treating it as suspicious. The man had some ID on him, but we're not releasing the name, not at this stage. He also had a newspaper cutting on his person. It was soaking wet but still just about legible, and it mentions you, Mr McIntosh."

The inspector looks at Jed as if expecting an answer. Jed nods to acknowledge what he's said.

"The cutting was to do with a Tom Carver's death in Tripoli," he says, in a tone that makes it sound like another question.

"I know the one," Jed replies. "But that paper has thousands of readers. Without knowing who you found, I'm not sure what there is to say."

"Well, you can start by telling me where you were between nine and eleven last night?"

"I was having a drink with a colleague in The Prince Regent on Liverpool Road. I got there at about half eight and left just before eleven."

"And where did you go then?"

"Home."

"Which is?"

"Just down the road from there. Richmond Crescent. You'll have the details on your system because I had a burglary on Saturday."

"That's a coincidence," Smith chips in.

"With what?" O'Brien asks.

The young detective flushes and starts doodling in his notebook.

Norah breaks the awkward silence, arriving with a tray of steaming mugs and spending a few minutes distributing them. Before leaving, she hands O'Brien a piece of notepaper, which he places carefully in front of him and reads as everyone sips their tea.

The inspector watches O'Brien over the rim of his mug, but then turns to Jed.

"This colleague you had a drink with, did she come back to your house?"

"He," Jed says. "And, no, he didn't."

"So, do you have anyone who can verify that you actually went home?"

Before Jed can answer, O'Brien intervenes.

"Let's cut to the chase here, gentleman. We are wondering if the body you found in the canal belonged to a young man going by the name of Gavin Mirren. Would that be the case?"

The inspector inhales audibly, signalling the annoyance of someone who is used to asking questions, not answering them.

"Let's assume that's the case, if you like. What's your point?"

"This is my point."

O'Brien holds out a copy of the death certificate. Walcott takes it, lays it on his lap and produces a pair of tatty black-rimmed glasses from his pocket, which he perches half way down his nose. After reading the certificate, he takes them off again.

"There could be any number of Gavin Mirrens," he says.

"There could be, but there aren't – not ones born around the time your corpse was born. We've checked."

"You have been busy."

"We received the certificate anonymously this morning. When I got your message, it wasn't rocket science to work out that we should check with Somerset House. One of my solicitors is on his way back from there as we speak. He phoned a few minutes ago to tell my secretary that there are no other birth certificates for people with that name who would now be in their late twenties or early thirties."

O'Brien pauses to allow his point to sink in. The inspector is motionless, staring at the certificate on his lap like he might have missed something.

"So, we have an identification issue," he says finally.

"We certainly do," O'Brien replies.

"Perhaps Mr McIntosh can help?"

Jed starts to say something but O'Brien holds a hand up to stop him. "No, he can't. The only person who can solve this little riddle for you is a man called Edward Chamberlain. Special Branch will probably know him. He says he's with the Foreign Office, but it's more likely he's a spook. I think you'll find he knows the true identity of your corpse. And I think it'll put you in a tricky spot. You won't have a cat-in-hell's chance of prosecuting anyone."

"Listen, Mr O'Brien, with all due respect, don't tell me my job."

O'Brien shakes his head, smiling. "Look, it's up to you. But the bottom line is, you can't murder someone who's already dead. And if that body really is someone else, I'll put money on Chamberlain stopping this from going any further. He won't want the murder of one his assets trailed through the courts. Especially if that asset killed the son of a British army major. You've seen the cutting. This man you've found was in Tripoli, and seen going onto the beach with Tom Carver the night he died. Are you getting the picture?"

The inspector nods in a cursory way and chews his lower lip. He'd walked into the room confident he had a good lead in a straightforward case, and now he has a political headache that's plainly way outside his remit.

"My only interest in all this is Jed's welfare and my own," O'Brien continues, sensing he's now in the driving seat. "Jed here has already had a spot of bother. We think the burglary at the weekend might have been Chamberlain's handiwork. And I had Chamberlain on my doorstep on Sunday – with a sidekick – making some not very subtle threats. So, I don't want to put you to any trouble, but you'd be doing me a great favour if you'd pass on a message when you've tracked him down. Just tell him that we don't want any more funny business from him. This death certificate is tucked safely away and, if anything nasty were to happen to either of us, this whole malarkey will definitely become public."

Walcott folds the death certificate neatly and slides it into the inside pocket of his jacket.

"I am getting the picture," he says, looking at his watch and buttoning his jacket. "But I've still got a corpse on my hands. And there are some messes even the likes of Chamberlain can't sweep under the carpet. The victim will, more than likely, have family – parents who are still alive or a wife somewhere who'll have something to say about this."

Jed lets out a gasp and everyone looks at him. "A wife?" he says.

O'Brien gives Jed a stern look, worried he's going to mention Hannah's name. "That's not our concern," he says. "Obviously, you have your job to do. I can see the problem. But Jed and I know nothing about Gavin's real identity. Jed's only met him a couple of times, and I've never met him at all."

"Okay, I'll have to look into all this," the inspector replies, patting the pocket where the death certificate is. He nods to Smith, and they both stand up.

O'Brien feels some sympathy for Walcott as they shake hands. It's painfully obvious that Chamberlain's amoral world of duplicity and dark arts is alien to him.

Turning to Jed, Walcott tries to sound like he's still in control. "I'm sure we'll be speaking to you again, Mr McIntosh."

O'Brien feels like saying 'I doubt it', but he manages to stop himself.

O'Brien stands at the window watching the two detectives picking their way through the shoppers in Chapel Market. The rain has stopped and shafts of sunlight are pouring through the gaps between the clouds, lighting up one end of the market but not the other.

"Poor old Walcott," he says. "The look on the man's face when I told him about Chamberlain. He came here thinking you were a prime suspect, and then it all fell apart. It's going to be a hassle for him. But it'll probably be taken out of his hands soon enough. He'll have to speak to his boss and up the chain it'll go, wheels within wheels. The Met's going to be furious with Chamberlain for putting them in an impossible spot."

"They won't be the only ones – plenty of people have reason to be furious with Chamberlain," Jed says.

"I know, but all in good time. I don't want you phoning anyone. Definitely not Ayesha, she's bound to be on their radar because of the cutting. And not Hannah either. I know she's going to be shattered, but you need to keep your head down."

"I was actually thinking of Tom's mother. His aunt, a woman called Dorothy Willis, approached me after the funeral yesterday saying her sister wanted to know the truth. The poor woman had just buried her son and – unlike her husband – seems to be sceptical about the official story."

"She's in for a hell of a shock. But let's not get ahead of ourselves. Don't be tempted to make any calls at all. None. It's too risky until we're confident Chamberlain's got the message. You don't want to end up with an axe in your skull like that fella they found in Sydenham."

O'Brien enjoys seeing Jed shudder at his reference to the gruesome story of a private eye who'd been found dead in a pub car park a few weeks earlier. It had been the talk of the office – and the subject of bad taste jokes – ever since.

"But how will we know if the coast is clear?" Jed says.

"Don't worry. It'll be obvious from the media coverage. Or, rather, lack of it. Once Chamberlain's heard we've got the death certificate, he'll bring the shutters down. He'll put the word out to Fleet Street that it's a matter of national security, and Bob's your uncle, they'll fall into line. You watch. In the meantime, you need to make yourself scarce, like I told you. Find a hotel and call me tomorrow morning first thing. We should have an idea of the lie of the land by then."

As Jed starts to reply, O'Brien goes through the door to Norah's office and talks to her in a muffled voice. A minute or so later, he comes back clutching a wad of notes.

"That's two hundred in cash," he says, handing it over. "It should be plenty for the hotel and a change of underwear."

248

O'Brien laughs, enjoying making light of the situation, while Jed – looking anxious and dazed – struggles to come to terms with the reality of his predicament.

"It's hard to take all this in," Jed says. "I mean, do you seriously think my life's in danger? Or that Ayesha could be a murderer? It all seems so far-fetched. I watched Ayesha going off for a run along the canal and, a few hours later, this guy masquerading as Gavin is found dead at Camden Lock. It doesn't look good, I know. But I just can't believe it."

"Do you think she could have done it? I mean, physically, is she capable of it?"

"Put it this way, I wouldn't like to be surprised by her on a dark canal path. She's nearly as big as him, and very fit. But it seems so crazy her taking the law into her own hands like this."

O'Brien smiles at Jed's faith in the British justice system. He's been around long enough to have seen its flaws, especially when affairs of state are at stake.

"She'd have been in a blind rage, Jed. She believed – probably rightly – that an undercover cop had killed her lover, and she will have assumed that the spooks would protect one of their own, why else was Chamberlain throwing threats around?"

"But if she *did* kill him, they're going to go after her, aren't they? Despite her having the death certificate as insurance."

"For her, the death certificate isn't insurance, it's motive, and of no use at all."

Jed shakes his head and smiles. "I reckon she's left the country. Simon said she went out in a hurry with a suitcase this morning..."

"Very wise. I'd do a runner if I was her. And, take my word for it, you need to get the hell out of here and lie low until further notice."

CHAPTER NINETEEN

Jed leaves the building without even going back to his room. The sizzling smell from the café as he passes is tempting, but – chastened by O'Brien – he walks briskly through the market to Penton Street.

Across the road, Thozamile is going into the ANC's offices and gives him a friendly wave. Since meeting after the bombing, when he came to see O'Brien, they'd occasionally chatted in the street, making small talk about the weather or football in a neighbourly way. Jed never really thought about what it must be like for your normality to include the possibility of being killed at any moment by a political enemy. But he does now.

On reaching the Pentonville Road, St Pancras' familiar Victorian clock tower comes into view, looming over the skyline in front of him. There's plenty of traffic but not many pedestrians. Jed's comfortable with that. Surely no one would try anything with so many cars passing? And fewer people on foot meant anyone following him would be more conspicuous.

His most pressing problem is to decide which hotel to go to. The ones his American relatives use when visiting London are bound to be way too expensive. The only other hotel he can think of is the Bloomsbury Ambassadors, which he's been inside once for a fund-raiser Hannah had dragged him along to. It's near Euston and will be as good as any, he decides.

As he approaches St Pancras, he buys a copy of the early edition of the *Evening Standard* and jogs up the steps to find the station buffet. He's desperate for something to eat and could kill some time checking the paper for a report on Gavin's body being found.

The buffet's hot food looks like it's been sitting there all week. Jed opts for a cheese roll and a cup of coffee and chooses a table in the corner furthest from the door, sitting with his back to the wall. As he does, he fleetingly finds his sudden cloak and dagger situation faintly ridiculous. But then he sees the headline 'Body found near Camden Lock' on an inside page of the *Standard* and is reminded of O'Brien's description of him as a 'smoking gun' for those who'll want to cover this up.

The report itself doesn't add much to what Walcott had said.

> *Police have closed off section of Regent's Canal near Kentish Town lock in north London after the discovery last night of the body of a man believed to be in his late twenties.*
>
> *The body was retrieved from the water by the emergency services after an anonymous 999 call. The Metropolitan police have not named the man, but they are treating the death as suspicious and have appealed for witnesses.*
>
> *About a dozen police officers were at the scene and had sealed off the normally busy towpath between Camden High Street and Kentish Town Road. A plastic tent was set up beside the lock and two emergency service personnel in an inflatable dinghy were also at the scene.*
>
> *The resident of a nearby house-boat, who witnessed the body being recovered from the canal, said the man appeared to be in his late twenties and was wearing a tracksuit and trainers.*

A spokesman for the Metropolitan Police said: "The emergency services received a call reporting that there was a body in the canal at 10.18 and went immediately to the scene. The man was taken to the Royal Free Hospital but pronounced dead on arrival.

"We are treating the death as suspicious and are awaiting the results of a post mortem examination."

The police say they will release the man's name once his family has been traced.

Jed puts the paper aside and takes a large gulp of the lukewarm coffee. Could Ayesha really have done this? And if she did, was it pre-mediated or an argument that got out of hand? Jed tries to picture what might have happened, conjure an image of her wrestling with Gavin on the towpath.

With surprise on her side, he could just about imagine Ayesha getting the better of Gavin. But how could she be sure where he would be and when? She knew he liked to run along the towpath in the evenings. It was about seven-thirty when he saw her leave. Perhaps, she went to his flat and waited, followed him when he came out. The report says the police were called at 10.18. It would have been dark but the footsteps of another runner on the towpath would not be out of the ordinary. He wouldn't think to look over his shoulder.

If it was Ayesha's doing, Jed assumes she'd consider it justice. And he struggles with that. All his legal training has conditioned him to believe you shouldn't take the law into your hands. But what do you do when the law-enforcers themselves think they're above the law? What avenues are left when those who are supposed to protect you from crime are themselves acting criminally, abusing their power in the name of national security? His father had suffered from it and was now close to death – without any redress or compensation.

Jed sees now why Ayesha had sent him away. She must have feared he would try to stop her. Or maybe she knew that it would be the end of his career if she'd implicated him.

If he had known, would he have been able to talk her out of it? What could he say? Let's go to the police and tell a detective like Walcott that she thinks her boyfriend has been murdered by someone they suspect is an undercover spy. He would have laughed in their faces and thrown them out.

But, implicated or not, she's left him in the firing line. Two men have now died in less than two weeks, and his boss thinks he could be next.

Jed looks at the snack he's bought. The cheese is shiny and curling at the edges. The roll's thin crust is cracked, exposing a fluffy white substance that looks more like something from Boots than a bakery. But he's desperate. He hasn't eaten all day and is beginning to feel light headed. He takes a large bite out of the cheese roll and, still munching, leaves to find a place that might serve something more nourishing.

Jed follows Euston Road towards the Rising Sun, where – as students – he and Hannah had sometimes drunk with other activists plotting tactics before NUS meetings in London. He feels bad about not phoning Hannah, putting his own safety first. She'll feel her life's imploded when she finds out Gavin deceived her. But does she even know what's happened to him yet? Ayesha surely wouldn't have just sent her a message or a copy of the death certificate like she did with him. But when would she have told her? Yesterday afternoon, Hannah was with Gavin at the funeral, leaning on him lovingly. Only a few hours later, he was dead.

But he doesn't want to think about all that now. He's going to stick to O'Brien's instructions, and sitting in the Rising Sun will only make him feel guilty about Hannah. He decides to go straight to the Ambassadors to see if they have a room for him. The sooner he's off the street, the safer he'll feel.

It proves to be a good move. Having splashed some of O'Brien's cash on an en suite room, Jed's soon sitting in an armchair eating steak and chips and flicking through the TV's Ceefax pages. A dead body in a canal would normally warrant an item, but Jed doesn't find anything on the London news pages. It's early days, but he feels relieved and decides to raid the minibar to celebrate.

After a nap, he's ready for a short walk round the corner to the Brunswick Centre to buy a shirt, underwear, and some snacks and lager to see him through an evening watching TV.

It's late in the afternoon, and people are already rushing home from work. A gloomy drizzle is descending on London. On the way to the shops a man bumps into him. It happens too quickly for Jed to take in what he looks like. He tells himself it was nothing, but that doesn't keep the paranoia at bay. He decides to cut the outing short. After buying some lagers at an off-licence, he abandons the idea of clothes shopping and dashes back to the hotel clutching the four-pack like he's a fleeing shop-lifter.

Once back in the room, he drops the catch, rips a can open and slumps into the armchair. His hands are shaking, but the lager begins to calm him. The previous night he'd needed the alcohol because Ayesha had rejected him, now he's drinking because she's put his life at risk.

When Jed wakes the next morning, his head feels as if it's been pinned to the pillow. He's slept so heavily that it takes him a while to come round. As he does, the sight of a hotel room is a disorientating surprise. He surveys the wreckage from the night before – empty lager cans, snack wrappers, a crumpled *Evening Standard*, greasy plates and mugs – and listens to the steady hum of the slow-moving traffic on Woburn Place.

Chamberlain's threatening face telling him he's 'off-piste' comes to mind, and he grabs the TV remote, just in time to catch the BBC London news. There's no report on a body in a canal. He flicks to Ceefax. Still no mention there either. He tries *Good Morning Britain* on TV-am. It's based in Camden Town. A death on its doorstep would surely get some coverage? But Ann Diamond is talking about an investigation into the murder of two Scottish girls. He hangs on for their news bulletin, but it's dominated by international stories – Gorbachev and Reagan shadow boxing over nuclear missiles in Europe, and Israel's coalition splitting over whether or not to talk to the PLO.

It's just after eight. He needs a shower but his heart rate is telling him he should check the morning papers first. He gets dressed sufficiently decently to go down to the hotel lobby to see if he can find any.

A miserable male receptionist with the grey and dishevelled look of someone who'd been up all night nods towards a rack and tells him not to take any back to his room. He doesn't need to – quickly rifling through the home news pages, he doesn't see any sign at all of the story.

Relieved, he goes over to a payphone booth, pushes two ten-pence coins in and dials O'Brien's personal line.

Norah answers. "You're still alive, then."

"I'm having a whale of a time," he replies sarcastically.

"I'll put you through."

After a buzzing sound and a few clicks, O'Brien comes on the line.

"Norah tells me you're enjoying the life of Reilly."

O'Brien thinks this is so funny his laughter triggers a deafening coughing fit. Jed holds the receiver a few inches away from his ear. He doesn't have the energy or inclination to explain that he isn't actually having a whale of a time.

"Have you spoken to Walcott?" he asks once O'Brien's finished.

"Not yet."

"There was a report in the *Standard* yesterday."

"Yes, I saw that. Looked like it was based on what the police put out straight away, before they came to see us."

"But I haven't seen anything since."

"Me neither. I'll phone Walcott now to check the lie of the land." The beeps start to go. "Come into the office."

"I'll be there in an hour," Jed shouts, but he's speaking to the dialling tone.

Jed feels a surprising surge of relief at the news that there's no news and bounds up the stairs to his room on the third floor.

By the time he gets there, the smell of perspiration soaking into the previous day's shirt tells him that having a shower is now urgent. He calls room service to order a Full English and coffee and goes into the bathroom. The shower head, dangling above the bath, appears to be an afterthought. Once undressed and under it, he finds there isn't enough pressure for more than a drizzle and, wondering if Reilly would have put up with this, he washes his hair in the basin.

By the time room service knock on the door, Jed's just about clean, dressed in his suit trousers and re-cycled shirt, and looking forward to the end of his confinement. He opens the door and attempts to take the tray, but the stooped man pushes past him briskly and sets it down on the desk, the door slamming shut automatically.

"Here you go, sir," he says, with a strong West country accent.

Jed pulls a pound note from his pocket, but the man still has his back to him. In the narrow area between the bed and the desk, they are barely a foot apart.

Jed is beginning to feel their proximity is strange when something hard and lumpy comes flying into his face. He falls back onto the bed – a cloudy image of an elbow revolving in his eyes – and lands with such force that he bounces onto the floor.

Jed's face down, his nose in the carpet. He pushes himself up into a crouching position, but he senses the man is right behind him. He stands up and tries to spin round in one movement. But he's too slow. The man is already lunging forward, his right fist flying in Jed's direction. It lands on his nose, sending him reeling against the wall. In an instant, he's pinned there, the man's left forearm pressing into his neck. He's gasping for breath. He tries to push him back, but the man is wielding a knife in his other hand, seemingly produced from nowhere.

"Don't even think about trying anything," he snarls, the blade barely an inch from Jed's mouth.

Jed's no hero, even when the odds are better. He's petrified. He puts his hands up. The man laughs in his face, spraying him with saliva, his breath reeking of tobacco.

Jed's certain it's the man he saw in Ayesha's street. He must be Chamberlain's sidekick. He's an inch or two shorter than Jed, but definitely heavier and stronger. His hair is unnaturally black. From such close quarters, Jed can see the grey roots coming through.

"Think you're clever, don't you?" he says, pressing harder on Jed's neck. "You think you can play games with us, send us threatening messages? Well, here's a warning – don't go flashing death certificates around or you could come a cropper. We'll be watching. Keep your nose out of things that don't concern you. If you don't, you won't live to regret it."

Jed opens his mouth, trying to reply, but nothing comes out. The man eases the pressure and lowers his knife, laughing in Jed's face again.

"You got the message?"

Jed's not sure whether to nod or shake his head. Yes, he's got the message. No, he won't go flashing the death certificate around.

The fear on his face must be enough of an answer. The man backs towards the door, the knife still in his right hand. With his left, he reaches behind his back, pushes the handle down and pulls the door open, without taking his eyes off Jed.

"It's alright, I don't need a tip," he says, as he backs out, sneering as if frightening Jed was the easiest job he'd ever had.

Jed doesn't feel good about that, but still being alive is compensation. He sits down on the bed. His hands are on his lap, shaking, the palms facing up. He stares at them. They seem completely detached from the rest of his body, out of my control, like two crabs on their backs, their legs thrashing in the air, trying to turn over.

As he sits there, blood starts dripping at even intervals onto the palm of his right hand. He counts the seconds between the drips like he's conducting an experiment. After the fifth, a small pool of blood has formed in his palm. His head is swaying gently, and the room has become milky.

Jed doesn't know how long he was unconscious for, but the next thing he remembers is opening his eyes and staring up at a smoke detector, its red light flashing evenly on the ceiling above him. He sits up and finds his legs are hanging over the edge of the bed exactly where he left them. He realises he must have passed out and slumped back on the bed.

His head's throbbing, but his hands are shaking less wildly. He gets up unsteadily and goes into the bathroom to check the state of his face in the mirror. There's a line of dried blood running down the ridge of his nose from a cut just above his left eyebrow. Under his nostrils, the stubble and blood have merged to form a lumpy red moustache. His upper lip and nose look swollen, but he's such a mess it's hard to tell how badly.

Jed licks his lips. The metallic taste of the blood is foul. He grabs the glass next to the bowl and fills it with cold water. Sipping cautiously, he goes back into the bedroom.

His fried breakfast looks repulsive. The egg yolks have gone hard and a skin has formed on the baked beans. He pours some coffee into a mug from the small white pot on the tray. It's still warm, and it's strong enough to drown the taste of blood.

Sitting down on the bed, Jed tries to take stock of what has just happened. There's only one thing he's certain of – the man mentioned the death certificate and yet he didn't kill him. He knows these two facts are connected, and he knows they mean something, but – in his battered state – he can't think straight.

CHAPTER TWENTY

"Norah, have you heard anything from, Jed?"

O'Brien says this sitting at his desk, shouting at the closed door to Norah's adjoining office. She opens it and stands in the doorway looking at her watch.

"It's gone eleven," she says. "It was well over two hours ago when he phoned. I'll call the hotel to see if he's checked out."

O'Brien thinks about that, sucking on his gums like a man who's taken his false teeth out. He's spoken to Walcott who had admitted that the inquiry had been 'suspended', spitting the word out like he resented the decision. The inspector hadn't mentioned Chamberlain by name – O'Brien didn't expect him to, they never confirm or deny that such people even exist – but he'd said he had passed on the message about the death certificate.

"Don't worry. Jed should be in the clear after what Walcott told me. He's probably been enjoying a leisurely breakfast."

"Taking advantage more like."

O'Brien smiles as she goes back into her room. Norah is always protective of the firm, scrutinising timesheets and expenses like her own money is at stake. It suits O'Brien. He can be the benign boss secure in the knowledge that she wouldn't let anyone abuse the rules. She'd been horrified when he'd asked her to go to the bank to get cash for Jed's hotel. The idea that such a large sum would be entrusted to someone so junior is alien to her. But he knows she is kind too, and that Jed is one of her favourites – that she would protect him as if he was her own son, and would be mortified if he was harmed in any way.

And she's screaming his name now, the sound echoing around the stairwell outside O'Brien's office. He rushes to the door to find the two of them standing on the landing, Norah examining swelling that has doubled the size of Jed's nose and cuts above his eye that are in the pattern of a knuckle duster.

"Sit yourself down in Conor's room, and I'll get some cotton wool and TCP to clean you up," Norah says.

O'Brien puts an arm around Jed's shoulder and steers him through the door to one of the armchairs.

"What in heaven's name happened to you? You look worse than Henry Cooper after six rounds with Ali."

Jed slumps into the chair and stares blankly at the wall as Norah arrives with the office First Aid kit and starts dabbing the wounds.

O'Brien sits down opposite and waits, studying Jed's face and regretting his Cooper quip. They really are nasty wounds, and he realises Jed must be suffering from delayed shock; if he pushes him for an explanation, he could break down.

Once Norah's finished removing the dried blood from his face and putting a plaster on the largest of the cuts on his brow, she goes back into her office and Jed starts talking, haltingly, about what had happened.

"It sounds like it was the same fella Chamberlain had with him when he came to see me," O'Brien says when Jed's finished. "Nasty piece of work. He must have been following you for days. He was probably on your tail from the moment you left the office."

"But I was very careful."

"Yes, but he's a pro, and he probably had back-up, maybe someone in a car."

"And he knew about the death certificate. He said so. Which means it isn't much use as life insurance."

"I wouldn't say that. You're not dead, are you? If Chamberlain wanted you killed, you would be – make no mistake about that. But he knows killing you risks the death certificate becoming public and the whole thing unravelling for him. This was likely meant as frightener, to put the fear of God in you. He doesn't just want to stop you flashing the death certificate around, he wants you cowering in a corner, not daring to do anything that might cause him bother."

Norah puts her head round the door. "Hannah's on the line, Jed, do you want to take it?"

Jed looks at O'Brien, who gives him a nod.

"I'll put her through."

Jed goes over to O'Brien's desk and picks up the receiver.

"Hannah, you okay?"

"Not really. Where the hell have you been? I've been frantic. I tried you dozens of times last night."

"Long story. You know what's happened?"

"That Gavin's dead? Yes. Can you come over?"

"I'm in the office. I've got a few things to do, but I'll be there later."

"What time?"

"About four."

Hannah doesn't answer. Jed can hear her breathing. "Okay, four," she mumbles.

The call doesn't so much end as dissolve. Jed holds the receiver for a few moments as Hannah weeps and the line goes dead.

"She sounds in a bad way," O'Brien says.

"It doesn't get much weirder. Your lover being killed, but turning out not to be who you thought he was… assuming she knows that part."

"Tread carefully, she might not. Who would she have heard from, apart from Ayesha? You might be the one who has to break it to her."

"And to the Carvers."

"Now let's not be hasty." O'Brien tries not to sound as alarmed as he feels. He was hoping Jed had forgotten about Dorothy and — apart from comforting Hannah — would go back to working quietly on some immigration cases.

Jed sits down in the armchair again and looks at O'Brien earnestly. "The thing is, I don't feel comfortable knowing what I know and not telling them, not when Dorothy asked me directly, told me that Tom's mother wants to know the truth. It wouldn't feel right keeping this to myself. And what have I got to lose, really? I mean, whatever I do now, I'll be looking over my shoulder for years to come. I may as well do the right thing."

"Steady on, Jed. I'm telling you, this beating was only a warning. Next time you could end up dead in a ditch or a car park somewhere. Make no mistake about it."

"But, once it's all out in the open, it would be too obvious who had a motive if anything did happen to me. They'd be leaving themselves wide open."

O'Brien laughs. "Wide open to what? You think someone like Chamberlain is ever going to be prosecuted for the things he does? These aren't the normal rules. You've seen what's happened with this body in the canal, whoever he is. All they have to do is say it's a matter of national security and that's it…"

"I know, as you said, the shutters come down. I get that, but I still couldn't live with myself, knowing the truth and not telling them. And there is strength in numbers. If I tell the Carvers and they take it up, it isn't just us carrying this secret around."

O'Brien hasn't ever seen Jed as determined as this. The beating seems to have galvanised him. He's usually too easy going for O'Brien's liking, as if nothing really rouses any anger in him. The new Jed is showing a bit of spirit, and he likes it.

"There's strength in numbers – I'll grant you that," O'Brien says. "I suppose I've always been careful not to antagonise the authorities, because I've seen how much grief they can give people who get on the wrong side of them. But every rule has its exceptions. There are times when you have to make a stand."

"So, you don't mind then? Because I was thinking of trying to see Dorothy now."

"If you think that's the right thing to do, then you should do it. But I'll come with you. I want to meet her. She's bound to be very angry about the possibility Tom was murdered, and once the Carvers start making waves, anything could happen. They'll have some clout. But, if we're going to go down that route, I want to be in the loop, and I definitely don't want you flying off to foreign places again without telling me."

O'Brien gives Jed his sternest look but, the truth is, he's beginning to warm to the fight himself.

The entrance to Ogilvy & Archer is about as far removed from O'Brien's pokey stairwell as you could imagine. It's the size of a tennis court with a marble floor, an oak reception desk, two lifts to the five floors above and a row of leather armchairs. Corporate literature is scattered generously on the coffee tables, and a servery to one side has jugs of coffee and tea and baskets piled with fruit, biscuits and other snacks for visitors.

Jed had called Dorothy from O'Brien's office and told her there had been some developments, warning that one of them was a rearrangement of his face. She hadn't wanted to talk on the phone and asked him to come to Ogilvy & Archer in the City for one o'clock. He said he'd be bringing his boss.

Ogilvy & Archer's is on King William Street near the Bank of England, and they'd taken a taxi, arriving in time for Jed to boost his sugar levels by raiding the snacks.

Dorothy appears promptly at one, making them jump from their seats when she calls Jed's name from half way across the marble floor. She's wearing a crimson business suit with a knee-length skirt and double-breasted jacket with padded shoulders. Her white blouse has a high ruffle neck with a gold choker resting below it. And her hair is up, giving a severe look that belies the impression Jed had given O'Brien of a kindly aunt.

"There you are," she says, as if finding them had been difficult. "My word, your face really is a mess. Tell me about it over lunch. Mr O'Brien, good to meet you. I've booked us a table at a nice little place across the road. I'm sure you appreciate that I don't want to discuss this on the firm's premises."

"Understood," O'Brien replies. "But, just for the record, O'Brien's is now treating this as the firm's business. Apart from anything else, we like to think our staff can look into something, in good faith, without getting beaten up."

"Absolutely. Quite right. But obviously we're in a different line of work here." Dorothy waves a hand at the reception area behind her and then nods towards the revolving the door. "Shall we go?"

The restaurant is on a narrow lane off King William Street. It is anything but a 'little place'. There are dozens of tables – nearly all of them are taken and nearly everyone seems to know Dorothy. The staff welcome her by name. At almost every table they pass, someone gives her a nod or a wave. At one table, a man stands up and says something, but Dorothy backs away, gesturing that he should call her, with her right hand shaped like a telephone – thumb to her ear, little finger to her mouth.

"Goodness," she says, as they sit down. "That man is a pest. He's always after free advice, as if I've got nothing better to do."

O'Brien is enjoying this. As a betting man, he'd put money on Dorothy beating Chamberlain in a fair fight. But this fight is going to be anything but fair, and he wonders how she'll react when they tell her what she's up against.

Menus land swiftly in their hands from the overly attentive staff.

"The smoked salmon is always good," Dorothy says. "But have something more substantial if you prefer. They do a delicious risotto with haddock, and their steaks are a safe bet."

O'Brien and Jed opt for steaks. Dorothy chooses the smoked salmon. Once she's given the waiter the order, she turns to Jed and peers at his wounds. "So, tell me the story – how did your face get like that?"

"I suppose you could call it a present from a friend of your brother-in-law."

Dorothy raised an eyebrow. "A friend, who would that be?"

"Chamberlain. The man – supposedly from the Foreign Office – who went to Tripoli with Major Carver and who has done his best to cover up what happened to Tom –

possibly, I would say almost certainly, because it was the work of one of his own operatives."

"Goodness, a spook, you mean. This all sounds rather far-fetched, Jed. Do you have anything to back it up?"

Jed produces the death certificate from his jacket pocket and hands it to her. She scans it cursorily and gives him a quizzical shrug. O'Brien is tempted to explain, but he decides to let Jed do the talking for now.

"Gavin Mirren – or, to be more exact, someone using that name – went to the conference in Tripoli with Tom. They were seen having an argument and going onto the beach together on the night that Tom died. But it turns out that this person lied to Tom and Ayesha about who he was – he'd never been a student at UCL, as he'd claimed, and the only Gavin Mirren born in roughly the right year – I mean, to be the age of the person who went to Tripoli – died sixteen years ago."

"So, have you confronted this man, whoever he is?"

"No, and that won't be possible now, because – the night before last – he was found dead in the canal at Camden Lock."

"Really? What on earth does Ayesha make of all this?"

"She's disappeared. I've no idea where she is. But it was Ayesha who obtained the death certificate and found out he'd lied about being a UCL graduate."

"Sorry, I'm confused. How did you get the death certificate if you haven't seen her?"

O'Brien can see Jed is reluctant to talk about Ayesha. "She had it delivered to our office," he says. "And it's possible she had something to do with this man's death because yesterday – according to her lodger – she left her flat in a hurry carrying a suitcase."

"Goodness. Avenging Tom's death with brutal efficiency."

Jed baulks at Dorothy's disapproving tone. "Well, we don't know that for certain. All we know is that he's dead, and she's disappeared."

Dorothy raises an eyebrow pointedly. "And what do the police have to say about this?"

"They started an inquiry, but it's been suspended," O'Brien says.

"Why would they do that?"

"Because we gave them the birth certificate."

O'Brien smiles as he sees Dorothy processing his implication that their action confirms that the man who went onto the beach with Tom must have been someone who's real identity the authorities want to protect.

She reads the death certificate for a second time. "May I keep this?"

"Yes, of course," O'Brien says. "The more of us who have a copy, the less likely it is that another one of us will end up looking like young Jed here."

Dorothy smiles, giving O'Brien a warm feeling that they are on the same wavelength.

With the food arriving, Dorothy pauses the questioning. It's obvious Jed needs a decent meal, and she watches him devour it with equally obvious satisfaction.

When his plate no longer shows any trace of food, she returns to the task of extracting every morsel of information from him. Demonstrating why the word 'forensic' is in her job title, she presses Jed for a description of the hotel where Tom stayed and the beach where his body was found. She wants to know everything the Libyan police said. She asks about the anonymous caller and what the argument had been about. She takes the name of the delegation leader and says they'll have to speak to more people who were there.

At every stage, she rigorously separates fact from speculation and doesn't seem fazed by the idea that 'Gavin' was an undercover spy and the mounting circumstantial evidence that he had a hand or two in Tom's death.

"I find Chamberlain paying you a little visit particularly interesting," she tells O'Brien. "Why would he go to the trouble of threatening you if there was nothing to hide?"

"Isn't my face hard evidence of that too?" Jed asks.

"On its own, no, sorry Jed. It's evidence that someone has taken a dislike to you for poking your nose around. But the man who attacked you could be anyone. What links him to Tom's death is that he accompanied Chamberlain when he visited O'Brien, assuming that it definitely is the same man. But all of this is still very circumstantial, and the trouble is, even if you can make it stack up, you can't prosecute someone who is already dead. You'd have to prove he was acting on orders, which is very likely of course, and then go after Chamberlain. But it is also possible this Gavin chap went rogue. And that is bound to be Chamberlain's defence."

Dorothy leans back in her chair to allow one of the waiters to clear their plates while another delivers three rich-smelling coffees with steamed milk. As they sit in silence sipping them, Jed's face begins to turn the inflamed red of someone who's been lying in the midday sun. He starts rocking in his seat. O'Brien grabs his arm to steady him. Dorothy waves to a waiter.

"Water please," she shouts.

A decanter and a glass arrive in seconds. She fills the glass and steers it into Jed's hands, cupping them with hers to guide it to his lips. He takes a tentative sip and then gulps the rest down.

"I'm feeling very hot," he says.

Dorothy stands up instantly. "Let's get you outside into the fresh air."

O'Brien helps Jed negotiate the narrow gaps between the tables, while Dorothy settles the bill. Once outside – in the quiet, shaded lane – Jed's face begins to return to its normal colour.

Dorothy puts a hand on his shoulder. "I don't think I've thanked you properly, Jed. You didn't have to put yourself in the firing line like you have. You didn't even know Tom. But I'm sure my sister will appreciate your efforts. What you've told me has put a very different complexion on things. It won't bring Tom back, needless to say, but I'm sure the family – even Henry – will want to get to the bottom of this. It might be nigh on impossible to prove that this man masquerading as Gavin Mirren actually killed Tom, but Chamberlain needs to be put on the spot. If nothing else, we'll create a bloody big stink..."

That brings a smile to Jed's face.

"Is there anything else you need from us?" O'Brien says, anxious to get Jed home or wherever he wants to go.

"Well, there's Hannah, of course. She was in a relationship with this man and may be able to shed some light on a few things. This must all have been devastating for her."

"We're not sure if she knows yet," Jed replies. "I mean, about his identity, the death certificate. I spoke to her earlier. She knows he's dead. But I didn't get into the rest of it. I'm going to see her now."

"Oh goodness, she's in for a shock. The poor girl won't want to be told that the man she's been seeing wasn't who he said he was – least of all by you, her ex. And you have to remember if they slept together, she will have consented under false pretences. Would she have done, if she'd known who he really was?"

Jed looks from Dorothy to O'Brien and back again with a perplexed expression. "Are you saying what I think you're saying?"

"Yes, I'm saying, you could argue that it was rape. Don't you agree, Mr O'Brien?"

"I do, you could most certainly argue that. She was deceived, and therefore does her consent actually count as consent? I think that needs testing in court."

CHAPTER TWENTY-ONE

Hannah folds the death certificate in half and slides it into a French dictionary on the shelves in her bedroom.

She nearly set it alight a few hours ago, thinking she would enjoy watching it burn. But she stopped herself. She realised that all she would be burning was a document about a poor twelve-year-old boy who'd been killed in a road accident. Putting a match to it suddenly seemed so disrespectful to him and to his poor parents who might one day find out his identity had been stolen.

She'd torn up some photographs of Gavin instead – a whole pack of them, taken on a clear February morning when they'd gone for a walk on Primrose Hill across silvery frosted grass. Pictures of him with London stretching behind, pictures of him pulling a silly face, pictures of the two of them – his arm around her – taken by a woman walking her dog who was so eager to get the shot right she'd made three attempts. All of them are now in the bin, torn into tiny bits, even the ones without him in. She wanted to eliminate any trace of that day.

But the image she can't get rid of, that has haunted her for two nights and two days, is of a man's body – someone she thought she knew – floating face down on the stagnant black water of the canal. It insinuates itself into almost everything she does or thinks. If she goes to the shops, one minute it feels as if the Gavin she thought she knew is by her side, the next all she sees is a corpse drifting on water. If the phone rings, her first reaction is to think it might be him and then the body is there again. If she closes her eyes, she can imagine him naked on top of her, until she sees him rotting in the water like a dead rat.

She's been picking over all that they did together, the months they'd been lovers, the first times for things.

The first time he'd asked her out – whispered it, when they were in a pub where a whole group of them were having a drink after a meeting. Did she fancy going for a meal the following evening? They'd met at an Indian place on Charlotte Street. The food was awful, tasteless lumps of chicken swimming in a tepid sauce. He'd finished hers and his. She was amazed at how much he could eat and yet be so lean, his torso firm and smooth when she slipped her hands inside his shirt as they kissed goodbye.

The first time they'd slept together, a few days later. She'd instigated it. She'd even bought some condoms. But she'd underestimated how awkward it would be the next morning, because she was still in the shared house and everyone was in, and he'd made so much noise. Her housemates had wanted her to tell them all about him when he'd gone. And she'd felt good about that, suspecting they'd seen her as a loser for chasing Jed. But now she knows that what she told them was a lie, a story invented to fool her.

The first time he'd said he loved her – when she was cooking a meal for him at the flat just after she'd moved in, only a few weeks ago. She'd lit some candles in the living room and turned the lights off. She wasn't trying to be romantic – it was only to make the flat seem less bare – but he must have assumed she was, and he'd put his arm round her in the kitchen and said the words. It had taken her by surprise, and the whole evening seemed like their best together. That's how she felt about it the next day. It had lifted her spirits. She'd had a lot on her mind, with the new flat and the new job and so many things to do and students to get to know, and he'd been attentive and asked questions. He was always attentive, so interested in everything – everything she'd been doing, everything people had said. *Interested.* Of course, he was interested. It was his fucking job.

Hannah feels sick now, not just emotionally but actually about to vomit. She goes to the toilet and throws up. It's mainly liquid. It's the middle of the afternoon, and all she's had all day is tea, mug after mug of it. She needs to eat, but the mere thought of it triggers the nausea again.

She lies down on the settee. With a bit of luck Jed, will be here soon. He might be a dick, but she's known him for nearly ten years – he's a dick she thinks she can trust. And there are only three people she trusts right now.

Her mother is another – she'll see her on Sunday when she goes to Brighton. There's no trace of him there. He wouldn't go with her to see Ally, and now she knows why. And her mother will be good. She won't ask questions. She'll let her take her time. And the weeding will be cathartic.

Ayesha's the only other person she really trusts. She's shown she'll do anything for her. She's sacrificed the life she'd made for herself in London. And now she's in Greece. Hannah knows that because Eleni came round earlier, sent by Ayesha. She brought enough food to fill the fridge and a message saying: "Ayesha is thinking of you and wants you to know she's okay". Eleni had explained that she's staying with a cousin of hers for the time being. She'd said she was worried about Hannah. But she won't be phoning. It's too risky. She'll keep in touch via Eleni.

Eleni's kindness in rushing there at Ayesha's behest was too much to bear. Hannah had found herself tearful for the rest of the morning, and every time she opens the fridge, and sees the food piled up, it sets her off again.

But she can hear Jed arriving now. It must be him. Why's he shuffling around on the landing outside? She opens the door. Without shoes she feels even tinier than usual, and Jed seems so tall. With his back to her, wearing a coat, for a moment, he's like *him*. A stabbing pain hits her in the chest, and she swallows hard.

"Jed?"

He turns around.

"Oh my God, what on earth happened to your face?"

Jed tries to smile, but the effort only exaggerates the size of his swollen upper lip. Hannah pulls him towards her. As she nestles her head into his shoulder, she feels him starting to sob, his tears running onto her forehead. They stand there motionless on the doorstep for a moment until Hannah lifts her head and wipes a tear from his cheek with her thumb. Putting a hand under his elbow, she leads him into the flat.

"Sorry about that," Jed says, sitting down on the settee. "It must be the shock. I couldn't bottle it up any longer."

"Who did this to you?"

Jed grimaces. "A thug who was sent to warn me off making any trouble."

"Trouble? There's already trouble. What do you mean?"

"It's a long story, and I can't really explain without telling you something else first. I think you need to sit down too."

Hannah takes the hard-backed chair at the table, but not because she's expecting any surprises.

"It's okay, I know about Gavin if that's what you mean."

"I know you know he's dead..."

"And I know he was a fake too. That he was never who he said he was. Ayesha told me the whole thing. She showed me the birth certificate. She told me about UCL, the argument with Tom, this supposed Foreign Office guy making threats. Presumably, the thug was sent by him."

Jed nods and looks thrown, like he had a whole speech prepared that he no longer needs.

"So, where's Ayesha now?" he says after a pause.

"She left the country. I doubt she'll ever be back."

"Where's she gone?"

"I'm not saying, Jed."

"You know though?"

Hannah nods. "Roughly. Not the exact address. She's keeping her head down until it's clear what the police are going to do. There's no sign yet that they see her as a suspect."

"And there probably won't be either. Chamberlain's taken control. He won't want any of this to be public. But do you think Ayesha actually did it?"

Hannah ignores that question. "More to the point, do I think Gavin killed Tom? Yes, I do. I think he was probably a murderer and definitely a complete bastard. The relationship was a sham, a shag for some pillow talk. He was using me to spy on all of us, especially Ayesha. I think she must have been the main target. And I think Tom was onto him."

"But when did you talk to Ayesha about all this? I saw you at the funeral, and you didn't say anything then."

Hannah hesitates. She doesn't want to get drawn into talking about the events of the evening after the funeral.

"Never mind that. It's not important when I found out or how."

"But the police might ask you if Chamberlain lets them off the leash."

"They might, but you're not the police, Jed. Back off."

Jed looks hurt, and Hannah hates not being more open with him, but Ayesha's last words to her when they were parting had been: "Don't talk to *anyone* about this, not even Jed." And she's going to stick to that for as long as she can. If he doesn't know, he doesn't have to lie.

Jed gets up and circles the living room. It's the first time he's visited the flat, and Hannah watches as he sizes it up.

"What do you think?"

"Nice pad."

Hannah tries to smile, but she feels sick thinking of how buying the flat had been so exciting, such a big moment for her.

"It is, but it's tainted. I can see him and smell him everywhere here. The bastard used to walk around naked like he owned the place, and all the time he was taking the piss, laughing at me, and enjoying himself like I was his fucking whore."

"Don't say that, Hannah. You were always too good for him. I thought that the first time I saw you together at Ayesha's flat."

"Fuck, Jed. That just makes me feel worse. Why didn't I see it? That's the point."

Hannah shakes her head and buries it in her hands, elbows on the table. Jed walks over and sits on a chair alongside her, his arm across her shoulders. The room darkens as a cloud blocks the sun, and somehow it makes Hannah feel calmer.

"Well, he's gone now, forget him, he's not worth the tears."

Forget him? She suppresses an urge to laugh bitterly. It's obvious Jed has no idea really what to say. But why would he? He doesn't know what she's about to tell him. And, even when he does, he won't be able to understand fully how she feels, because she doesn't. Her body is in turmoil, its chemistry explosively unsettled, but she doesn't know what's natural and what's not, what's sickness from betrayal and what's sickness from the embryo growing inside her.

"Forget him?" She lifts her head, turns to look Jed in the eye and puts a hand on her stomach. "He's in here, Jed. I can't forget him. I will never be able to forget him. There's a life in here that's come from him. And the terrible thing is, I don't know if I'm going to be able to love it. Which means I don't know if I'm going to be able to have it. But, whatever I do, whatever I decide, there's no refuge from him now. He might be dead, but the anger won't go. It'll be with me for the rest of my life."

CHAPTER TWENTY-TWO
ONE MONTH LATER

Jed isn't sure about the colour she's chosen. The paint manufacturer calls it 'fern'. It's too dark for his liking, but he's only a conscript, drafted in to help Hannah decorate her flat.

She's a tough task master. It's the second of the three days he's taken off to do it, and he has already slapped two coats of lavender emulsion on the walls of the main bedroom and he's close to finishing the first coat in the living room. The quality of his work is questionable, but she doesn't seem to mind as long as he keeps up a good pace and doesn't mess up the skirting boards and door frames that she's already painted with white gloss.

At one point, yesterday afternoon, she screamed "for fuck sake, Jed" when she discovered the fern encroaching on some woodwork. She ranted at him for several minutes, saying he was useless, careless and countless other things. And then she dissolved into tears.

That seems to have been the pattern since she found out about Gavin. One minute she's hyper active, the next she's crushed and listless. She is mostly nicer than usual to Jed, but occasionally she attacks him fiercely for what he regards as nothing much at all.

The tablets seem to be helping to even out the mood swings. She had been reluctant to use medication, but her GP persuaded her it would help, at least until she feels the benefit of counselling. The GP has arranged a rape specialist – accepting without hesitation that it couldn't be viewed as anything else – and Hannah has already had two sessions.

But she doesn't talk to Jed much about what happened, or her pregnancy, even though they had probably spent more time together during these past four weeks than in the four years since they officially stopped dating. His role is mainly practical – and purely platonic.

He sleeps at her flat – on a single mattress in her tiny second bedroom – more nights than at his own house. But neither of them has any appetite for their usual banter, never mind rekindling anything remotely romantic. That relationship now seems like a relic of another life.

Jed tells himself that he stays with Hannah because he wants to keep an eye on her, like a good trooper on duty. But the truth is it's often easier to crash in her spare room than to trek home, and he's still wary of Chamberlain springing another thug on him.

His more objective self knows the latter is unlikely. He's now small fry for Chamberlain compared to the growing problem he has with Dorothy and O'Brien. Dorothy phones Jed regularly to check details of what happened or to tell him about letters she's fired off and people she's roped into the campaign.

Their first success was to secure an injunction preventing the cremation or burial of the body in the canal. The hearing had been held in camera and the judge would not disclose the real name of 'the deceased', but he agreed to give Dorothy's lawyer more time to prepare a case. Her latest call was to tell Jed about what she called "a political breakthrough". He'd tried to get her to tell him what it was, but she would only say that something would be in the papers "very soon".

Jed checks his watch, carefully avoiding dripping paint on it. It's just after midday. Hannah has gone to Belsize

Park for a coffee with Gloria, her favourite student. They've been spending a lot of time together and would normally meet at the flat but Hannah wanted to get away from the smell of paint. She's been gone more than two hours now. Jed isn't worried because he knows Gloria will walk her back to the flat, even if she doesn't come in. He's getting hungry though, and stock levels in the fridge are not what they were because Eleni's visits are less frequent now that things are, in her eyes, settling down.

He's just finishing the first coat of fern when Hannah arrives back waving a copy of the *Guardian*. She's wearing her usual Parka and looking wet and windswept, her hair hugging the shape of her head like a shiny brown helmet. She runs her fingers through it, trying to separate the strands. That only makes her look even more bedraggled, but she's beaming about whatever's in the paper.

"You should see this," she says, spreading it out on the second-hand oak table he'd helped her choose a few days earlier.

She's pointing at a report on an inside page headlined, *'MPs join call for inquiry into Tripoli death'*. They stand side by side reading it.

> An all-party group of MPs is backing calls for an inquiry into the death of a journalist whose body was found on a beach in Tripoli in April.
>
> Oliver Haines says the Freedom of Speech APPG supports the call because new evidence has emerged to suggest that Tom Carver, who was attending a conference in Tripoli, may not have died as a result of an accident.
>
> Carver's family is understood to have obtained a document and other information from reliable sources that cast doubt on the original version of events. They

282

claim another person from Britain was on the beach, and that this person was using a false identity and may have been involved in an undercover policing operation.

"We have written to the Home Secretary calling on him to commission an entirely independent investigation into this tragic death," said Holmes. "The new evidence provided to me by the family is compelling, and I am making it available to the Home Secretary in confidence."

The Tripoli conference, which was attended by peace campaigners from Europe and the US, was being held to mark the anniversary of the controversial US bombing of Tripoli. Carver, 27, was reporting on the event for the British-based magazine, Third World Voice.

Carver's aunt, Dorothy Willis, says the family is convinced that another British person was involved in her nephew's death and that there has been a cover-up.

"The Foreign Office has questions to answer about why it discouraged a proper investigation into Tom's death," said Willis

"The other British delegates to the conference came home on the day Tom's body was found and could easily have been interviewed by the police here. But, as far as we know, no one was.

"The family is keen to hear from anyone who was in Tripoli with Tom about the events of that night to establish what really happened. We won't rest until we know the truth."

Hannah and Jed stare in silence at the story for much longer than it takes to read it. For Jed, seeing their case presented in black and white for the first time – even in such guarded terms – is somehow a relief. He knows there's no rational reason for feeling like that, because they never doubted themselves, but it feels good to be believed and to see that belief declared in public. They aren't losing their minds. This isn't a paranoid fantasy.

"The MP's comment is a bit weak," Hannah says.

"What do you expect? He probably wouldn't have said anything at all if Dorothy hadn't let the Major loose on him. Dorothy said that even the *Guardian* was wary. They didn't want to mention the body in the canal until they had some kind of confirmation it was, you know…"

"A deceitful undercover rapist. Yes, I do know."

"What Dorothy's hoping is that some media coverage will flush out more evidence. People will come forward, and the government won't be able to portray it as a conspiracy theory."

Hannah touches her tummy and smiles.

"This definitely isn't a theory. And it could be – what do they call it? – the smoking gun. Did Dorothy tell you she'd phoned me?"

She hadn't, and Jed's irritated she hadn't because they had agreed to give Hannah more time before popping the DNA question.

"She did? When was that?"

"Yesterday. She wanted my blessing for a letter she was going to send the Met mentioning that I'm pregnant and requesting a DNA test on the corpse."

"What did you say?"

"Yes, of course. Why wouldn't I? I mean, I know he's the father because I didn't shag anyone else, but if it helps expose him and nail Chamberlain, then why not? But I'm not ready to go public yet. That would be too much. I told her she can only use my name for the letter – for now."

Hannah starts turning the pages of the paper. It's dominated by General Election campaigning. Margaret Thatcher is claiming Labour's plan for a minimum wage would destroy jobs. Neil Kinnock wants to know why other countries could do it and not Britain. The election is only ten days away, and the polls are all over the place, but all of them show the Conservatives leading.

"She's going to get in again, isn't she?" Hannah says.

"Looks like it, but the poll in yesterday's *Observer* was close. And Adam says the response on the doorstep in Islington South is good. But then he said that last time, and Chris Smith only won by about three hundred votes."

Jed senses Hannah isn't really listening. She's wandered across to the window and is watching people walking up the hill from the Underground station. The rain has stopped, leaving puddles glistening in a sudden burst of June sunshine.

"Let's go for a walk," she says. "The smell of paint is getting to me again."

"But what about the decorating?"

"I'm the boss. You've earned a break. And I haven't got any food in – we can grab something while we're out."

It isn't up for discussion. Hannah has started to button her Parka for a second outing. Jed makes a brief effort to clear up, tossing his brush into some soapy water in the sink and putting the lid back on the paint tin. But Hannah is already at the lift keeping the doors open with her foot by the time he's put on his coat.

Outside, they turn right, cross Adelaide Road and continue in silence past the Roundhouse. Jed is surprised Hannah's leading them in the direction of Camden Lock. He hasn't been there since the day the body was found. He doesn't think Hannah has either. He assumes she'd have said something.

"Are we going where I think we're going?" he says.

Hannah nods but doesn't offer an explanation. When they reach the canal, they turn right onto the towpath and come to a stop fifty yards along, where the water is wider.

Hannah stops dead and stares at the water, her gaze angled at a spot a few feet from the edge.

"That's where he was floating," she says.

Jed replays the words to himself, but he's still not sure if he's misheard.

"You mean, you were here."

Hannah nods, not looking him in the eye.

"So, you saw what happened?"

Jed turns so that he's facing Hannah – feeling annoyed that she hasn't told him this before and wanting an answer – but her eyes are still fixed on the water.

"I was here, standing right here, where I am now," she says. "I'd been waiting for over an hour. It was dark, but I saw him in the distance. He was wearing his usual fluorescent yellow running bib. As he came under the bridge, I could see that Ayesha wasn't far behind. I called to him. I shouted 'Gavin'. And he didn't respond. Why would he? It's not his name. Then he saw me and looked anxious. Not pleased to see me at all. It was as if he knew something was wrong. By the time he reached me, Ayesha had closed the gap to twenty yards or so and was walking. No one else was around by then. It was nearly ten. He said 'what's up?'. I said, 'who are you?' And he pretended to be confused. So, I said, 'you're not Gavin Mirren are you?' And he said, 'what are you on about?'. But, by then, Ayesha had caught up with him, and she pulled out the death certificate and held it up to his face. You should have seen the look in his eyes. The hatred in them when he'd read it. He glared at Ayesha. I thought he was going to hit her. But then he turned to me, all creepy and sleazy, and said 'Babe, you don't believe this crap, do you?' In that moment, I could have killed him. I wanted to."

Hannah turns to look at Jed, her eyes watery but her expression more severe than he's ever seen it. He still can't quite believe what he's hearing. He'd assumed that Ayesha had acted alone. It had never occurred to him that Hannah had been there.

"I really could have killed him," she repeats, as if wanting Jed to be clear on that.

"But Ayesha did instead," Jed says.

Hannah shakes her head vigorously. "No, no, actually, she didn't. Probably no one will ever believe it. But that was never our plan. We wanted to confront him, that was all. And it had to be in a fairly public place because we were worried about our own safety. If we wanted to kill him, why would we do it right here where people out walking might see us?"

"So, what happened?"

"He kind of lunged towards me. I'm not sure what he was trying to do, but it made me jump to one side, and he lost his balance – tripped or something – and fell sideways onto that." Hannah points at a steel stump right on the edge of the canal path. "His head landed directly on it, and made the most terrible noise, and he kind of bounced off it straight into the canal. It happened in a split second, and we both knelt down, but we couldn't reach him, he was drifting away from us, face down and not breathing, no movement, no air bubbles, nothing. And Ayesha just said 'we have to get help, but no one's ever going to believe us'."

Jed puts his arm around Hannah and gives her a long hug, but they're partially blocking the canal path and people are passing, giving them sideways looks.

"Let's get away from here," he says, releasing her and nodding sideways in the direction of Regent's Park.

They walk without talking for ten minutes or more. The sky is still clear, and Jed is happy to prolong their outing. He has a host of questions backing up in his head, but he wants to give her time.

"It was Ayesha's idea to call 999," Hannah says finally. "I was too stunned to think straight. Oddly, and I know this is going to sound strange, I felt cheated. I'd felt like killing him, but, all of a sudden, he was dead and it just made everything worse. We went to the phone box. Ayesha did the talking but she didn't give her name and, when we walked back across the bridge, we could see a few people had gathered, but they couldn't reach him either. And we just walked on."

"And you've kept all this bottled up for four weeks?" Jed's tone is sympathetic but, inside, he's hurt that she didn't confide in him.

"I had to Jed. Ayesha insisted that she'd take the blame if it came to it. And she didn't want you to know that we'd planned to confront him together because she was worried that you'd be compromised – it would wreck your career. She said that she had nothing to lose. She wanted to leave the country anyway. She'd had enough, the whole thing – with Gavin and Chamberlain – had made her hate being here."

"So why are you telling me all this now?"

"Because things have moved on. Because Ayesha's safe, and we can do the DNA tests, and I'll make a statement, and we'll find a way to expose all this, however long it takes. But Jed, what you must know, is how grateful Ayesha is to you. She's told me that. She told you to go that evening only because she felt you'd risked enough.

She was upset afterwards knowing that she'd probably never be able to see you again to explain."

Jed bites his lip, to stem the tears welling up inside him. He's had such confused feelings about why Ayesha had pushed him away, and what he'd assumed she had done. Had it been an act of pure revenge? Was it premeditated or did things get out of hand? Did it count as justice, the only kind available to her? Did it even matter what he thought?

None of that has turned out to be relevant, and he feels foolish for even thinking what he had, for rushing to judgement. But Ayesha's behaviour had been odd that evening, as if she was on a mission, and Hannah had so many reasons to be distressed that it never, for a moment, occurred to him that her being there and actually seeing him die might be one of them.

"What do you think Ayesha will do now?" Jed says.

"She's going to stay in Greece for the time being. She's living near Athens with a cousin of Eleni's and she's earning some money as a tour guide."

"But doesn't she want to go home, back to Beirut?"

"Not yet. Eleni says her parents are going to visit her in Greece sometime this summer, but Ayesha doesn't want to live in Beirut, not while Israel is occupying half the country. Not after what happened."

"You mean her uncle being killed. She never finished telling me about that."

"I don't just mean that. But, yes, that was a big thing for her because he was like a second father. Apparently, he'd lived with them when she was growing up. And she took it really badly when he was killed, when the Israelis bombed the PLO's offices in Beirut. Their planes pounded it for hours, a seven-storey building, reduced to rubble with two hundred people inside, Ayesha's uncle among them. And they never recovered his body. So that must have been devastating, by any standards, but what happened a few weeks later was even worse. It completely broke her."

Hannah looks at the sky and then her watch. Clouds have gathered and it's grown much darker as they've walked. They've reached the point where the canal turns right and runs through the middle of London Zoo. Giraffes are peering incongruously over rooftops only a hundred yards further on.

"I think it's going to rain again," Hannah says. "Let's go over to Prince Albert Road and back across Primrose Hill. It'll be quicker that way."

They walk up a path leading away from the canal and follow Prince Albert Road until they reach the entrance to Primrose Hill. The traffic is heavy, and it's too noisy to talk. But once they're near the top of Primrose Hill, Hannah stops, takes her Parka off and spreads it on the damp grass.

"This'll do – I think the rain will hold off for a bit," she says, patting her coat to invite Jed to sit next to her.

The clouds are grey and so low it looks as if the Post Office Tower and Centre Point are holding them up, but there are shafts of sunlight coming through in the distance to their right, offering some hope of the rain being kept at bay.

"What was it then, that finally made her decide to get out of Beirut?" Jed says, gently.

Hannah is sitting cross-legged with her eyes half closed, her back straight, taking deep, even breaths of the cool air. When she starts talking, her tone is matter-of-fact. Jed soon realises why. It's not a story that needs embellishing.

"You know that Ayesha was a maths teacher. Her day job was at an elementary school for Lebanese kids. But, after work, she'd go to Shatila."

Hannah looks at Jed to see if she needs to explain.

"The Palestinian refugee camp," he says, "Where her grandmother, mother and uncle lived when they first arrived in Beirut in forty-eight."

"Yes, she'd taught there for years, as a volunteer, and she'd got to know the children and their families really well. And even after her uncle was killed, she carried on teaching at the camp. But things had changed because the PLO's forces in Beirut had been evacuated to Tunis, as part of a deal with the Israelis, and no one was left to guard the camps."

Jed knows what she's talking about now. He remembers reading the reports and the outcry about it.

"And the Israelis sent the Phalangists in," he says.

"That's right. It was carnage. They went on a killing spree. Ayesha went there afterwards, having heard the rumours, and saw boys with testicles hacked off and girls who'd been raped and killed, their throats cut. It's hard to get your head round it. All the children in Ayesha's class were killed, except one — a girl called Samira — who she thinks escaped. She found her mother and baby sister shot dead, but Samira was nowhere to be seen, and Ayesha searched frantically for her for hours but couldn't find her. And, afterwards, she just fell apart. She couldn't speak for days. And her parents were so worried about her they arranged for her to come to London, to get away and recover."

"And still nothing's been heard of Samira?"

"No, but Ayesha's determined to find her. Eleni says she's been talking about that a lot. And I'm going to see what I can do from here."

Hannah turns to Jed to signal she's finished, as if saying, 'and that's Ayesha story'. But he's looking into the distance across the West End to Big Ben, his thoughts drifting to what Chamberlain might be up to. Somewhere in those buildings over there he's moving among the great and the good, covering his tracks, justifying his actions if he needs to, which is unlikely, because it's doubtful anybody in those corridors cares very much about the collateral damage – the death of a troublesome journalist or the abuse of a woman or even the loss of their own asset – as long as it doesn't cause any political fall-out or damage Britain's 'interests'.

"What are you thinking?" Hannah says.

Jed's eyes have been drawn to the west now. In the distance, the shafts of sunlight have been replaced by a curtain of rain, advancing rapidly. Every so often, thunder echoes faintly.

"I'm thinking that those black clouds to our right are far too close for comfort."

"Let's go," Hannah says, jumping to her feet and pulling her Parka on in one seamless movement.

They walk briskly towards Chalk Farm, both checking over their shoulders from time to time to see how close the black clouds are getting. As they cross the bridge over the railway lines into Euston, rain starts hitting the pavement in large blobs, landing with increasing frequency. They break into a jog, but it isn't enough. By the time they reach Adelaide Road, it feels like someone's emptied a giant tank of water on them.

Hannah starts running faster. Jed is anxious she'll trip. He assumes she's decided to have an abortion – she hasn't told him yet – but he doesn't want it to be on the pavement. He stays right on her shoulder until they reach Haverstock Hill and the entrance to the flats. Once inside, gasping for breath, they laugh like kids who've escaped an imagined baddie.

Hannah takes her Parka off in the lift. Again, her hair is like a shiny brown helmet. She shakes her head, showering Jed with water. They laugh, and he feels an urge to kiss her, but he holds back, worried he'll upset the equilibrium they've found.

The smell of paint is overpowering as they enter the flat. Hannah gasps and shoots straight into the living room to open a window. Jed notices some post under his feet in the hall and picks it up. It's mainly junk mail. But one of the envelopes has no stamp. It's addressed only to 'HANNAH'.

"That'll be from Eleni," Hannah says, taking it from him. "She must have come round."

Jed knows the system. Eleni communicates with Ayesha through a travel agent in Athens and is under strict instructions not to use the phone or post to pass on messages or news to Hannah.

He watches her rip the envelope open. As she starts to read it, she pulls him closer so that he can see too.

> *Hannah,*
>
> *Exciting news. The Red Cross has located Samira. Their office in Athens told Ayesha that she's in Damascus. She was adopted by a Syrian family. Ayesha's flying there to see her at the weekend. She's thrilled. She wanted you to know straight away. She sends her love. I'll come over tomorrow with some food.*
>
> *Love, Eleni.*

Jed waits for Hannah to read the note again, slowly, seemingly savouring each word in turn. He can see she's welling up, but, at the same time, her lips are twitching like she wants to smile.

"Trust Eleni to bring food into it," she says, laughing, watery eyes sparkling. She wipes a tear from her cheek with the back of her hand and leans into Jed as he puts an arm around her shoulder.

"She knows we have to stay strong," he says. "And we can't fight back on empty stomachs."

ENDS

Newport Community
Learning & Libraries

Acknowledgements

Writing a novel would be impossible without the support and collaboration of other people.

It has been a work in progress for nearly five years during which time my wife, Kim, has been a sounding board and given numerous suggestions. Her comments on an early iteration prompted a radical rethink that has, I think, made it a much better book.

The penultimate draft was read by Betty Hunter, Frieda Park, Jennifer Larbie, Brian Filling and Steve Hoselitz, and I am enormously grateful to them for taking so much trouble in sharing their thoughts, all of which have influenced the final outcome in one way or another.

The final stages of the process were aided by the professionalism of Simon John, who designed the cover, and Katrin Lloyd and Kate Doheny-Adams, who did the proof-checking and type-setting. My thanks also to the team at Freshwater for handling the marketing and to the Books Council for Wales for providing a wide range of support.

While all those mentioned have been hugely helpful, I am ultimately the author of every word in the book – any errors or deficiencies are entirely my responsibility.

OVER THE LINE
by Steve Howell

First published in 2015, *Over The Line* tells the story of an Olympic poster girl who comes under suspicion because of her links to the steroid-fuelled death of a childhood friend. A gritty and poignant thriller, it's a story of suspicion, denial and betrayal set in and around the drug scene in a south Wales gym.

On the eve of the Olympics, Britain's poster girl, Megan, seems destined for a gold medal. But detectives investigating the death of Matt want to find out what she knows. In panic and riddled with angst, Megan disappears, only to resurface arm-in-arm with Will, an old boyfriend who was banned from rugby after failing a drugs test.

Her coach, Liam, doesn't know what to think. He wants to trust her but has to wrestle with his doubts under growing pressure from the police and media. As layers of Megan's past are peeled away, she has to face up to some big mistakes - but the biggest of them is a surprise even to her.

'With each passing month, the themes in Over The Line become more relevant.'
Sean Ingle, The Guardian.

'The heroine of British athletics, tainted by doping and death. Couldn't happen? Read Over The Line and decide. Absorbing.'
Michael Calvin, author and former Independent on Sunday columnist.

GAME CHANGER
by Steve Howell

Game Changer is an insider's account of one of the most dramatic elections of modern times.

In 2017, when Theresa May unexpectedly called a general election, most commentators thought she would win by a landslide. But, over a tense and turbulent eight weeks, Labour closed the gap to deny May a majority with the largest increase in Labour's vote share since 1945.

'Game Changer is a vivid account of what it was like to be in the engine room of Jeremy Corbyn's remarkable election campaign.'
Dennis Kavanagh, Emeritus Professor of Politics, University of Liverpool. Author of Thatcherism and British Politics.

'If you're interested in how Corbyn did better than expected in the general election, you should read this book.'
Tim Shipman, Political Editor, Sunday Times and author of Fall Out.

21/5/21

Newport Library and
Information Service